INCUBUS 4

By Brandon Varnell
Art by Orendi Laran

This book is a work of fiction. Names, characters, places, and incidents are the products of the author's imagination or are used fictitiously. Any resemblance to actual events, locales, or persons, living or dead, is coincidental.

Incubus, Volume 4
Copyright © 2022 Brandon Varnell & Kitsune Incorporated
Illustration Copyright © 2022 Orendi Laran
All rights reserved.

To see Brandon Varnell's other works, or to ask for permission to use his works, visit him at www.varnell-brandon.com, facebook at www.facebook.com/AmericanKitsune, twitter at www.twitter.com/BrandonbVarnell, Patreon at https://www.patreon.com/BrandonVarnell, and instagram at www.instagram.com/brandonbvarnell.

If you'd like to know when I'm releasing a new book, you can sign up for my mailing list at https://www.varnell-brandon.com/mailing-list.

ISBN: 978-1-951904-46-3 (paperback)
978-1-951904-47-0 (eBook)

DEDICATION

This page is made in dedication to my amazing patrons. Without them, my characters would never get lewded by so many wonderful artists:

Zach Ulbright; Damen Hailey; MillerLite97; cj savage; Kconraw; Charles Savage; Gingy; Mana & Steel; Brendan Kane; Derek HEATH; Max; calob Rose; randgofire23; MrRedSkill; Thomas Oconnell; Yuno; Chett Nialo; Jordan McDonald; Eric Bailey; Robert Shofner; Joshua Hasbell; Mike Dennehy; Alex Burt; Green and Magenta Beast; Tanner Lovelace; Zak Whitaker; Jessy Torres; Daniel Glasson; pheonixblue; Forrest Hansen; Edward P Warmouth; TheGothFather72; Christopher Gross; Adam; Joshua Kern; Edward Grindle; IronKing; Sho_36; Brendan Smiley; Mark Frabotta; Raymond T; Michael Erwin; Samuel Donaldson; Armando Pastrana; Nathan S; Thomas Jackson; Sean Gray; Chace Corso; ToraLinkley; Forrest Hansen; Rafael; Philip Hedgepeth; Chopper; Jacob Wojno; Aaron harris; max a kramer; victor patrick bauer; William Crew; Jacob Flores; Michael Moneymaker; Seismic Wolf

CONTENT

CHAPTER 1 - 01
CHAPTER 2 - 31
CHAPTER 3 - 57
CHAPTER 4 - 85
CHAPTER 5 - 110
CHAPTER 6 - 135
CHAPTER 7 - 165
CHAPTER 8 - 195
CHAPTER 9 - 217
CHAPTER 10 - 239

CHAPTER 1

ANTHONY'S VISION WAS BLURRY, war hammers were battering his skull, and his body had become sluggish to the point where even lifting his hand required monumental effort.

If he included that time when Director Azrael had captured him, this was the second time he had been poisoned. As an incubus, a creature who sustained himself on mana, he had a certain level of resistance to poisons. That did not mean, however, that he was immune.

Especially if the poison was not magical in nature.

"You want me... to help you... kill... someone?" As he spoke those words, Anthony tried to figure out when this woman had poisoned him. He hadn't given her any opportunities. She had never drugged any of his food or drinks when she joined him for lunch at the Institution of Magical Sciences, and he never saw her outside of school, so how could she have poisoned him?

Unless...

Anthony vaguely recalled an intruder sneaking into his apartment, kissing him, and shoving something down his throat. The object had dissolved after he'd swallowed it and nothing had happened, so he had honestly forgotten about it. Professor Incanscino had also looked over him and not found anything strange. His trust in that woman was such that he was incapable of thinking she could miss anything.

But it seemed even his esteemed professor could make mistakes.

"That's right." Selene was no longer smiling. Her eyes were narrowed, hands clenching and unclenching as though just thinking about the person she wanted to kill caused her to feel unbearable hatred. Her entire body shuddered from the overwhelming emotions bombarding her. Anthony could see her hatred manifested physically through her body language.

"Why should we help you?!" asked Brianna.

The redhead already had her double-bladed sword out. The Geminius Sword shone in the light of so many neon signs as she pointed it at Selene.

Despite Brianna's obviously threatening stance, Selene appeared unbothered by the other woman. In fact, she wasn't even paying attention to Brianna. She was staring at Anthony. She had been this whole time.

"Why should I… do what you want?" Anthony asked.

A coy smile caused her lips to curl as if she had been waiting for him to ask that question.

Selene said, "Don't you want me to remove that poison from you? While it isn't deadly, it also isn't something that you can just get rid of. That poison was made from a combination of herbs that can only be found in my personal garden. They've been infused with the darkness element to enhance their effectiveness. I am the only one in the entire world who can make the antidote for you."

Selene walked over to them, hips swaying hypnotically from side to side. Anthony was sure he would have appreciated the sight, even though her body was covered by a cloak, but he could barely even see. His vision had become fuzzy.

"This poison is one that makes your entire body feel heavy like you are being weighed down by a mountain. It will give you headaches, exhaust your strength, and make it so you can never function properly again. It is also self-propagating. It is a poison that latches onto the host and drains their vitality in order to continue existing."

Brianna was still right next to Anthony, her blade drawn, feet spread apart and knees bent as though ready for action, but she wasn't attacking. Perhaps she knew that attacking when she didn't know how to cure this poison was a bad idea. That said, her grip on the Geminius Sword had tightened so much her knuckles had turned white.

Selene knelt before him. The wide smile on her face remained. It was like she took sick amusement in his suffering.

"You know, I originally didn't want to do this. My original goal was to simply seduce you and convince you to help me afterward. I figured you were the kind of man who would do anything for his bondmates. However, immediately after I joined your college, you became wary of me. You never let me get any closer than was necessary to maintain an amicable relationship, so, you could say that what is happening right now is all your fault."

Anthony wanted to speak, but all he could do was groan. The poison was beginning to affect him more as time went on. He could barely even think straight, so the most he could do now was listen to this woman blame him for what was happening.

Damn... her... if I manage... to heal from this... I'll make sure she... regrets it...

Selene's smile widened as she stood up. "I'll give you some time to think of an answer. That said, I suggest you make a decision soon. That poison might not kill you, but it's perfectly capable of putting you into a coma you'll never wake up from."

Selene turned around and began walking away. At this point, Brianna finally seemed unable to stop herself. She brandished her sword at Selene.

"Hold it! Do you really think I'm going to just let you walk away after all this?"

Selene turned only her head to look at Brianna from the corner of her eye. A smile touched her lips. It seeped with a sort of cold amusement.

"Let me walk away? My dear girl, you have no choice but to let me go. I am the only one who can remove the poison from Anthony's body, so you cannot kill me, and if you lock me up, then I definitely won't want to help you."

Brianna clenched her teeth as Selene continued walking away before, quite suddenly, her body became covered in darkness and burst into bats. They weren't real bats, however. Even Anthony could tell they were made purely from mana. The bats flapped their wings like they were real and scattered into the air.

"What a... a pleasant woman..." Anthony muttered bitterly. He couldn't believe he'd been so careless. While Selene's words that he was responsible for what happened to him were not true, he did feel a certain amount of responsibility regarding his current state. He should have been more vigilant.

"Are you okay?" Brianna asked as she knelt by his side. She placed a hand on his shoulder, but he could hardly feel it. His body already felt like there was a mountain sitting on his shoulders.

"I... don't think so..." Anthony admitted. "Damn it. I was really careless... this time."

"All of us were careless," Brianna said softly. "None of us could have imagined this would happen. Anyway, let's get you back home."

Brianna slung his arm over her shoulder and hauled him to his feet. Anthony sagged against her. He had no strength to move. Even so, Brianna didn't seem bothered by this at all as she began walking resolutely to the nearest maglev station.

They were fortunate it was so late and there were very few people out and about, which meant no one really paid attention to them at the station or on the maglev. Anthony spent all of his time on the maglev resting against Brianna. His eyes felt so heavy like they were being forced closed by an invisible hand.

The walk home was long and laborious. Anthony's strength had already disappeared, and he couldn't focus enough to activate Physical Enhancement. He didn't know what kind of poison was running through his body, but he could tell it was incredibly strong, even if it was non-lethal.

"About time you two returned. Do you know how long we have been—Anthony?! What's wrong?!"

The first person who greeted him and Brianna upon their return was Secilia, who had stood up to greet them, only for her eyes to widen with shock when she saw the state he was in. Her feet thumped against the floor as she rushed over to him. Marianne, who had been sitting on the couch, also stood up and ran to his side. When she caught a glimpse of his sweat-covered and pallid face, the blood drained from her face as she brought a hand up to hide the shocked O-shape that was her mouth.

"He's been poisoned," Brianna said through gritted teeth. "I'll tell you about it later. For now, help me get him to bed."

"Yeah. Okay."

Secilia took Anthony's other side to take some of the burden off Brianna. His bondmate could have used Physical Enhancement, but she probably wanted to spare him some dignity by not carrying him in her arms like a princess.

Marianne trailed behind them as they took Anthony into the bedroom and laid him on the bed. His entire body was soaked in sweat. His skin felt cold, but his body felt like it was burning up. He closed his eyes and tried to calm down with several deep breaths, but it was no use. His breathing was so labored that he was struggling to take in oxygen.

"Now that Anthony is in bed, tell us what happened," Secilia said. Her expression was more serious than normal as she stared at the redhead, who looked overwrought with nerves.

She and Brianna were sitting on the edge of the bed, while Marianne stood by the foot of the bed, looking uncertainly between the two. Anthony wanted to reassure the vampire girl, but he couldn't. His mouth refused to form words.

Brianna sighed once before nodding. "Don't worry. I'll tell you what happened."

Anthony found it hard to focus on Brianna's words as she talked about how Anthony's body suddenly began losing strength, and how they had been confronted by Selene Dracul, who wanted him to kill someone for her in exchange for the antidote. Secilia was silent as Brianna explained everything to them. Marianne had gasped when Brianna mentioned Selene showing up. Anthony found that odd, but he couldn't speak, so he let it slide.

"So that's what happened." Secilia crossed her arms and gnashed her teeth. "I can't believe someone managed to poison Anthony, and it was Selene?! When did she have a chance to do that?!"

"Do you remember when Anthony was attacked by an assailant who snuck into the apartment?" asked Brianna, though she didn't give Secilia a chance to answer before continuing. "That person was not only able to sneak into our bedroom without anyone noticing, but she was able to quietly dismantle my barrier without me noticing. I first thought his attacker was a magician since they are clearly well-versed in magic, but now I believe it was Selene."

Anthony had come to the same conclusion. Her being the attack also explained why she had been able to use the darkness element. It was a common type of magic among vampires.

"I see. That does make a lot of sense." Secilia glanced at Anthony, then looked away, perhaps unable to continue staring at him

while he was in such a sorry state. "What should we do now? How
can we cure him?"

"I don't know." Brianna reached out a hand and began stroking
Anthony's hair. Her hands felt cool against his burning skin as she
brushed away the bangs sticking to his forehead. "We might... we
might have to agree to do what Selene wants in exchange for having
her remove the poison."

"Are you crazy?" asked Secilia, standing up and glaring at the
redhead. "Do you really think we can trust a woman like her? If she's
willing to go so far as to poison someone just so we agree to do her
bidding, then she's obviously not the kind of person we can trust.
Even if we agree to kill someone for her, she probably won't remove
the poison completely. She might even keep a little bit of poison inside of Anthony to keep a constant bargaining chip available whenever she wants him to do something for her."

"I know that! But what else can we do?" asked a now frustrated
Brianna.

"I might be able to build a machine that can remove the poison
from Anthony," Secilia said.

"And how long will that take?" asked Brianna.

"... Probably a few weeks?"

"So you want him to stay like this for several weeks?"

"Of course not! But I don't want us to agree with Selene's demands, especially when we don't even know who she wants us to
kill."

"Neither do I, but it's not like we have a choice! We can't leave Anthony like this! If you really care about him, you should be willing to do anything you can to help him!"

"What do you think I'm doing right now?!"

The conversation was quickly becoming heated, with accusations and exclamations flying around. While Brianna and Secilia traded snipes often, they had never argued to this extent. Anthony wanted to step in. He wanted to tell them they needed to stop. But he couldn't. With the poison running through his body, sapping him of his strength, all he could do was lay there.

He felt useless.

It was at this point in time that the quiet Marianne raised her hand. "Um... I might be able to help him."

Brianna and Secilia stopped arguing and turned to her. When their gazes landed on her, Marianne nearly stumbled back in fright. Her entire body went stiff like a plank as she broke out in a cold sweat. The other two either didn't notice or didn't care.

"You can remove the poison?" asked Brianna.

Marianne shivered and her eyes darted about like she wanted to run away, but she nodded instead and said, "You... you probably already know this, but high-level vampire nobles have a very strong regeneration factor. We can heal from almost any wound. We can even regenerate lost limbs if we consume enough blood."

"I do know of this ability," Brianna said with a frown. "But how can that help Anthony? It's self-regeneration. All that means is you can heal yourself."

"Um… as a vampire noble, my own body can heal itself as long as I consume enough blood," Marianne tried to explain. "I should be able to suck the poison out of Anthony, then dismantle the poison inside of me by drinking his blood."

Brianna and Secilia grew silent. Tension seemed to fill the room. Anthony couldn't possibly know what those two were thinking. His head was spinning as he tried to retain a grip on his consciousness, but he at least heard what Marianne had said.

"Do it," he rasped, using the last bit of his strength to speak.

"Anthony?" Brianna looked down at him in shock.

Anthony stared at Marianne through half-lidded eyes. "Do it. It's okay. I… I trust you."

"R-really?!" Marianne's eyes lit up like beacons in the middle of the night. She seemed a lot happier than he felt his words deserved. "Okay! I'll start right now!"

Marianne hurried over to his side and leaned over the bed. She opened her small mouth, fangs glinting in the light. Brianna and Secilia remained silent. It was unknown whether they approved of this method or not, but this was also one of the only choices available to them.

"Um…" Marianne stopped just as she was about to bite his neck, looked at Brianna and Secilia, blushed, and said, "C-could you two please not watch me. It's… embarrassing."

They gave the vampire girl an intense stare but eventually turned around. Once they did, Marianne's eyes flashed and a smile caused her lips to curve delightfully. It only lasted for a moment before the shy and embarrassed look came back.

Marianne leaned down again, her mouth so close to his neck that Anthony could feel her breathing on him. A shiver made its way down his spine. It wasn't a shiver of fear, but one of pleasure, of anticipation. Even when poisoned, his incubus nature could not be quelled. Anthony didn't wince when Marianne sank her fangs into his neck. It didn't hurt, not even when her fangs broke his skin. It actually felt oddly pleasant, like when Secilia would bite his neck and suck on it to leave a mark. Her soft lips pressed against his skin and her tongue flicked out to lick away the blood that leaked from the puncture marks.

He couldn't feel his blood being drained, but he could tell somehow that she was, indeed, draining him of blood. It wasn't long before his body began feeling lighter. The mountain that had been weighing him down seemed to disappear as if it had never existed. At the same time, Marianne's body jerked and spasmed, shuddering several times as though she was in pain. Once she had sucked out all of the poison, her body slumped onto the bed.

Anthony sat up. Marianne's head slid off his neck, down his chest, and came to rest on his lap. Her eyes were closed and her breathing was a touch shallow.

"Anthony?" Brianna turned back around. "How do you feel?"

"I feel a lot better." Anthony raised his hands and clenched his fingers. "It's as if I was never poisoned, to begin with." He looked down at the girl whose head rested on his lap, reached out, and began stroking her hair. "Marianne really saved me this time."

Brianna nodded in agreement. "She did. I don't know what we would have done if she wasn't here."

"Hmph. I could have saved Anthony if I was given enough time," Secilia muttered as she crossed her arms.

"Time isn't something we have at the moment," Brianna said.

Secilia had nothing she could say to refute Brianna's words.

Now that Anthony was feeling better, he didn't believe staying in bed was appropriate. He climbed out of bed, lifted the unconscious Marianne into his arms, and set her down on the bed instead. He put her on the other side since the side he had been laying on was soaked with sweat. He didn't want her catching a cold. After which, he sat on the edge and began stroking her hair again.

Secilia was the first to notice his expression. "Are you thinking of making Marianne your bondmate?"

"I am," Anthony confirmed.

"I'm not so sure that's a good idea." Brianna didn't quite dismiss the idea, but she seemed reluctant. "Remember that her entire reason for coming here was you. Her mother sent her all this way because she wants to use your power to benefit herself."

"But isn't Elizabeth Tepes the most peace-oriented of the three Vampire Warlords?" said Anthony. "I don't think it would be wrong to ally myself with her. And besides, I like Marianne. She's a bit... odd, but I can tell she's a genuinely good person."

"Hmph. You're just attracted to her because she's pretty," Brianne muttered.

"There is that too," Anthony admitted.

It was impossible to deny that Marianne was gorgeous. She didn't have Brianna's bountiful figure, but her lithe and graceful body looked like something made by a master sculpture. Her snow-white skin, her beautiful silver hair, those gorgeous features. Every inch of her could drive a man wild with lust. Even her tiny feet were like works of art.

"So you're gonna fuck her?" asked Secilia.

"Why are you always so crass?" Brianna muttered.

"Because I can be."

Anthony sighed and stopped the two from arguing before they could really get going. He had no desire to listen to them quibbling right now.

"I'll talk to Marianne about it within the next few days." He paused long enough to smile at the two. "Why don't you two get ready for bed? I'm going to stay here for a while longer."

The expressions Brianna and Secilia wore when he said that made them look out of sorts, but they didn't say anything against his decision. Anthony kept his eyes on them as they wandered out of the room. The door shut, the sound of their footsteps receded, and only then did he turn around to look at the woman lying on the bed.

"You can stop pretending to be unconscious now," he said.

"Hee hee. When did you realize I was faking?" asked Marianne as she opened her eyes. Unlike before, when she had looked embarrassed and uncertain, her eyes now contained a glint of amusement.

"Shortly after I picked you up," Anthony said. "You don't seem to realize this, but I am studying to be a doctor. I can easily tell when someone is unconscious based on how they're breathing and their pulse."

"I see. A doctor, huh? In that case, would you like to play doctor with me?" Marianne lifted her skirt, revealing an expansive amount of her unblemished, milky legs. She would have looked like the epitome of confidence.

If only she wasn't blushing.

"Maybe later." Anthony beamed at her before his smiling expression disappeared, replaced with a more serious look. "Before that, I'd like to ask you something."

"You want to ask about my abrupt personality change, right?" Marianne wore a knowing smile as she placed her hands in her lap and clasped them together. She squeezed her fingers hard enough to make her knuckles turn white. "Let me guess, you think this personality change is because I have multiple identity disorder?"

"That was the first thought that came to mind, but I don't think that's the case anymore," Anthony observed Marianne for a moment, putting his thoughts and theories in order before speaking. "When someone has multiple identity disorder, they tend to have memory problems. There will always be gaps in their memory, but you... you don't seem to have those. When you woke me up the other day, your personalities switched partway through. It was like you were trying to put up a strong front but lost your nerve at the last second. What's more, you perfectly remembered what happened after your other personality appeared. That wouldn't be possible if you had multiple identity disorder."

"You're a pretty smart guy." Marianne leaned back on the bed and sighed. She looked a lot more mature at that moment than she did when her other personality came to the front. "You are right, of course. I don't have multiple personalities. The personality you see before you is something I crafted for myself, to protect myself."

"Protect yourself from what?" asked Anthony.

Marianne shook her head. "Sorry, but while I do like you, I don't trust you enough to tell you that. What you're asking about is my deepest and darkest secret. If you want to know about it, you'll have to earn my trust."

"Well... I guess that makes sense," Anthony said with a sigh. "How can I earn your trust?"

"That's a good question." Marianne's smile revealed her fangs, which glinted in the lamp light by his bedside. "I'm not going to tell you. If you want to earn my trust, you'll have to use your own intelligence to do so."

Anthony frowned and wanted to tell her that she was being unreasonable, but before he could, the expression on Marianne's face changed, becoming less confident and more uncertain. Before long, the shy and easily embarrassed Marianne who was always apologizing had replaced the strong and confident one.

"Um... I'm sorry," she said in a soft voice. "I know I'm being unreasonable, but..."

"No. I don't think you're being unreasonable," Anthony interrupted the girl, causing her head to snap up and stare at him. When he saw the shocked expression she wore, he shrugged. "It seems clear to me that something happened to you in the past and it caused your trust in people to plummet. I'm willing to work hard and earn your trust."

"Th-thank you," Marianne mumbled. "You're very kind."

"Well, I try to be," Anthony said with an uncertain smile. He stood up. "Anyway, get some rest. You can sleep on our bed tonight. Bri and I will take the couch."

Marianne looked like she wanted to say something, but Anthony was already walking out the door.

***

The weekend came and went. Anthony had been wracking his brain all Sunday to try and figure out how he could earn Marianne's trust, but the truth was, he really had no idea what to do. It wasn't like those stories where the prince rescued the princess and his altruism automatically earned her trust. This wasn't fiction.

Anthony arrived early to Professor Incanscino's class that morning, sat down in his usual spot, and closed his eyes as he pondered the matter of Marianne. He was curious to know what had happened to her. There were not many people he knew who could create a fake persona to use. People with multiple identity disorders were a lot more common.

As he was pondering the matter of Marianne, the door opened and Selene walked in. She wore a wide smile as she walked up the steps. That smile left, however, when she lifted her head and caught sight of him. He and Selene stared at each other for a good while.

"Anthony." Her lips twitched into a bewitching smile. "You look well."

"Thanks. I feel pretty good. You also look like you have been well. Did you have a good weekend?"

"Good enough, though it could have been better if someone could just go along with my schemes."

While their conversation seemed sincere and friendly to any on-lookers, there was an underlying current of tension in Selene's voice. She had obviously not expected him to be back on his feet so soon. Even now, as she sat next to him, he could feel her stealing glances at his side profile.

More and more people arrived. Professor Incanscino was the last. She walked up the lectern, set her purse and water bottle on the table, and turned to face the students.

"I hope all of you have been studying hard. We'll be taking a quiz today. Turn on your laptops and log into your student profile. You should all have a notification in your inbox. It will have the link to your test."

While several students groaned, Anthony was not one of them. He logged into his student profile, opened the message in his inbox, and clicked on the link, which brought him to a very obvious quiz.

Even though a lot was going on in his life right now, Anthony still made time to study and do his homework. The first few questions were simple yes or no answers, but the further along he got on the test, the more elaborate the questions became, like the one asking him to describe the five symptoms of someone who had mana poisoning and how to treat it. Even then, all of the questions were ones he could have found in his textbooks.

It took him a total of forty-nine minutes to complete. During that time, Anthony kept feeling a pair of eyes on him, watching him like a hawk. It was Selene. He did his best to ignore her, finished his test, and pressed the submit button that sent the test straight to Professor

Incanscino's inbox. After that, he waited until class was over before ignoring everything and heading straight to his teacher.

"Professor Incanscino."

"Did you need something, Mr. Amasius?"

"I did. I'd like to talk to you about an important matter."

The other students barely gave them a cursory glance as they left. It wasn't all that unusual for him to stay after class to speak with Professor Incanscino. The only one who stared at him was Selene, who looked like she wanted to say something, but she chose not to in the end. The vampire woman exited through the door alongside the others.

"Hmph. You want to ask me about Selene, right?" When Anthony nodded, Professor Incanscino snorted. "That conversation is going to take a bit more time than we have available right now. Come to my office after school. We can talk then."

"Okay."

Anthony knew better than to push the issue, so once he received her words, he left the lecture hall. He expected Selene to be waiting for him, but she wasn't present when he entered the hallway. It was as if she had disappeared.

Anthony came alone to see Professor Incanscino. They both sat on their respective couches, facing each other. Professor Incanscino was no longer in her business suit, which she only wore when acting in her capacity as a teacher, and was now dressed in her white gothic lolita outfit. She also wasn't wearing shoes. Her white stockings stretched across her feet and legs. Because of how tight they were, he could make out each of her tiny toes.

"You came because you have questions regarding Selene Dracul," Professor Incanscino began. "I am guessing she made a move on you by this point?"

"Actually, she tried to poison me."

"Oh?" Professor Incanscino straightened in her seat. "I am assuming this is the same person who snuck into your apartment and shoved something down your throat? I didn't expect her to act so impulsively. Tell me what happened."

Anthony related all of the relevant information he had to Professor Incanscino. The diminutive woman listened as he told her about his confrontation with Selene and how she had demanded he help her kill someone after the poison had spread through his body. It took no longer than an hour to finish.

"Hmmm. It was probably a type of poison that she enhanced with her own magic to act as a parasite," Professor Incanscino said at last. "This kind of poison is nigh undetectable to even the best scanners because it mimics a person's blood vessels. Scanners can't tell the difference between the poison and the actual blood vessels themselves."

"I've never heard of a poison like that," Anthony said.

"I'd be surprised if you did. It's very rare. Anyway…" Professor Incanscino quickly shifted gears. "What's important right now is not that she poisoned you, but what she wants from you."

"She said she wants me to kill someone, but I have no idea who she might want me to kill," Anthony said.

"Hmph. You haven't done enough research into Selene's past then." With her blonde ringlets spilling over her shoulders, Professor Incanscino crossed her arms and leaned back. "Are you aware of the relationship between Selene and her father?"

"Of course not." Anthony shook his head.

"You really haven't done any research at all, have you?" Anthony felt his cheeks heat up when Professor Incanscino gave him one of her deadpan stares. "I would have expected you to have at least looked up information about her. Don't you have someone capable of hacking almost any database in the world? And anyway, this is pretty common knowledge." She paused long enough to make him feel embarrassed. "Selene and her father hate each other."

"Why is that?" asked Anthony.

"I don't know, but about two years ago, Selene and her father had a huge fight that ended with Vlad Dracul's main mansion being completely destroyed. After that, Selene vanished and hasn't been seen until now."

"And... what were Vlad and Selene fighting about?" asked Anthony.

"No one knows." Professor Incanscino reached up and flipped her hair over her delicate shoulders. "Nobody knows what exactly happened back then. Vlad hasn't released any statements concerning the matter, but about two days after his mansion was destroyed and she disappeared, he disowned her. Selene is the youngest of his children. He has three, by the way. Two sons and Selene. It could just be that she has daddy issues."

"Please don't make jokes," Anthony said.

"Who said I was joking?" Professor Incanscino gave him a sharp smile. "In either event, the person she wants you to help her kill is most likely Vlad."

Anthony didn't even know what to say to that. She wanted him to help her kill a Vampire Warlord? Was she crazy? No, scratch that. The woman was obviously insane. She had tried to seduce him, and when he refused to allow her to even try, she attempted to poison him. If it wasn't for Marianne's help, he'd have probably been forced to go along with that woman's insane scheme.

"Was that all you wanted to ask me?" asked Professor Incanscino.

"Yes," he said after a while.

"Then you can leave. I have to grade your papers."

At the woman's blunt dismissal, Anthony stood up and left her lavish office. He closed the door behind him, entered the elevator, and thought about what he had learned as the elevator descended to the first floor.

Selene Dracul was estranged from her father and wanted to kill him for reasons Anthony couldn't fathom. Who would want to kill their own parent? It would have to be someone who either had a very good reason or was certifiably insane. Or both. There couldn't be anything else. The question now was: What should he do about this?

It was obvious that he would have to deal with Selene eventually. She was clearly desperate to have his help. She would try something again to convince or force him into going along with her plans. He needed to be ready for whatever she tried.

The elevator door opened. Anthony stepped outside. Just as he was about to begin walking down the hall, something powerful like a bolt of lightning hit him in the chest. He stumbled, raising a hand to press it against his chest. He expected to see a wound there, but there was nothing. He blinked in confusion for several seconds. What just happened? It was only after a moment passed in silence that he realized this feeling wasn't coming from him. Emotions that were not his flooded through the bond he had with Secilia; shock, fear, anger, and anxiety slammed into him like a hurricane.

Once he figured out what was happening, he stopped hesitating and sprinted toward Building #4, which was dedicated to engineering. Secilia was in danger. He couldn't afford to waste even one moment.

***

Secilia bit her lip as she manipulated the large pair of robotic arms with one hand and typed several lines of code into a holographic monitor with the other. A series of beeps issued from the monitor, which showed all of the programs she was installing into the magical matrix for the weapon she was building. Meanwhile, the robotic arms were in the process of welding together said weapon.

A set of gloves and boots.

They didn't look like much on the outside. If anyone were to see them, they would have said these looked just like a regular set of gloves and boots with metal plating covering the outer layer. The inner layer was made from a synthetic fabric that appeared to be black. No one would ever know that lining the inner layer of each article was a matrix powered by microscopic mana stones.

"There. They're all done. Phew."

Secilia stopped manipulating the arms and finished installing all of the necessary programs. The holographic monitor vanished, the robotic arms stopped their work, and Secilia picked up the gloves from the workstation with a satisfied smile.

"Now to test them out."

The first thing Secilia did was put on the gloves. They were the focal point of her work. The boots were more or less accessories meant to complement the gloves. After slipping the gloves on, she moved her fingers to make sure the metal segments wouldn't hinder her movement. Clicking noises issued from the gloves as the metal segments clacked together.

"Okay. Activate: Martial Skill."

"Activating."

The voice that issued from the gloves was female and pleasant on the ears, if a tad artificial sounding. Several glowing lines appeared across the gloves like circuits on a motherboard. They didn't extend past the gloves, which only covered up to her forearms.

Secilia was just about to put on the boots when the door to the engineering room slid open. She turned around, wondering who it could be, and froze when she saw Selene walking in with a hard look on her face.

The vampire woman was wearing tight black pants, black boots, and a black shirt. Every article of clothing conformed to her lithe and graceful body. Secilia wouldn't have been surprised if someone said it was spray-painted on.

"What are you doing here?" Secilia asked on instinct. "Wait. That's a stupid question. Don't tell me you want to kidnap me to blackmail Anthony into doing your bidding?"

"You're pretty smart." Selene's voice was a dark growl, which perfectly matched the sinister scowl on her face. "That is exactly what I am here for!"

Before Secilia could even retort, Selene had vanished into a shadow and reappeared out of Secilia's own shadow. Her hands had become claws, which she raised above her head, then brought down as if to tear Secilia's face off.

"Defense Mode!"

"Defense Mode: Activated."

The gloves glowed a bright blue as Secilia's arms were raised, crossed over each other to form an X. Selene brought her claws down, but they scraped off the metal of the gloves, and then they were flung wide as Secilia's arms swung out. The sudden surprise counter caused Selene's eyes to widen as she stumbled backward.

Secilia wasn't done.

"Attack Mode!"

"Attack Mode: Activated."

As if her body was being moved without her will, Secilia darted forward and attacked Selene with a series of rapid-fire punches. All of them were dodged. Selene, with her supernatural speed and reflexes, shifted on the balls of her feet as she backpedaled. A fist to the face was avoided when she tilted her body. A powerful jab missed

when Selene moved left. No matter how many attacks Secilia threw
out, none of them found their mark.

Selene jumped back, her expression a lot more cautious than before.

"I had not realized you were such a powerful combatant. I
thought the only one among Anthony's bondmates who could fight
barehanded was Brianna."

"Hmph. You should never judge a book by its cover," Selene
snorted.

"Is that so? I'll be sure to keep that in mind from now on."

Selene darted forward once more.

"Defense Mode!"

"Defense Mode: Activated."

Appearing like a ghost within a burst of speed, Selene swung
her arm wide like a lion clawing at her prey, but Secilia raised her arm
and blocked the blow, then twisted her wrist and knocked the attack
away. Selene once more stumbled.

"Attack Mode!"

"Attack Mode: Activated."

Secilia shifted into a basic combat stance, tucked her left fist into
her torso, and thrust it forward with speed and power that her small
body should not have been capable of. Selene's eyes went wide. Yet
even though she was surprised, she still evaded the attack. It passed
her by as she shifted her body left.

Unwilling to just let herself be countered like that, Selene thrust
out her hand and knocked the gloved arm back. Secilia, having never
expected such a daring counter, stumbled. Selene took advantage of

this to attack again. She didn't claw at the other woman. Instead, she launched a powerful kick that caught Secilia in the side.

With a cry of pain, Secilia's feet left the ground as she was thrown back. A gasp escaped her mouth as she landed on her side, skidded across the ground, and struck one of the many machines located inside of the room. A loud clang reverberated around her. She grimaced as her ears rang, but the pain in her ears was nothing compared to the pain in her side. It felt like her ribs had been snapped after someone smacked her with a baseball bat.

"Now I get it," Selene said as she began walking over to her. "You don't actually know martial arts at all. It's those gloves you are wearing. They somehow allow you to use martial arts without having to be taught. Very impressive. I've never seen anything like it before. But even if those gloves of yours can let you use martial arts, your weak body still isn't well suited for hand-to-hand combat."

Secilia grimaced as she slowly climbed to her feet, holding a hand to her ribs. Sharp pain stabbed her side. She tried to ignore it, but that was like trying to ignore someone shooting you in the face with a water gun.

"I'm not surprised you figured that out," she hissed. "My combat gloves are still in the testing phase. These are just a prototype. I plan to improve on them eventually and turn them into something that will let me protect myself if someone like you ever tries to attack me when Anthony and Brianna aren't around."

"Smart plan. Too bad they aren't ready right now," Selene said with a sharp smile seconds before she launched herself at Secilia.

"Defense Mode!"

"Defense Mode: activated."

Selene swung her clawed hands, but Secilia activated Foresight alongside her gloves and used her ability to see one second into the future to avoid the attack. She stepped back. As the claw swept past her with room to stare, she darted forward and slammed a fist into Selene's gut. The attack startled the vampire and caused her to grunt in pain. However, this did not stop Selene from clasping her hands, raising them above her hand, and bringing them down like a hammer on Secilia's back.

"Hurk!"

It felt like her body had been hit with a wrecking ball. Secilia was slammed into the ground so hard the floor dented underneath her. Her vision went black, then came back, then faded out again. She tried to focus, but it was too hard. She was losing consciousness quickly.

"Hmph. If Anthony hadn't been so stubborn, I wouldn't have had to resort to these methods. Well, there's nothing I can do about it now. I'll just have to use you as my bargaining chip," Selene said. It sounded like her voice was coming from far away, even though her boots were right in front of Secilia's face.

Selene leaned down and made to grab Secilia, but just before she could, the doors exploded like someone had placed an explosive on them. From within the burst of power, a figure flew into the room and rushed straight for them.

"Don't you dare touch her!"

"Shit!"

With a curse, Selene leaped far away from Secilia, who could not see the person who had rushed into the room, though she definitely recognized his voice. A powerful explosion of air howled around her. Selene, who was still in her line of sight, screamed as the blast of wind smacked into her, sending her tumbling to the ground.

A pair of shoes stepped in front of Secilia. She still couldn't move, but she knew those shoes belonged to Anthony. Relief washed over her.

"I didn't expect you to arrive so quickly," Selene said as she climbed back to her feet.

"You're pushing it, Selene," Anthony warned. "I can deal with being poisoned, but attacking my bondmate is unforgivable."

"Desperate times call for desperate measures." Selene spread her arms. "I had no choice but to try and take her. This is all your fault, you know. If you'd just let me seduce you, none of this would have happened."

"You can't blame me for being cautious, Selene Dracul."

Selene's eyes narrowed as she hissed at him. "Do not call me that!"

"Not fond of your last name? That's too bad. I'll call you whatever I damn well want."

Selene looked like she was about to attack again, but then she paused and turned her head. Her face paled. Before Secilia could wonder about that expression, the woman looked back at them.

"It seems the Time Witch has noticed me. I'll leave for now, but don't think this is the last you've seen of me. I'll come back, and whether I have to use words or force, I will get you to do what I want."

"Good luck with that," Anthony said, his voice snide.

Selene grimaced as she quickly vanished into her own shadow, disappearing from view. Anthony waited for several seconds to make sure she was really gone. Then he turned around and knelt beside Secilia.

"You okay?"

"N-not really." Secilia coughed a bit as sharp pain filled her lungs. "I think… she might have broken one of my ribs."

"In that case, I'll take you to the hospital."

Anthony scooped Secilia into his arms, lifting her as easily as if he was lifting a body pillow. Even though her chest still hurt, the moment she was in his arms, Secilia felt safe and secure. The warmth from his powerful arms and muscular chest filled her body. She relaxed into him, closing her eyes and smiling as he carried her out of the engineering lab.

CHAPTER 2

THE ACADEMY ISLAND HOSPITAL FOR MAGICAL CATASTROPHES was not the only hospital in existence on Academy Island. There were many smaller hospitals, which dealt with non-magical wounds like broken bones, stitches, and non-magical-related illnesses. The Institution of Magical Sciences didn't have a hospital, but it did have a nurse's office, which possessed all of the machinery and equipment necessary to be considered a fully functional hospital.

Since Anthony didn't want Secilia dealing with the pain any longer than necessary, he took her to the nurse's office located in Building #2.

"Her ribs are indeed broken," the nurse said. "Two of her ribs have been shattered. I am not sure how such a thing can happen. Were you hit by a hovercar?"

The nurse was a woman in her late thirties who didn't look a day over twenty. Her dark skin contrasted against the white uniform. She had long hair that was black and a bit frizzy, kind of like she had an afro but her hair had grown too long to maintain it.

"S-something like that," Secilia said with a laugh, only to hiss and wince as she pressed a hand against her side.

Secilia was sitting on the hospital bed as the nurse looked her over using a simple medical scanner. It looked like a miniature vacuum. A small holographic screen appeared above it, displaying Secilia's skeletal system. That scanner could also be used to display her organs, nervous system, veins, and basically every human body system in existence. This was a relatively new piece of tech that had shaken the medical world two years ago. It was still considered the best piece of scanning equipment today and was widely used in hospitals around the globe.

The nurse did not look too happy with her answer, but she didn't say anything more about the subject and instead said, "Healing your bones would normally be an easy process with magic, but it looks like whatever caused these bones to shatter had mana suffused into it. Before I can fix your ribs, I need to disperse the mana inside of you."

Setting the scanner aside, the nurse had Secilia lay down, placed her hands over his bondmate's ribs, and created a magic formula. It was not a complex formula. He recognized the spell as one that doctors and nurses with an aptitude for magic were taught. While there were plenty of methods that could be used to disperse the mana inside Secilia, using a spell like this was one of the fastest.

As the magic circle activated, the area around Secilia's side began glowing a bright white. Following that, what appeared to be a dark miasma emerged from her skin. The miasma wasn't thick, but there was enough to startle Anthony and Secilia. On the other hand, the nurse merely furrowed her brow as she channeled more mana into her spell, causing the magic circle to spin. The miasma also began spinning, forming what appeared to be a small cyclone as it soared into the magic circle and disappeared like mist dispersing in the summer sun.

"Okay. Now that the mana has been dispersed, I can heal the wound."

The magic formula the nurse was using changed, the symbols and patterns becoming different. This was another healing spell, though it was more complex than the previous one. Anthony knew the spell, though he could not use it himself. That was the bad thing about being an incubus. Even if he wanted to, he could not use any spell that was not related to the seven cores within his body.

As the healing spell worked its magic, Secilia sighed in relief, her body relaxing, the tension on her face vanishing. It was a clear sign that her ribs were healed.

"You are free to leave now. I don't know what you did to so thoroughly break your ribs, but try to be more careful from now on," the nurse said.

"Don't worry. I have no intention of going through that again," Secilia mumbled as she climbed off the hospital bed. She reached out to Anthony and grabbed his hand. "You heard the lady. Let's go home."

Anthony nodded as they left the nurse's office, the building, then the campus altogether. They walked to the nearest maglev station and hopped onto a maglev. It wasn't crowded, so they found a small section of the bench to sit on. Secilia leaned into his side and used his shoulder as a pillow.

"I contacted Bri and let her know what happened," Anthony said.

"You know, I've noticed that you call Brianna 'Bri,' but I'm still Secilia. Why is that?"

"Because there aren't any good pet names that can be used to shorten Secilia." Anthony would have shrugged, but he didn't want to knock her off his shoulder. "In either event, she and Marianne know what happened and are waiting at home. I also let Professor Incanscino know."

"You tell that tiny professor everything, don't you?"

"Of course. She is my benefactor... why are you looking at me like that?"

"... No reason."

Secilia had been wearing a deadpan stare when Anthony explained why he told Professor Incanscino about anything and everything that went on around him. Of course, her being his benefactor was only part of the reason, but he didn't want to get into his other reason.

Once the maglev stopped at their station, they got off and walked the rest of the way home. They entered the apartment, slipped off their shoes, and walked into the living room. There they found Marianne sitting on the couch with her feet propped on the edge. She had wrapped her arms around her knees and was watching the screen with rapt attention.

"In just two weeks' time, a peace conference will be held between the Prime Minister of the Atlantic Federation, the King of Britannia, the Vampire Warlords Elizabeth Tepes and Vlad Dracul, the

Beast King of Russia, the Nine-Tailed Fox of Japan, and the Three Succubus Queens. The peace conference is going to be held at Academy Island this year, due in large part to its independence and neutrality. This is a big event where a large number of world leaders will be gathering. I can already feel the anticipation in the air…"

"It looks like something interesting will be happening soon," Secilia said, her words causing Marianne to snap her head towards them.

"I've heard the peace conference happens once every two years." Anthony scratched his chin as Marianne unwrapped her arms from around her legs and stood up. "I didn't realize it would be taking place here though. I think the last time they had the peace conference, it took place in the Americas because it's not controlled by any government, making it neutral territory."

"Neutral. Right. You mean lawless."

Anthony shrugged at Secilia's comment and sarcastic expression.

"Welcome home, you two," Marianne said as she curtsied to them.

"Thanks," Anthony said with a smile. "I hope you weren't too bored while we were gone."

"Not at all." Marianne appeared a little more relaxed than usual as she smiled at them. He might even go so far as to say she was excited. There was a sparkle in her eyes. "I used most of the time between when you left for school and now to clean."

"I can tell." Actually, he couldn't tell, but that was because the apartment had already been spotless when he left thanks to Marianne.

"Thank you for helping us keep this place clean. None of us are what you'd call good at maintaining cleanliness."

"What are you saying? I'm the epitome of clean," Secilia said.

Anthony gave her a look. "You're the dirtiest one here."

"Rude."

Marianne's cheeks turned bright red as she beamed at him.

Secilia snorted as she walked further into the room and sat on the couch. While Marianne looked at her curiously, Anthony ignored her.

"It looks like your mom will be coming to Academy Island within the next week or so," he said.

"Yes!" The sparkle in Marianne's eyes became so bright Anthony could have sworn there were stars in them. "I know it's technically only been a few days since I saw my mother, but it feels like it's been a really long time."

"Well, you have been through a lot."

Anthony went over to the couch and sat down as well before patting the spot beside him. Marianne hesitated before shuffling over and sitting on his left. She didn't sit so close they were touching, but she still sat closer than someone who was "just a friend" would sit. He wondered if that was a sign but discarded the thought. He was planning to bond with Marianne soon, but there was a time and place for such things.

"I almost forgot this peace conference would be happening again. So much has happened in the past half a year that I haven't even thought about it," Anthony said.

"I think most of the stuff that happened to you only happened within the last two months, wouldn't you agree?" said Secilia. While it sounded like a question, she didn't give him time to answer. "There was Brianna trying to kill you, me kidnapping you, and now the incident with Marianne. All that happened within just two short months."

"Hmm. I suppose that is true," Anthony acknowledged.

"The peace conference, huh?" Secilia stared at the holographic TV. The man speaking on it was currently detailing the history of the peace conference, how it came about, and its importance to the world. "If I recall, this peace conference is one that most of the major powers within the world come to, to re-sign the Demonic Covenant."

Marianne nodded. "There are several major powers who will be in attendance. The Atlantic Federation, Russia, the European Federation, Japan, Britannia, and Academy Island. Of those powers, the European Federation is the most fractured. It's more like a land of warring states. Mother is one of the powers, but there's also Vlad Dracul who owns the west, and the former Vampire Warlord Cane who rules the south. The Succubus Queen Naamah rules her own small province close to Cane's former domain, Angrat Bat Mahlat is the ruler of Babylon, and Eisheth Zenunim rules over most of Africa. To the east is the Ogre Overlord's domain. He and Cane never participated in the peace conference."

The news played softly in the background as Marianne explained more about the various world powers. Some of it he knew, but some of it he didn't know. Back when he was Lilith's bondmate, they had occasionally traveled out of the Americas and journeyed through most of Eurasia, though they'd never gone to Russia, Japan, or the Ogre Overlord's domain.

Lilith had been well-known in many nations and could often come and go as she pleased. This was not only because of her power but also because she was an independent demon with enough power to rival the strongest factions in the entire world. No one wanted to have her as an enemy.

Thanks to her connections, Anthony had met quite a few powerful figures like Naamah, the King and Queen of Britannia, and the Prime Minister of the Atlantic Federation. Of course, he had also had the displeasure of meeting Cane. He'd even met Elizabeth Tepes, who seemed to have a special friendship with Lilith. When they were traveling through Europe, they had stayed in one of Elizabeth's private estates, though he'd oddly never met Marianne before today.

Lilith often did her best not to involve him and his brother in anything political. Her other bondmates had told him that she was very overprotective of him. Some of them had jokingly complained that it wasn't fair how she favored him so much.

"I hear ogres are a violent and warlike race," Anthony said.

"They are," Marianne confirmed with a nod. "They love war and hate peace, which is why they never participate in the peace conference. While Shuten Doji is hailed as the strongest ogre who unified the eastern part of Europe and Asia, the truth is his entire domain is just a large warzone that he created for his own amusement. Because of that, eastern Eurasia has been labeled a warzone and no one among the other nations is allowed to travel there. Mother used to send diplomats to try and negotiate with Shuten Doji, but none of them ever returned."

Shuten Doji was the name of the Ogre Overlord. Like the Beast King, the Vampire Warlords, and the Succubus Queens, he was one of the most powerful demons in existence.

The news regarding the peace conference ended and the newscaster began discussing less important topics. Secilia used this as an excuse to change the channel. She put on an action show where the plot seemed more like a thinly veiled excuse to make every object under the sun explode.

"This Shuten Doji sounds like a problem child," Anthony mumbled.

"Problem child?"

"… Never mind."

After Marianne gave him and Secilia a small lesson regarding the powers that be, the vampire decided to prepare dinner. Secilia and Anthony faced off against each other in video games for the better part of an hour.

Brianna returned home around the time Marianne was adding onions, garlic, and carrots to a large pot, but she only sat down on the couch and began working on her homework. It seemed she had to write an essay on the history of the Demonic Covenant.

Marianne finished cooking dinner. She had made braised lamb shanks with rosemary. He didn't know where she got the lamb, so he asked about it. Apparently, Marianne had gone shopping earlier that day and bought the ingredients needed to cook dinner with the money he had given her.

Dinner was eventually finished, the dishes were washed, and they all stayed up relatively late into the night sitting on the couch and watching movies. It was an odd turn of events for Anthony. He had always lived alone until meeting Brianna, but now he was living with three beautiful women—two of whom were his bondmates. If asked whether he could have imagined himself living this way back when he was still trying to resist his incubus nature, he would have said no.

Hours after dinner, Anthony lay in bed, completely naked. Secilia, also naked, lay with her body pressed against him. Light traces of sweat still remained on their skin and the heavy scent of sex clung to the air. Anthony was gently caressing Secilia's naked hips as he thought about several important matters.

"I need to get a nylon rope," he muttered. "Or something similar." Closing his eyes, he let out a tired sigh and released one last word before falling asleep. "Tomorrow."

***

Just like he had promised himself, Anthony traveled to a specialty shop the next day. School was already over. Secilia was at home, having been escorted by him, and he was alone this time.

It felt a bit odd being by himself now. In the last two months, Anthony had grown used to living beside Brianna, Secilia, and now Marianne. They had become his new norm. Being by himself no longer felt natural.

The Castle was a large store located in a seedier district of Academy Island, which contained mostly love hotels, dance clubs, and bordellos. It was only about two stories in height, but it was wider and longer than any other building present. Just looking at it from the outside, Anthony could not immediately guess that it was a sex shop, but the large sign above the door—"The Castle: For All Your Fetish Needs"—gave away exactly what this store sold.

Taking a deep breath, he walked inside.

While the outside might have made it look like an ordinary store, he could tell what this shop sold the moment he walked in. Mannequins dressed in lingerie and dominatrix outfits were on full display. Several aisles were catering to self-pleasure devices like dildos, fleshlights, and strap-ons. Another aisle had shelf upon shelf filled with oils, lubes, and scented lotions. He even saw an aisle for various types of sauce like chocolate that was meant to be smeared on someone's body and eaten off.

"It's like I stepped into Heaven," he murmured, then paused. "Or sin."

"Welcome, dear customer," someone said to his left.

Anthony turned around and caught sight of a woman with straight black hair, pale skin, and a buxom figure. She wore a dress that trailed down to her ankles. A slit running up one side allowed him to catch a glimpse of bare leg. He couldn't tell how old she was, but that was because this woman was not human. Her pointed ears, perfectly symmetrical face, and ridiculously curvy figure gave her away.

She was a succubus.

Well, a succubus running a sex shop seemed natural, at least.

Before he could ask her a question, the succubus continued. "My name is Catrina. I'm the owner of this shop. Hmmm... I do not recognize you. Is this your first time here? Please, do not hesitate to let me know if there is anything I can do to help you out."

"Actually, there is something you can do to help me," Anthony began. Since she had so kindly offered aid, he wasn't going to turn her away. "I'm looking for several strands of thin rope made from jute, hemp, or linen. Um, they should be around .23 inches in diameter and eight to nine feet long."

"Ah." The succubus woman's eyes lit up as she listened to him. "You are interested in shibari, aren't you?"

"How'd you guess?"

"Ropes made from those materials are generally used for S&M, but S&M here in the west generally uses more domineering items like shackles, chains, and chokers." Catrina studied him as a strange flash flickered across her vision. "What do you know about shibari?"

"Not much," Anthony admitted.

"Then I believe I should first tell you that shibari is actually a word that gained popularity here in the west. Shibari is quite possibly a misuse of Japanese vocabulary. The word itself denotes a generic form of tying in Japanese. It simply means 'to tie.' The actual Japanese word used to describe erotic bondage is 'Kinbaku,' which involves tying a person up using simple yet visually intricate and aesthetically pleasing patterns. The word 'shibari' somehow came into common use here in the west at some point to describe the bondage art, Kinbaku."

Anthony listened to the woman with rapt attention. He didn't know if this information would be in any way useful, but he believed it was appropriate to learn what he could about the activity he wanted to try.

Catrina gestured for him to follow her and began walking down an aisle. It was an aisle filled with all kinds of BDSM items like shackles, manacles, ball gags, and so on. As she led him down the aisle, Catrina continued talking.

"In Japan, the most often used type of rope is a loose laid, three strand jute rope. It's referred to as 'asanawa' and usually translated as 'hemp rope.' The word 'asa' is translated as 'hemp' and 'nawa' as rope. That said, this is technically a more generic form of the word hemp and refers to a range of natural fiber ropes rather than one pertaining to a specific plant. The most often used rope in shibari is jute."

"Why is jute the most often used rope?" asked Anthony.

"Probably because it's soft and won't irritate the skin if someone is bound by it," Catrina stated before leading him to a section with various kinds of rope. There were a lot of different colored ropes too, from pink to black to red to blue. Catrina went to the black rope. "I'm assuming your lover has pale skin. In which case, I would recommend this black jute rope. It has the six-millimeter diameter you're looking for and is thirty feet in length—more than enough for you to use. You won't even need to buy more strands, which would be less cost-effective."

"Okay."

Since Anthony had no idea what he was getting into, he simply agreed with Catrina. She smiled as if she knew what he was thinking.

Grabbing a bunch of rope, she coiled it up and handed it to him, then began moving again.

"Since you've also never practiced shibari before, it would be in your best interest to grab a few books on the subject," she said. "There are many people who want to begin practicing bondage without actually studying the subject. This often results in their partner getting hurt from malpractice. If you wish to avoid that, it is imperative that you learn about Shibari and its various practices before attempting to do anything yourself."

"That makes a lot of sense. What books would you recommend?" asked Anthony.

In response to his question, Catrina led him to an aisle filled with books, which made him feel very odd. He knew they were all related to sex, but part of him simply couldn't associate books with a sex shop.

Catrina grabbed several books, which she began stacking into his hands: *Bondage: A Practical Manual for Beginners: Shibari and Kinbaku, Shibari You Can Use: Japanese Rope Bondage and Erotic Macrame, Essence of Shibari: Kinbaku and Japanese Rope Bondage,* and *The Seductive Art of Japanese Bondage.*

Anthony stared at the books being stacked onto his hands. They weren't very big. The largest one looked like it was maybe two hundred pages, but it would still take a long time to read through all of these.

"To start off, I would recommend *A Practice Manual for Beginners,*" Catrina suggested. "That should give you a starting point to begin practicing shibari. Once you've studied that, you can move on to the other books, which introduce more complex concepts and patterns that are used in shibari."

"I understand. I'll start with that then."

Anthony was very glad this woman was so helpful. He was already beginning to feel overwhelmed by how much reading and studying he would have to do. All he really wanted was to tie up Secilia and have his way with her.

Had he known in advance that so much research would be involved, he might have not come here, but now that he had, his desire to tie up Secilia was even stronger.

He paid the woman for the items and left the store with a large bag in hand. Because this type of shop specialized in products that were not quite acceptable to be displayed in public, they didn't have a delivery service like other stores. The bag was also nondescript. No one would know he'd just bought bondage equipment unless they looked in his bag.

As he left the seedier part of the city and merged with the flow of traffic, traveling to the nearest maglev station, a sudden feeling that he was being watched washed over him. He turned his head and frowned when he saw a smiling Selene striding over to him.

"I thought I told you not to come near me and mine ever again," Anthony said, his voice hard.

Selene didn't seem bothered by his vicious words at all, and in fact, she smiled all the wider when she heard him speak. This made his frown grow even more stern, but she ignored that too.

"I never thought I'd see you exiting a sex shop. Then again, you are an incubus. I suppose it is only natural for you to grow curious about such places."

"What do you want? Spit it out now, or I'll just ignore you."

Anthony was not in the mood to deal with this woman at all. He already felt a good deal of hatred for her because of what she had done to Secilia. The only reason he didn't attack her right now was because they were in public.

"I want you to help me kill someone," Selene said, the smile leaving her face.

Her words made Anthony smile, but it was a cold smile. "You must be dreaming if you think I would ever help you with anything, much less killing someone."

He began walking away. Selene, however, was not willing to leave things at that and followed him.

As they walked side by side, the eyes of many people were drawn toward them. It was, perhaps, natural. Selene was a gorgeous woman who could make any straight man turn their head and stare at her, and Anthony was admittedly an attractive young man with a supernatural allure that caused women of all ages to do the same.

Anthony still wished they would stop staring.

"I know you are angry at me for what I did... and I am sorry about that," Selene admitted, though she sounded reluctant to his ears. She took a deep breath. "However, you are the only person I can turn to. There is no one else who can help me."

Despite his anger, Anthony would admit that he was curious to know who she wanted him to kill. It wasn't often someone came to him with a request to help them kill someone. This was, in fact, a first for him.

Yet for however curious he was, Anthony was even more disgusted by the methods Selene had used to try and coerce him into doing her bidding. First, she tried to seduce him. When that didn't work, she poisoned him and tried to coerce him with a cure. When Marianne cured him of his poison, she attacked Secilia in an attempt to kidnap the woman and use her as a hostage to force him into doing what she wanted. Her methods were all despicable and only made his dislike of her grow even more.

"Maybe if you had come to me earnestly and honestly from the beginning, I would have at least heard you out." Anthony paused long enough to glare at her. The hatred in his eyes set the woman rocking back on her heels. A startled look finally appeared in her wide eyes. "But instead of simply coming up and asking me for help, you tried to force me. Even worse, you hurt my Secilia and tried to kidnap her."

Secilia had already been kidnapped once by Mendez. His protective nature had been running hot ever since that moment, so even the slightest action taken against Secilia would have invoked his wrath.

"There is no way I would ever help someone like you. You tried to manipulate me, but more importantly, you hurt my bondmate. Let me make one thing clear. If I ever catch you anywhere near one of my bondmates again, I will kill you," he said, and this time, his voice was a snarl so vicious Selene actually trembled in place as her already pale features became even paler.

Anthony glared at the woman before snorting and walking away. She didn't follow him.

***

Brianna still wasn't home when he returned, but Secilia and Marianne were present. It looked like Secilia was teaching Marianne how to play the video game system he owned.

The system itself was pretty old. It wasn't a VR system but one that you played by watching the holographic TV. Players wore a set of gloves, which they could use to manipulate their avatar. The movement of the hands and fingers corresponded to the movements of the character. For example, if a player wanted to run, they had to pump their hands back and forth as if they were running. If they wanted to use a weapon, they could grab at where their weapon was located on their avatar's body—their hip, for example. The system was very easy to use, but since it wasn't VR, the experience was a bit limiting.

Marianne seemed to be having fun at least.

"You're back. About time." Secilia was the first to notice his presence. She glanced at the bag in his hand as he slipped out of his shoes. "What did you buy?"

"Nothing much," Anthony said. "Just some accessories I needed for something. Anyway, would you mind following me for a moment? There's something I wanted to talk to you about."

"Um. Okay."

It was clear that Secilia had no idea what he wanted to talk about, but she dutifully followed Anthony to the master bedroom. Once they were inside and the door slid shut, he waved his wristwatch over the monitor, and the locking mechanism activated.

"Anthony?" Secilia asked uncertainly.

Anthony set the bag down by the door, turned to Secilia, and closed the distance between them. Before she even had a chance to squawk, his mouth was hampering hers with a hungry kiss. He didn't stop there. Anthony reached behind Secilia, grabbed a handful of her butt cheeks, and lifted her off the ground.

Although she was surprised by his sudden actions, she soon got over her surprise and reciprocated. Her kiss was passionate, if a little uncertain, and her tongue danced against his, sending arcs of electric pleasure straight to his brain. She wrapped her arms around his neck and her legs around his waist as Anthony pushed her back against the wall.

Their breathing became heavy as the intensity of their kiss grew ever more passionate. Anthony wasn't even bothered by the saliva dripping down their chins as he pushed his body against her. Secilia's muffled moans, the scent of her body, and the feeling of her pressed fully against him were all that mattered.

He wanted more.

Anthony did not let Secilia leave that wall, but he did set her down so he could remove her shirt and shorts. She was wearing a standard pink shirt today. Her shorts were the kind that rode so high up her hips that her butt cheeks were almost showing. He lifted the shirt above her head, revealing her white bra, and then knelt in front of her and undid the buttons and zipper before sliding the shorts down her stocking-clad legs.

He didn't just remove her shorts. He also removed her under-wear along with it, exposing her beautiful pussy to the world. He gazed at her slightly wet lips with a hungry gleam in his eyes.

"Anthony... haaaah... you're being unusually aggressive toddaaaaayyy! Oooooh!"

Secilia's words were lost and her eyes went wide as Anthony leaned up, pressed his tongue against her snatch, and dragged it across her from top to bottom. Her lips parted for his tongue. The taste of her pussy was divine, and he needed more. He wrapped his arms around her legs to keep her in place and dined on her like a man who had gone without a meal for several decades.

"Haht! Haaa! Anthony! You're tongue! Haaa! Haaa! S-so deep...!"

With such a passionate kiss, there was no way Secilia could keep quiet. Her moans became louder, her breathing heavier, and her body began shaking. She pressed her head against the wall and released that beautiful music that drove Anthony insane. His desire for her sky-rocketed and caused him to swirl his tongue around her clit. Secilia, who had just undone the front clasp on her bra, shuddered from head to toe and released a loud scream as she orgasmed.

"Haaah... haaaah... haaaaah... Anthony... what...?"

Secilia's body was slumping against the wall, but she didn't fall because he was keeping her in place. When he looked up, it was to find his bondmate, her body covered in a glistening layer of sweat, hair matted to her forehead, and her breasts, now free from their con-fines, heaving and jiggling as she tried to regain control over her breathing.

Anthony stood up, removed his shirt, his pants, and his underwear. He was now wearing nothing more than his socks, which he simply couldn't be bothered with. Now more or less naked, he pressed his body against hers. His cock became wedged between her lips now puffy with arousal.

"I want you right now," he said.

Secilia's eyes widened and her already flushed cheeks gained several more shades of red. This was one of the few times he'd ever been so demanding. Even when they had rough sex, he was still gentle. This new demeanor seemed to shock her, but more than that, her pussy became even wetter at the commanding tone in his voice. Clear liquid dripped down her inner thighs.

"If you... if you want me... then you should... just take me," she said, her breathing growing even heavier, headier, and needier.

"Turn around," he commanded.

Secilia shivered as she turned around, presenting her beautiful ass to him. Her butt cheeks were perfectly round and springy. Anthony licked his lips as he placed his hands on her rear. Secilia released a soft whimper as he began massaging her butt cheeks.

"Anthony... Ahn!"

If Secilia had been about to say something, she stopped the moment Anthony thrust himself inside of her. It was a single, swift action. Her pussy conformed around his cock, lips spreading open to make way. The sensation of being inside of her was pleasant, but while some part of him wanted to bask inside of her, another part just wanted to fuck her silly.

So that was what he did.

Anthony did not set a steady rhythm or a gentle pace. He pulled his dick out until just the tip was still inside, then rammed it inside of her before repeating the process. Secilia released a sound that was halfway between a scream and a moan. Her breasts became sandwiched against the wall from the power of his thrusts.

"Hnn! Hrrn! Hyk! Haaaa! Ahn! F-fuck! This is93677918haaa! Ahn! Haaa! S-so intense!"

Those were the few words Secilia was able to get out as he continued his fast and powerful thrusts. Her pussy was not as tight as Brianna's, which made it easier to deliver such thrusts. At the same time, the feeling of her walls rubbing against him as he pushed himself as far into her as it could go created an incredible sensation he'd never felt with anyone else. Rather than a vice, her cunt felt more like a soft sleeve that he was sliding into.

No longer content with just this, Anthony pulled Secilia back until her back was pressed against his chest, grabbed her thighs, and lifted her into the air.

"Ahhhnn?!"

Secilia's cry was of both pleasure and surprise. Anthony paid only a little attention to it as he walked over to the full-body mirror that led to the closet space and stood before it.

"Look at how lewdly your legs are spread right now," Anthony whispered into Secilia's ear. His voice was a low growl that caused Secilia to moan and shudder. "See how your pussy is spreading for my cock? How does it feel to see this? How does it feel to have my dick thrust inside of you?"

"It feels... it feels good... haaah... aaaahn... haaaah... haaaaah..."

Secilia's eyes were half-lidded as she looked at their reflections in the mirror. Anthony was behind her, holding her up by her legs and leaning back slightly so she wouldn't fall forward. Her legs were spread wide, allowing them to perfectly see himself spreading her apart as he plowed her from behind. Her juices were leaking from her lips, trailing down his dick, balls, and thighs. The sight made Secilia's pussy clamp down around him and pulsate as she orgasmed again. More of her juices drenched his thighs and the floor, creating a small damp spot that would have to be steam cleaned at some point.

Anthony still wasn't done.

He maintained his vigorous thrusting, his abdominals flexing with every thrust of his hips. His back muscles were straining as he maintained this position and his arms were becoming a little sore, but he had no intention of stopping now. Maintaining this position as he continued to fuck her, Anthony began kissing her neck with rough, passionate kisses. Secilia leaned her head back and moaned.

Anthony had no idea how long he continued with his current actions. Time lost meaning when he was with his bondmates. The feeling of being inside of her, of their bodies pressed together, of the bond between them flaring up and creating a feedback loop that enhanced the pleasure each of them was experiencing, all of it combined to create a moment in time that he wished could go on forever.

It was unfortunate that everything had an end.

Anthony's end came when his balls tightened. He released a sound that was like a low roar as he thrust his length so far into

Secilia's wet crevice that it felt like he had poked her cervix, then shot load after load of cum deep inside of her. Secilia's toes curled, her thighs tightened, and her pussy twitched and pulsed around him as she orgasmed again.

Anthony felt mana flowing into him through their bond, filling him up, capping him out. At the moment, he couldn't take in any more mana, so if there was any excess, it would simply leak into the atmosphere.

A sense of exhaustion came over him as he walked backward until his legs hit the bed. He allowed himself to fall back, bouncing once. Secilia lay on top of him, her body heavy as she breathed in and out. It was the nasally sound of someone who was having trouble catching their breath.

Secilia eventually recovered enough to turn around. She curled her legs onto the bed as she straddled his hips and pressed her face against his sweaty chest. Anthony was sure he smelled, but Secilia rubbed her face against him like a cat seeking affection. She kissed him once, then lifted her head to gaze at him.

"Did something happen?" she asked. "I certainly don't mind the rough sex, but you were a lot more aggressive today than I've ever seen you."

Anthony sighed as he placed his hands on Secilia's lower back, stroking his fingers along her spinal cord. She bit her lip and arched her back like a cat did when its owner was petting it.

"I ran into Selene today," he admitted.

"Ah," was all Secilia said.

"She's still trying to convince me to kill someone for her, but all I could think about was how she hurt you." He sighed and looked away. "It made me angry."

"And being angry made you horny and full of lust." Secilia nodded several times as if it all made sense. "I understand now. That's an incubus for you. Any powerful emotion is enough to turn you into a horndog."

"That is an awfully rude and racist thing to say about incubi," Anthony said. "I'd go on strike, but you'd probably just laugh at me."

"I definitely would."

Anthony raised a hand and placed it against Secilia's cheek, stroking her cheek with his thumb. Secilia closed her eyes and leaned into him.

"After confronting Selene and remembering what she did, I guess I was just feeling a little possessive. Sorry about that."

"Hey, I'm not complaining." Secilia grinned at him. "Any time you feel like taking your frustrations out on something, feel free to come to me. I am more than willing to have sex like this again."

"Mmm. I will."

Anthony leaned up, placed one arm behind himself, and pulled Secilia into a kiss. This one, unlike his previous ones, was a lot more tender, filled with his love instead of his lust. Secilia sighed into the kiss. She threaded her fingers through his sweaty hair and scraped her nails against his scalp. It was a wonderful feeling. However, the moment they began kissing, Anthony became hard again.

"You incubi really are the horniest creatures I've ever met," Secilia murmured as she rubbed her nether lips against the long, hard, hot rod trapped between her thighs. "I hope you realize I'm not having sex with you right now. I feel too raw."

Anthony nodded seriously. "I know. Pay it no mind. That thing has a mind of its own."

"Hmph. Mind of its own, my ass. You're just a lecher."

"Says the woman who created a puddle on the floor."

"It wasn't a puddle!"

Before their banter could really get going, someone knocked on the door.

"Um, er, ah... A-Anthony? Secilia?" It was Marianne, and she sounded embarrassed. "I, um... I know you are busy with, er, stuff... b-but dinner is ready now. A-also, Brianna is here. Could you two please, um, make yourselves presentable and come out? Thank you!"

They didn't get a chance to answer Marianne before the sound of her footsteps faded. A moment of silence passed between them as Anthony looked at the clock.

"Whoa. It's already that late?" Anthony mumbled like he could believe it.

"I guess we were in here longer than either of us realized," Secilia said. "That's an incubus for you. You've got stamina like a stallion."

"If you're trying to create an adequate simile to describe my sexual prowess, then that was a horrible attempt."

"You shut your whore mouth, or I'll shut it for you."

"... Yes, dear."

CHAPTER 3

ANTHONY SPENT MUCH OF THE FOLLOWING WEEK doing everything he usually did, with the addition of also studying up on shibari. Even now, the sight of Secilia tied up caused his body to burn. He often wondered if he might have found his fetish, but he didn't think it was that, not really, because otherwise, wouldn't he have already discovered his enjoyment of bondage back when he was Lilith's mate?

While he didn't know what sort of feelings were spurring him on, that did not stop him from fervently learning what he could about Shibari, which induced him to read three of the four books he bought in rapid succession. He only had one more book left to read: *The Seductive Art of Japanese Bondage*. Anthony was fairly confident that he could perform shibari now. However, he was waiting for the right time to bring this matter up with Secilia.

In the meantime, he stuck to having normal sex with Secilia and Brianna.

That probably… wasn't a good thing.

"Ahn! Ah! Ah! Haaa! Haht! Hrrrnnn! Oooooh!"

The sound of flesh slapping against flesh echoed around the room as Anthony's thighs smacked against Brianna's ass as he took her from behind. She was standing. However, she was bent over the bed, arms being held behind her back by him, torso arching as he gently pulled her back, and he was churning her insides with his gentle but powerful thrusts. Red hair draped over either side of her body like a curtain. Her back glistened with sweat.

The scent of sex was heavy in the air.

Anthony did not know how long they'd been having sex. It could have been a few minutes or a few hours. All he knew was the feeling of her tight passage squeezing him like a vice, rubbing against him in ways that made him delirious with pleasure, the scent of her sweaty body filling his nose, and the sight of her exhausted frame shaking and heaving as he brought her to yet another orgasm.

"Nnnggg!"

Brianna's body spasmed, her back arched, and drool leaked down from her chin as another orgasm hit her. How many did this make now? Ten? Fifteen? Anthony grunted as her pussy convulsed around his cock and shot his fourth or fifth load of cum inside of her. He jerked his hips a few times. Once he stopped cumming, he lowered Brianna's upper body onto the bed and pulled his dick from her with a wet pop.

Standing back, Anthony spent a long moment studying Brianna. While her torso was on the bed, her jelly-like legs were dangling over the edge, her feet resting on the floor, twitching with the after-effects of so many orgasms. Even her toes were periodically twitching as if all the nerve endings in her feet had been struck by an electric shock.

Her back, legs, and ass were covered in a thick layer of sweat. Her shoulders heaved as she gasped for breath. She had closed her eyes, which meant he could see her long and beautiful eyelashes. Sweat also coated her scalp and face, causing her bangs to stick to her forehead.

A combination of their sexual fluids was leaking from her pussy. His dick grew hard again.

Because he simply needed more, Anthony placed a hand on Brianna's shoulder and turned her onto her back. Brianna's half-lidded eyes were glazed over. It didn't look like she was all there. She only came to when he started rubbing his dick against her outer labia once more.

"Anthony... please... I can't... can't go another round with you... I'm too tired..."

As she spoke those words in between her pants, Anthony's body shivered as an internal struggle took place inside of him. He was so horny. Granted, this was nothing unusual. He felt like he was becoming hornier with each passing day, which perhaps was one of the reasons he'd begun reading up on Shibari. He wanted to find something that could satisfy his sexual urges.

At the same time, for as sexually active as he was, for as high as his libido was, he didn't want to be the kind of boyfriend who would not listen to his girlfriend... girlfriends. Anthony wanted to place their needs above his own. He took several deep breaths and tried to calm down. It didn't work, not really, but since she was asking him to stop, he couldn't say no.

"Okay. I'm sorry, Bri. It seems I went overboard again."

Brianna shook her head, but it was clear from the fluttering of her eyelashes as she struggled to keep her eyes open that she was exhausted.

"It's... fine. I know... this is just... how you are. You need this. Sorry, I can't... be of more help..."

"No, you help me plenty. I'm the one who needs to learn self-restraint."

Anthony was careful not to let his dick rub against Brianna's nether lips as he leaned over and gave her a gentle kiss. The content sigh Brianna released as she kissed back made him feel relieved.

"Anyway, I'm gonna take a cold shower. Maybe that will cool me down."

"Mmm."

Anthony went over to the door, though he didn't leave right away, but instead turned toward Brianna as she lay on the bed, her thighs and calves hanging over the edge, feet resting against the floor. He had to turn away again. A fire exploded inside of his belly, urging him to claim her once more.

Now somewhat fearful of this intense lust, Anthony went into the shower and turned it onto its coldest setting. The freezing cold water was intense enough to make him feel like he was bathing in a tub of ice. He shivered as goosebumps appeared on his skin, but the freezing cold chill brought clarity and caused his burning body to calm down. It worked. That was all that mattered.

After taking a quick shower, Anthony grabbed some cloth and a bucket, which he filled with lukewarm water. He went back into the bedroom where Brianna was. She was still on the bed, in the same position she had been in when he left, but she was completely conked out. It looked like she'd fallen asleep while he was taking a shower.

Anthony went over and knelt beside her, placed the bucket on the ground, and grabbed the cloth. He wrung it out until it was damp, then began cleaning her body. He started with the gap between her thighs since it was dripping with his cum, but then cleaned off her inner thighs, calves, and feet. He also wiped the sweat off her chest and back.

Brianna didn't respond much when he was cleaning her legs, but she did produce several erotic moans when he cleaned her large chest. Her breasts were pretty sensitive. Her nipples stiffened under his touch, but he focused entirely on just making sure she was clean. He even rolled her over and cleaned her back.

Once Anthony had wiped Brianna down, he lifted her into his arms and placed her fully on the bed, allowing her head to rest on the pillows. He pulled the covers over her body. It was warm, so she probably didn't need it, but he thought she'd be more comfortable with her modesty protected like this. After placing a single kiss on her forehead, Anthony got dressed in simple black pants and a white shirt before leaving the room.

He wandered into the living room. The sounds of the holographic TV playing made him look over to find Secilia sitting down and watching the news. The holographic screen was depicting a person walking out of an airplane. It was a man whose face was covered in thick fur that reminded him of a lion's mane. He had golden eyes, lion ears on his head, and a body so muscular that Anthony worried his military-esque uniform might tear.

"Just this morning, the famous Beast King of Russia, Ivan Sil'yazhelyy, arrived on Academy Island for the upcoming peace conference with his wife and daughter."

As if the words "wife and daughter" drew attention to them, Anthony glanced behind the man as he walked down the boarding ramp. Two people were following him.

One of them was a woman whose age was hard to guess. She didn't look much older than twenty and could have passed for the other woman's older sister, but the way she carried herself made her seem older and more mature. Her hair was cut short. It also had a leopard print pattern and the ears on her head looked like those of a cheetah. She wore a long white gown with a dip in the front that displayed her large chest. She was even more bodacious than Brianna. Her pneumatic knockers were practically bursting from her clothes.

The person next to her looked more like a girl than a woman. She had long hair that trailed down to her butt. It reminded him of threads spun from gold, an intense golden color that was brighter than the sun. She had the same golden eyes as her father. Likewise, her ears were also those of a lion's.

Her golden hair framed a face that he would have called cute but seductive. The confident smile plastered on her face offset the youthfulness of her features. She had a small nose, cute pink lips, and a round chin. However, that smile, which bordered on a smirk, gave her the look of someone whose confidence in herself could probably be taken as a form of arrogance.

She had a body that could rival her mother's, though her breasts weren't as big and her hips weren't as wide. Unlike the woman beside her, this girl was wearing a military-esque uniform similar to her father. It had epaulets on the shoulders, was predominantly blue in color with red lining the hem and sleeves, and seemed to be similarly straining against her body. It looked like the buttons would pop off her chest, though for a different reason than her father.

"I see you finally deigned to leave your bedroom," Secilia said from where she sat. Her expression as she watched him sit down was quite... something. "You know, I've been thinking about this for a while, but we should invest in insulators to keep any sounds that come out of the bedroom from reaching us. I don't mind listening to you make Brianna scream, but poor Marianne over there is burning up."

At the mention of her name, Marianne squeaked. Anthony glanced at the girl to find that she was setting the table. Her cheeks were dark, stained as they were with all the blood rushing to her face, and her lips quivered. When she noticed him looking at her, she busied herself with her work and tried to pretend she hadn't noticed his gaze.

"You bring up a good point," he said with a sigh. "I'll look into getting some kind of insulation that can block out sound."

Because he couldn't stand to see Marianne doing all the work, Anthony stood up and began helping her set the table.

"Y-you don't have to do that," Marianne said.

"Maybe I don't, but I want to help." He smiled at her. "We're all living here, so we should all do our part. Isn't that right, Secilia?"

When he called the dark-haired young woman out, Secilia raised her hand and flipped him off.

Marianne's expression froze, but then a grateful smile appeared on her blushing face. "Then, um, thank you for the help."

"I feel like I should be the one saying that," Anthony said. "Anyway, since it smells like you're cooking breakfast, leave setting the table to me."

Anthony set the table as Marianne scurried back into the kitchen. He didn't know what she was making, but the scent of eggs wafting over to him was tantalizing and made his mouth water.

I wonder when I should ask Marianne to become my bondmate...?

He'd been thinking about making Marianne his third bondmate for a while now, but he was a little worried about scaring her off. She could act confident when needed. However, she could only keep her facade going when in public and didn't include acts of seduction. She'd already tried several times to confidently seduce him, only to become too embarrassed each time.

Though it is cute.

It was during this time that Brianna stumbled into the room, walking with a pronounced limp. Her eyes were still lidded. She looked tired, but she wandered over to the table and sat down, though her entire body slumped forward as she rested her head against the table.

"Looks like someone got fucked good," Secilia said when she saw the state Brianna was in.

"Mmm." It was a testament to how tired she was that Brianna didn't react by blushing and blasting Secilia for her crude language. Anthony once again felt a small pang of guilt. He knew he needed more bondmates, but it wasn't like bondmates just fell from the sky, and the only one he could conceive asking to become his next bondmate acted like a frightened rabbit being cornered by a tiger.

Marianne came out from the kitchen with breakfast, which Anthony was surprised to discover was an open sandwich with scrambled eggs and smoked salmon. It was lightly seasoned with salt and pepper. She also made a coffee with lots of cream and sugar for Brianna, who accepted the beverage with a tired smile.

"So what is the plan for today?" Anthony asked.

"I have school," Brianna muttered with a tired sigh. She took a sip of the steaming beverage in her hands. Nothing happened at first, but she seemed to feel better after a couple more sips.

"I want to test out some new equipment I made," Secilia told him. "I've created some prototypes I never got to really test out because I was attacked by Selene. Speaking of, have you seen her recently?"

Anthony shook his head. "I haven't seen her since our confrontation last week. She hasn't been attending classes either."

Selene tilted her head and considered his words. "Her identity as a student was probably just a front to get close to you. Now that you've summarily rejected her, she has no reason to attend."

"I know."

Anthony sighed and ran a hand through his hair. He was, in some ways, grateful that Selene seemed to have backed off, but it also made him nervous. She didn't seem like the kind of woman who gave up easily. Her silence made him feel like, rather than giving up, she would do something even more extreme to make him comply with her demands. He was worried Brianna, Selene, or even Marianne would get caught up in her schemes.

"What about you, Mari?" asked Anthony.

"Me?" Marianne blinked several times and pointed at herself. "I'm planning to go shopping. We're almost out of food."

"In that case, I will go with you," Anthony said.

"Y-you don't have to do that."

"Actually, I wanted to talk to you about something important, and going with you to help shop for groceries gives me a good excuse, so let me tag along, okay?"

"Well... okay. So long as you don't mind."

Anthony and Marianne looked at each other for several long moments. The world itself seemed to move out of focus. Even Brianna and Secilia seemed to disappear from Anthony's vision.

Marianne had been living with them ever since they rescued her, but the two of them had never really spent any time alone together. Anthony was afraid of pushing too hard. He didn't want to come onto her too strongly because he feared being rejected by her. At the same time, he knew they needed to at least speak soon. The two of them had been dancing around each other for the past week.

"Looks like we've become a pair of third wheels," Secilia said to Brianna.

"I do not know how two people can both become a third wheel, but this is a good thing," Brianna said. "Anthony should have spoken with Marianne last week."

Secilia shrugged. She couldn't disagree.

***

While the vast majority of Academy Island was all city, there were several sections of the island that had not been turned into a metropolitan jungle of steel and glass. These areas were designated as nature preservation zones and located around the outskirts of the island. They were covered in thick vegetation. Trees and a variety of plants grew without care, creating a canopy that made it hard to see through.

Nature preservation zones had been created not only to preserve nature and animals but also to prevent further damage to the ozone. Academy Island studied everything under the sun, not just magic and technology, but also zoology and various other branches of natural science. Thanks to the creation of these nature preservation zones, the quality of Academy Island's air remained high.

Near the southern peninsula existed a rocky cliff covered in that vegetation. To the unknowing eye, it looked like nothing more than a natural land formation. The cliff was several hundred yards high. Waves crashed against the cliff far below. There was absolutely nothing about this area that seemed out of place.

Unless someone traveled beneath the surface.

In an underground bunker far below, an old man was standing in front of a streamlined jet alongside several people dressed as members of the Academy Island's Private Security Forces. Each person stood straight, snapped at attention. They looked like soldiers getting ready to be drilled by their instructor. In their hands was the latest assault rifle from Armas Weaponry—a company located in the Philippines that specialized in the creation of high-grade weaponry.

Felton stood with his hands behind his back. He waited and watched as several workers moved a boarding ramp to the jet's door, which opened seconds later to reveal a man standing behind it. The man who walked down was the same one he had been talking to last week. He looked even older than Felton himself. His aged skin was wrinkled and possessed sunspots. Despite his old age, he still walked with his back straight and had clear eyes that possessed a sharp intellect.

"Lord Christoph, it is good to see you again."

Felton bowed to the man before him, but the one called Lord Christoph merely chuckled like a doting grandfather as he raised a hand.

"There is no need for that. You and I have been comrades for many years. How have you been, Felton?"

"I have been kept busy," Felton admitted. "Working on the Board of Directors for this wretched island has left me unable to find any time for other pursuits."

"You are doing the honorable task of sowing the seeds for humanity's rise. It might be black and rancid to work alongside these monsters, but I believe it will all pay off in the end. Your commitment to our cause will be glorified for generations to come."

"Thank you for your kind words."

The soldiers who were with them fell in line as Felton and Christoph walked out of the hidden docking bay and down a long hallway. Their footsteps echoed back to them.

This underground base was one of several that belonged to the Sons of Liberty. It wasn't large, but it did possess several floors, a couple thousand people worth of personnel, and a large armory where all of their weapons and ammunition were located. Felton had created this base and several others in preparation for the coming extermination.

They eventually reached a small lobby. It looked like a sitting room. The metal floor shifted to soft red carpet, lounge chairs had been arrayed around the room, and several tables sat between them. There was even a bar with several different drinks available. While Christoph sat down, Felton went over to the bar and poured himself and his companion a glass of brandy.

"Thank you," Christoph said as he took the offered glass. "It has been a long time since I had a good glass of brandy. I see you still carry the good stuff."

"I enjoy a nice drink every so often, so I make sure to stay stocked." Felton sat down in the chair opposite his compatriot, glass in hand. He took a slow sip, allowing the liquid to burn down his throat, then set the glass on the table and stared at the older gentleman. "Now onto business. I've been smuggling weapons and personnel into Academy Island for the last five years. We now have five thousand troops at our disposal, along with several tesla tanks, attack helicopters, and fighter jets."

"Five thousand isn't a large number," Christoph warned.

"It's not, but it should be enough for what we have planned," Felton replied.

Christoph leaned back in his chair. "And what is the plan?"

"I'm currently in charge of setting the stage for the peace conference," Felton began, swirling the brandy around in his glass. "I
plan on having my men plant several high-grade explosives underneath the conference hall. When the signing takes place, we will activate the explosives and blow the entire peace conference apart."

"That might kill many of the people in attendance, but it won't
be enough to kill the main players. The Vampire Warlords, Succubus
Queens, the Nine-Tailed Fox, and the Beast King are powerful individuals. It will take more than a few explosives to defeat them,"
Christoph said.

"I'm aware. This is just the opening act." Felton took a sip of
brandy before speaking again. "After bringing chaos to the peace conference, our men will storm the area and begin systematically eradicating everyone present. Our men are equipped with anti-magic bullets, silver bullets, and magic piercing rounds. The helicopters also
use anti-magic rounds, and the tesla tanks are great for dealing large-
scale damage to the surrounding infrastructure. They can easily penetrate through the flesh of therianthropes and will break the magic
barriers of the Vampire Warlords and Succubus Queens. Without
their leaders, the remaining demons will be much easier to eradicate."

Christoph said nothing for a long while. Felton was not bothered
by this and used that time to sip down the remainder of his brandy.

His compatriot was someone who calculated and thought about
everything before speaking, especially on important subjects such as
this. Christoph had not lived to the ripe old age of eighty-five by being
stupid. His cold calculations had led to him being able to integrate
himself into a society he hated without anyone knowing he was a

terrorist, or that the Sons of Liberty was an organization dedicated to the eradication of demons and not a humane charity group.

Of course, even with his careful calculations and planning, there were still some who knew what the Sons of Liberty really was, but they lacked the evidence to prove it. If anyone tried something against him, it would look like the strong bullying the weak. Christoph could use his vast influence to turn public opinion against his enemies. He was a master of emotional manipulation.

"Yes, that is a sound plan," Christoph said at last. "It's simple, but no plan survives first contact with the enemy. This should work as the opening salvo, and we can adapt the plan as needed once it's underway."

"Those were my thoughts exactly," Felton said.

"I should warn you, however, that you will be cut loose should you fail."

"I know the risks."

"So long as you are aware. We cannot have anyone suspecting the Sons of Liberty are anything more than a peaceful organization, not until our enemies are eradicated and there's no one else to oppose us."

"Yes, I understand. Don't worry. If I fail in my task, feel free to cut me loose. Better to sever a limb than gouge out the heart."

"I could not have said it better myself."

The two compatriots smiled. They were on the same page.

"It seems we are finally nearing the era in which we humans will reign supreme." Christoph smiled. "I believe this calls for a toast."

Felton also smiled as he poured them both some more brandy.
As their glasses clinked together, he thought about all the hard work
he had put into this one moment. Finally, after years of toiling away,
he could begin ridding the world of all the filth that infested it.

***

While grocery stores had fallen out of favor because most people simply didn't have time to prepare home-cooked meals, that didn't
mean they no longer existed. Some people still believed in more tra-
ditional values. A few families still enjoyed sitting down together and
eating a meal cooked with love instead of something prepared for the
sake of convenience. It was because of these people that grocery
stores still existed today.

The one Anthony and Marianne were shopping at was small. It
had several aisles filled with produce, poultry, fish, dairy products,
and bread. There were canned goods, brand-name sauces, packaged
pasta, and so on. Only a few people were located in this store, which
explained why it wasn't very large. They probably didn't get more
than a few hundred customers a day. That wasn't a lot for a store located inside of a city with a population of nearly 1.5 billion people.

"What are we getting?" asked Anthony as he pushed a small cart
in front of him, following behind Marianne.

Marianne looked at the holographic display on her wristwatch.
It was brand new, black, and had a sleeker design than his own. Pro-
fessor Incanscino had helped her acquire it despite how she wasn't an
Academy Island citizen.

"Um… we need packaged pasta, tomato sauce, ground turkey, flour, milk, eggs…"

Anthony listened as the girl listed off several dozen items. No wonder their food expenses had increased so much. This was going to make it more difficult to budget their expenses in the future. Anthony wondered if he should try applying for a job, but between school, training, sex, and trying to be a good boyfriend, he really didn't have time for that.

"That's quite the list. I'll just follow your lead and help push the cart," Anthony said.

"M-mm." Marianne nodded, but she didn't look at him, almost like she was afraid of something.

Shopping for groceries took a lot longer than he expected, almost half an hour, but they eventually found everything on the list and made it to the front.

This store didn't have a self-checkout lane. Instead, the cash register was operated by an older woman with graying hair and a few wrinkles around her mouth. As she looked at the two of them, a smile blossomed on her face.

"It's so nice to see young couples like you two," she said. "There is so much bigotry in this world. Seeing a human dating a vampire does this old woman's heart good."

Marianne flushed bright red. "Oh… we're not—"

"Thank you." Anthony smiled at the woman, interrupting Marianne. "We appreciate your sentiment. I agree. It's a good thing when people can accept each other."

It wasn't a surprise that the woman had mistaken him for a human since he was reining in his pheromones. Without those, no one would be able to tell he wasn't human. Most people would probably assume he was just an abnormally attractive man, though a few might suspect he was something else.

Marianne looked at him, but he paid her strange expression no mind as their groceries were rung up. After paying for their food and having everything placed inside of a sealed container that would keep the food fresh on their way home, they left.

Neither of them spoke for a while. Marianne kept stealing glances at him from the corner of her eye, and Anthony was content to let her do so until she felt the need to break the silence.

The sun had risen into the sky and the morning fog had completely vanished. The midday sun caused the atmosphere around them to heat up. All the steel and blacktop pavements absorbed heat and made the city a lot hotter than if they lived somewhere less populated.

I really wish they'd create pavement that kept cool... but I suppose that would be asking for too much.

There had been attempts in the past to create cool pavement, but they all ended in failure. There simply wasn't a material, man-made or otherwise, that could adequately reduce heat. He remembered one attempt where they built air conditioners underneath the roads. That had been one of Academy Island's dumber ideas.

"Um, Anthony?" Marianne finally spoke up. "Why didn't you let me correct that woman? She thought you and I... she thought that we were..."

"Dating. I know." Anthony's words silenced Marianne. "The reason I didn't stop her is because I honestly don't have a problem if she or anyone else makes that assumption about us."

"Ah?"

He turned to study Marianne as the girl looked at him with wide eyes and flushed cheeks. The expression on her face was priceless. He'd definitely remember it for all times.

"Why are you so surprised?" he asked. "You and I have been living under the same roof for the past several weeks. While we haven't done a whole lot together, I do enjoy spending time with you."

"You do?" Marianne's eyes brightened. Their luminescence reminded him of stars.

"Of course I do. To be honest, I've thought about asking you to become my bondmate for a while now, but I was never certain if doing so would be appropriate." Marianne stared at him with wide eyes. Since his thoughts were already out in the open, there was no point in holding back. "I know you came all this way in order to find me, that your mother wanted you to convince me to become your ally before someone else snatched me away. You probably feel a little guilty about that." Marianne lowered her head. "But I'm actually glad she sent you to me." Her head snapped back up. "You've been a big help around the house. I'm sure you've noticed, but none of us are any good at housework. Your kindness and compassion is something I find very attractive, and if I'm being honest, that confident facade you sometimes put up is really attractive too."

Marianne said nothing as he spoke, but the color in her cheeks was growing consistently darker the longer he talked. She was a lot like Brianna in that she didn't take compliments well.

"In short," Anthony continued, "I like you."

"Oh. I... I, um..." Marianne stumbled over her words.

Anthony sighed and raised his free hand to place it on her shoulder, startling her. "You don't have to answer me right now. I came at you with this pretty suddenly. Think about whether or not you have any feelings toward me and answer me then. Okay?"

"Mmm. Okay." Marianne nodded once. She seemed a little calmer. That was good since he was worried about frightening her off.

They began walking again. The atmosphere wasn't as uncomfortable as before. Despite Anthony confessing how he felt to Marianne, neither of them was bothered. The cute vampire girl was even wearing a happy smile as she walked by his side.

Just as they turned a street corner, a shadow flew over their heads. The two looked up in time to see a woman falling from the sky. She flipped around like a professional acrobatic, body spinning, and landed on the ground just a few meters from them. Anthony and Marianne stopped upon seeing her.

The woman stood to her feet, lion ears twitching on her head as a breeze caused her long, golden hair to billow. She was dressed in regular clothes. Her jeans had one long pant leg and another that was short. She wore a shirt that had tears in it, but the tears looked like they were designed that way as opposed to looking like someone had torn up her outfit. As she turned to face them, her chest bouncing like a pair of beach balls sitting on her ribs, her bright golden eyes locked onto them.

She paused.

"Mari?" Her eyes grew bright as a happy grin appeared on her face, the woman who Anthony now recognized as the one he had seen alongside the Beast King walked over to them. "Man! I feel like it's been forever since we last saw each other. How've you been? Life treating you well?"

The woman spoke with a thick Russian accent. It was hard for Anthony to understand her, but the accent added to her allure.

The sudden familiarity this woman displayed toward Marianne startled Anthony. That said, as the woman strode toward them with bold steps, he expected his companion to hide behind him... which was probably why he became surprised when Marianne stepped forward with a confident smirk on her face.

"Sasha, it really has been a while, hasn't it?" Marianne reached out and clasped "Sasha's" hands. "I saw you on the news this morning. I had no idea we would be meeting each other so soon."

"Ha ha ha! Me neither! I didn't realize you were even on Academy Island yet!"

While the two girls were talking, Anthony studied Marianne, whose expression had completely changed from her normally shy demeanor. Her bearing now exuded an aura of confidence that was almost overpowering. It looked like she had adopted her other persona for this meeting.

"I've been here for over a week now," Marianne replied to the woman's comment.

"A week?" Sasha's eyes widened, but then they narrowed as she shifted her gaze over Marianne's shoulder and locked eyes with him. "Could the reason have something to do with that gorgeous man behind you?" Her expression flickered before a fanged grin appeared on her face. "I get it now. This man must be... your lover, right?" Marianne smiled but said nothing. "Oh ho. So that's how it is. I never expected you to get yourself a man so soon."

Since he had been brought into the conversation now, Anthony walked forward until he was standing beside Marianne.

"I'm Anthony. It's nice to meet you, uh... Sasha?"

"Ha! All my friends call me Sasha, but my real name is Alexandra Sil'yazhelyy." She stuck out her hand. "It's a pleasure to meet the man who can make my best friend fall for him."

"It's nice to meet you, too."

Anthony took Sasha's—Alexandra's—hand. Her grip was firm and strong, not at all like some of the dainty women he knew. Now that he was looking at her more closely, he could see that her body was packed with muscles. Her biceps and triceps were well-defined and powerful, and her forearms a little thicker than he expected. Likewise, her legs were muscular, and he could see a six-pack peeking out from a slit in her shirt.

This was something he wouldn't have noticed if she was still wearing that military uniform she'd worn on the news.

"Hmmm... you have a very odd smell." Before he could ask Sasha what she meant, the woman leaned forward and began sniffing him. "I can smell several women on you." Her eyes narrowed. "I hope you're not cheating on my bestie here. I should warn you, if I find out that you haven't been faithful to her, I will tear you a new asshole."

Anthony wondered what he was supposed to say in a situation like this. Should he tell her that he was an incubus? That was technically supposed to be a secret, but there were already so many people who knew about it that he wasn't sure it mattered. Actually, he was surprised this woman didn't already know who he was. If Elizabeth Tepes could find out his identity, it stood to reason all the major powers already knew about him.

Before he could say anything, several black hover cars suddenly swerved into the street. Sasha narrowed her eyes and bared her fangs when she saw them.

"Awww, shit! Hey, Mari! This lover of yours knows how to run?"

"Don't worry. He's capable of keeping pace."

"Good! Then let's get out of here!"

Anthony really had no idea what was happening, but before he could even comment, Sasha had latched onto his and Marianne's hands and began hauling butt. She ran away at what seemed like her top speed. The hover cars followed.

Left with no other option, Anthony activated Physical Enhancement, which gave him more than enough physical strength and endurance to keep up with Sasha. He looked over at Marianne, worried that she might be lagging behind. He was surprised, however, when he saw that she was actually flying instead of running. Well, that was a vampire for you.

The hover cars were right behind them, traveling at a speed that must have been at least 120 kilometers per hour. Despite how fast they were going, Anthony, Marianne, and Sasha were traveling even faster. They were also more maneuverable. Rather than sticking to the main road, they darted down several side streets, cut through alleys, and even entered a park.

"Who the heck are these people chasing after you?!" Anthony asked, shouting to be heard over the roaring wind.

"Ha ha ha! Those are my bodyguards!"

"Why are you running from your own bodyguards?!"

"'Cause I don't need them! They'll just get in the way of my fun!"

Anthony gave the woman an aggrieved look that she couldn't see because she was facing forward. He turned his head toward Marianne, but she just gave him a hopeless smile, as if to say that was just how Sasha was.

The hover cars eventually disappeared from his view, meaning they probably lost them. Sasha led him and Marianne into another park—Anthony wasn't sure which one—and only stopped after they couldn't see anything but trees and grass.

"Whew. That should keep them off my back for a little while," Sasha said before she turned an admiring gaze toward Anthony. "Mari was right. You're pretty damn fast. Physical Enhancement, huh? That's a nice ability, and it looks like you're better at using it than most people."

"It was the first ability I learned how to use." Anthony shrugged.

"You seem pretty strong. I'd love to face you on the sparring mat at some point," Sasha said, her eyes sparkling a little as if the idea of fighting him was exhilarating.

He looked at Marianne.

"Sasha is the number one strongest youth in Russia," Marianne explained, her confident persona still in place. "She's won numerous national and international mixed martial arts championships, including the Youth League MMA World Tournament. That was... I wanna say four years ago now?"

"Five years," Sasha corrected. "I fought in the Youth League back when I was fourteen." Which meant she was currently nineteen years old, the same as him. "In any case, now that we've lost those losers, I want you and your boyfriend to show me around."

"We'd love to, but we actually have to get back home." Marianne looked at the storage container in Anthony's hand. "We were actually shopping for groceries before you showed up."

"Shopping for—you mean you two live together? For serious?"

"For serious," Marianne said with a very serious expression.

"Wow. I had no idea you two were already cohabitating." She gave Anthony another once over, as if she was looking at him in a new light, then grinned. "Damn, boy. You work fast."

"Thanks," Anthony said, his voice dry.

"Then I guess I'll tag along with you two," Sasha decided without their input. "I want to see what kind of place Mari and her boyfriend live in."

Anthony felt some hesitation toward letting this woman see his place. She had, after all, threatened to tear him a new asshole if she caught him cheating on Marianne.

"Sure," Marianne replied with an easygoing expression. "We don't mind letting you see where we live. We can even introduce you to Anthony's other lovers."

"Right. Right. I'd love to meet Anthony's other lovers!"

Sasha didn't even realize what she was saying until she had already said it. Silence reigned within the park for several long seconds as the woman went over the words she and Marianne had just spoken. As the realization dawned on her, she looked back and forth between Anthony and Marianne.

"... Heh?"

She sounded confused. Anthony didn't blame her. If he had heard that his best friend was one of several lovers, he'd have probably felt the same way.

"Heh?!"

"You did that on purpose, didn't you?" Anthony asked.

"Of course not." Marianne sniffed. "I was only telling the truth. She was going to find out eventually, so I thought it was better to be open about it than lie."

"That's... yeah, you bring up a good point."

Sasha didn't seem like the kind of woman who enjoyed being lied to. Marianne knew her friend well enough to know that it would lead to disaster and a lot of drama, so she'd decided to simply be open about it. Still, he was surprised she could say that without becoming embarrassed.

Once the confusion wore off, Sasha, like an erupting volcano, shouted so loudly that her voice echoed across the park, causing the animals within to run as far from the area as they could.

"WHAT DO YA MEAN YOU'LL INTRODUCE ME TO HIS OTHER LOVERS?! CHTO ZA KHREN' PROISKHODIT?!"

CHAPTER 4

"HA-HA-HA! I see! I see! So you are an incubus and Marianne is one of your bondmates! So that's how it is!"

It was late afternoon when Anthony arrived home with Marianne and Sasha in tow, and after getting home, he had Sasha sit on the couch and explained the situation to her. It didn't take long. In fact, the explanation was straightforward. He was an incubus, Marianne was one of his bondmates, and he had two more bondmates, both of whom were fortunately not home during his explanation.

Of course, there was the small fact that Marianne wasn't really one of his bondmates. They had yet to consummate their relationship, and he still wasn't sure what their relationship even was. At the same time, he did have the intention of having her become his bondmate, so it wasn't like they were stretching the truth too far. He had even confessed to her just before Sasha interrupted them.

Marianne came out of the kitchen as Anthony was explaining their situation to Sasha, a pitcher of freshly brewed iced tea in one hand and a tray with three cups in the other. She set the tray down, poured tea into all three cups, then handed one to Sasha, one to him, and kept the last one for herself. Afterward, she sat next to Anthony, close enough that their thighs were touching, which was far closer than she usually sat.

Her cheeks were an almost unnoticeable shade of red.

"Now that I think about it," Sasha continued after laughing herself hoarse. "I do remember hearing about an incubus living somewhere on Academy Island, but I didn't pay the news much mind since it didn't concern me." Her eyes became focused like laser pointers as she locked onto him. "So *you* are that incubus. I guess it really is a small world."

"I don't think the world is that small, but Lilith once told me that power attracts power." Anthony thought back to his time with the woman who saved his life and taught him what it meant to love someone. Every lesson she had ever imparted was something he kept close to heart. "This is the reason powerful people always end up meeting."

"Power attracts power, huh? Yeah, I guess that does make sense." Sasha pondered his words before nodding. "I rarely ever get a chance to meet regular people, but I've met plenty of powerful people in my life. Father is surrounded by them. His allies, his enemies… all of them possess extraordinary power."

"So I'm guessing you are here for the peace conference, Sasha?" Marianne asked, smoothly changing the topic of their discussion.

"I couldn't care less about attending this peace conference," Sasha adamantly said, shaking her head and causing the long locks of her golden hair to sway. "However, Father and Mother said it was important that I, as their daughter, make an appearance with them, so here I am." After saying this, a glimmer entered her eyes. "Of course, now that I know you are here, I don't mind being forced to come all this way. I even got to learn something very interesting."

Anthony took a sip of his iced tea as Sasha and Marianne conversed. It was cold and unsweetened. The cool liquid helped quench his parched throat.

These two are quite close.

Anthony observed the duo as they happily chatted about everything from what they had been doing since the last time they met to what brands of clothing they were most into. He was surprised to learn Sasha liked fashion since she didn't seem to be the type, but her knowledge of brands and designs was extensive. It just went to show he couldn't judge a book by its cover.

One thing Anthony did notice was that while Marianne appeared happy, and he was certain she truly was excited to see her friend, she kept her public facade up around Sasha, never letting it drop. He thought it strange that she would not act like her true self with a friend.

"I think it's about time you tell us why you were running away from your own bodyguards," Marianne said.

Sasha grinned. "Isn't it obviously because I wanted to explore on my own? Bodyguards just get in the way. You can't experience a new place if you're constantly surrounded by dudes in suits. Everyone I come across looks at me with fear when they're around."

Marianne wore a smile that was at once amused and aggrieved. "That does sound an awful lot like you."

"Ha-ha-ha! Of course, it does! You know I hate being confined!"

Marianne and Sasha spoke for almost an hour until the door to the apartment opened and someone walked in. It was Brianna. Anthony, Marianne, and Sasha turned to look at the woman. A strange silence fell over the group of three.

"I'm home," Brianna called out.

The redhead slipped off her shoes, carefully set them on the rack, and was just about to wander further into the apartment—only to stop when she realized they had a guest. She froze. Her eyes locked onto Sasha, but then she looked from Sasha to Anthony and Marianne. There was a question there.

"Bri..." Anthony stood up and walked over to the redhead. "Welcome home."

"Thank you. It's good to be home..." Brianna frowned as she glanced once more at Sasha, who was eyeing her like a lioness staring down a gazelle, then looked back at him. "Who is that?"

"This is Alexandra Sil'yazhelyy," Anthony introduced.

Brianna's reaction when he introduced Sasha by her full name was even more pronounced than when she had discovered there was an unknown woman in their apartment. Her entire body froze solid as if she was a block of ice. Then a shudder traveled through her body from her head to her toes, followed by the blood draining from her cheeks. Anthony was worried because her response seemed a little too overboard, but then Brianna came into herself, took a deep breath, and calmed down.

Her eyes became like blades.

"I never expected the Beast King's infamous daughter, Bloody Alexandra, would one day be drinking iced tea in my apartment," Brianna said, eyes still locked onto the woman in question.

"And I never expected to one day be meeting my friend's lover and fellow bondmates, and yet here we are." Sasha's reply was mild, but there was a sharp tone to it. "Also, I don't much like the nickname 'Bloody Alexandra,' so I'll thank you not to use it. You can just call me Sasha."

"I understand," Brianna said. "From now on, I will call you Sasha—wait. Lover?"

As those words penetrated her brain, Brianna looked at him, her eyes seeking an explanation. Unfortunately, he didn't have one to give right now. He couldn't say anything with Sasha present, so he mouthed, "I'll tell you later." Brianna frowned at him but nodded.

As their silent conversation was happening, Sasha was studying Brianna with her bright golden pupils. They were incredibly striking. Anthony had never seen anyone with eyes quite like hers. At the same time, while her eyes were beautiful like liquid gold spun into the shape of two orbs, they also looked dangerous. There was a deadly quality to her eyes that would have made a normal person shudder in fear.

"Custodes Daemonium, huh?" She turned to Marianne. "It seems your lover has quite the interesting taste in bondmates. I never would have imagined he'd be able to seduce a woman belonging to that organization."

Marianne gave an ambiguous smile. "Anthony is certainly an interesting man."

"Seeing someone from Custodes Daemonium makes me want to test myself against them."

"Please don't. The last thing we need is you destroying an entire city block because you lost control of yourself while sparring."

After Brianna entered, Anthony got a cup from the kitchen and poured her some iced tea as she took his place on the couch. Since the couch wasn't very big, he did not have any room to sit there, but that was okay. He decided it would be fine to let the girls do some "girl talk" or whatever while he worked on his homework.

He got out his laptop, sat before the table, activated the holographic screen and keyboard, and began typing up his latest report on the historical use of Feng Shui in healing and how it could be applied to modern medical techniques.

Secilia arrived about half an hour after Brianna did. She accepted Sasha's presence a lot more readily than her fellow bondmate had, but Anthony thought the reason for that was because she wasn't as knowledgeable about Sasha as Brianna was. As a member of Custodes Daemonium, Brianna knew a lot about all the major powers in this world, including the people involved with them. On the other hand, Secilia knew practically nothing and probably didn't even care to know.

Sasha didn't stay too much longer after Secilia returned home.

"I'm sure Father and Mother are thoroughly pissed off at me by now, so I'll have to show up and pacify them," she explained. The way she said that so calmly threw him off. Also, the idea of the Beast King of Russia being "pissed off" was a terrifying prospect, so the fact that she could be so collected impressed him.

"Be sure to give your parents my regards," Marianne said.

"I will. It was good seeing you, Mari."

"You as well. It was nice to catch up."

After giving a simple farewell to him, Brianna, and Secilia, Sasha exited the door and disappeared. They heard her footsteps thumping down the hallway, but soon even those vanished from their senses.

Marianne stood in front of the door for some time. After a moment, she placed a hand against her chest, took several deep breaths, and then all the tension in her shoulders evaporated as she slumped down.

"Haaaaah… that was one of the hardest things I've ever had to do," she said, her voice no longer calm, confident, and collected. Now she sounded like a demure and easily embarrassed young woman. The sudden change threw off both Brianna and Secilia, who had yet to really see her ability to switch from one personality to another.

"You okay, Mari?" asked Anthony as he leaned over and placed a hand on her shoulder.

Marianne jerked as though startled by the contact, but then she turned her head and smiled at him. Her cheeks were flushed, and her eyes were a tad wet. However, she seemed mostly okay.

"I'm fine. I am just not used to maintaining my public mask for so long," she confessed.

Anthony tilted his head. "Why do you even need to be using that public mask of yours? Isn't Sasha a friend?"

"She is," Marianne said softly. "But at the same time, she is not. Sasha is someone who respects the strong and derides the weak. I met her at another peace conference several years ago that was held in the neutral kingdom of Romonica. Back then, I was using my public mask to appear strong and graceful, which I guess is what attracted her. If she found out that I'm really just a weak and easily embarrassed girl, I'm sure she'd hate me."

"Hmm…"

Anthony wanted to tell this young woman that she shouldn't have to worry about that, that he was sure her friend wouldn't dismiss her just because of such an inane reason, but he didn't know Sasha enough to say what kind of response she would have after learning that Marianne wasn't as strong as she made herself out to be. On the other hand, Marianne seemed to know a lot about her. That was why he kept silent.

"Alexandra Sil'yazhelyy is not only one of the most powerful women on the planet, but she is well-known for her hatred of weakness," Brianna chimed in. "I remember hearing about her first MMA tournament on the news. During her very first match, she beat the person she was fighting against until they were a bloody mess. Not only was she laughing as she did so, but she mocked her opponent for being a weakling."

"She sounds like a real piece of work," Secilia muttered.

"Well, in either event, it's getting kind of late. Do you want me to help you get started on dinner?" he asked, holding out his hand to her.

Marianne stared at the hand for the longest time, then slowly, tentatively, as if afraid of being burned, reached out and placed her hand in his. She gave him a tentative smile.

"Yes, please."

As Anthony pulled Marianne to her feet, he felt two sets of eyes on him. Turning, he found both Brianna and Secilia staring in his direction. The two girls were sitting on the couch together. The looks on their faces made him self-conscious. He felt blood rushing to his cheeks and turned his head to hide his expression. During that time, Secilia leaned over to Brianna and spoke in a voice just loud enough for him to hear.

"Anthony is becoming quite the player, isn't he?"

"He does seem to be getting better at smooth-talking women."

"Hmph. It looks like we're gonna have to keep our guard up around him."

"I can hear you two, you know." Anthony sent them a mild glare.

Secilia stuck out her tongue. "Good. I was worried we weren't talking loud enough."

Anthony rolled his eyes but didn't comment as he followed Marianne into the kitchen. While she began getting ingredients out of the fridge and cupboards, Anthony grabbed the plates, utensils, and cups. He brought everything over to the dinner table in the living room and set it up. Brianna asked if she could also help, but he turned her down. The kitchen wasn't that big, so having more than two people working in there would just make it more crowded than it needed to be.

Several hours after dinner found Anthony sharing a bed with an exhausted Brianna. The young woman's nubile body was slick with sweat as she rested snugly within the crook of his arm. Naked breasts pressed against his side. Nipples rubbed against him with each inhale.

Her eyes were closed and she was taking deep breaths, but he could tell she hadn't gone to sleep yet. Brianna had these really cute snoring noises she made whenever she was asleep.

"Hey, Bri. What do you know about Alexandra?" he asked.

Brianna blinked her brilliant blue eyes. She shifted a little, her leg rubbing against his and sending a jolt straight to his brain. He bit his lip as a surge of desire welled up inside of him. Damn it. They'd just had sex, but he was already horny again.

"Alexandra Sil'yazhelyy is the daughter of Ivan Sil'yazhelyy and Svetlana Sil'yazhelyy," Brianna began, her voice a soft murmur. "She was born with extraordinary strength. Her accolades in martial arts are world-renowned. However, not as many people know that she's also one of the most ruthless individuals in the entire world and has an intense hatred for traitors. About one year ago, a faction within Russia rebelled against Ivan's rule, and Alexandra was the one who took care of them. She stormed the rebel base by herself and slaughtered every person there. That moment was how she earned her nickname 'Bloody Alexandra.'"

Anthony felt a shiver crawl up his spine as Brianna's words invoked an image of the boisterous and friendly Sasha storming a fortress like a blood-crazed maniac. He imagined her destroying the entrance, rushing into the base, and tearing people limb from limb with the incredible strength she possessed as a therianthrope. It was not what he'd call a pleasant mental image.

"The base not only had five thousand people in it, but there were also two former generals of Russia who'd grown dissatisfied with their lack of status." Brianna paused for a moment before switching gears. "A long time ago, I hear Russia was a communist country, but ever since the Beast King came to power, it's become a dictatorship. Ivan Sil'yazhelyy rules with an iron fist and those who dissent are destroyed with extreme prejudice. This is how he was able to take complete control of Russia within just two short years."

Russia was one of the nations Anthony had never been to. Back when he was traveling with Lilith, she had avoided that nation. According to her, the Beast King was not someone she ever wanted to meet.

"I'm guessing the two generals were also killed?" said Anthony.

Brianna nodded. "They weren't killed right away, though. Alexandra captured them both and made examples of them."

"I somehow don't like the sound of that," he muttered.

"I'd be worried if you did." Brianna sighed as she closed her eyes and nuzzled his shoulder. "Alexandra brought them back to the capital, broke their limbs, hung them naked from a flagpole, and left them there for two weeks. I'm told they died from a combination of the cold and dehydration."

"And you said that was two years ago?" Anthony asked.

"Yes."

He scrunched up his face. "So, this happened back when Sasha was... seventeen. Damn. She really is vicious, but she didn't seem to be a bad person when I was talking to her."

Brianna shrugged. "I never said she was bad. Sasha is a fanatical patriot, the kind that can be incredibly dangerous if crossed. However, while she might not be outright evil, she is definitely not a woman you should underestimate under any circumstances."

"I'll make a note of that."

"Good. Now, I'm going to bed. Goodnight, Anthony."

"Night."

The moment she said the words "goodnight," Brianna's breathing grew much deeper and she began releasing those cute snores of hers. He stroked her shoulder as he listened to her snoring. He continued listening to her adorable snoring before he also closed his eyes and began slowly succumbing to sleep. His last thoughts, oddly enough, were not of his bondmates, but of Marianne's friend.

Alexandra Sil'yazhelyy. What a terrifying woman.

***

Because of the upcoming peace conference, Lucretia had been forced to double down on her work. She had already split her time twice to create two extra time clones. One of those clones was in charge of attending school—she didn't like the idea of having someone replace her—while the other clone was involved in the standard work she did for the Academy Island Private Security Forces.

Meanwhile, she was working on the peace conference itself.

There was a lot that went into planning a pace conference. As someone whose job was to ensure the safety of the people attending the conference, Lucretia needed to create guard formations, plan contingencies in case of emergencies, and handpick the people who would be attending the ceremony as security detail.

She had already handpicked the people who would be attending the ceremony, the guards who would be traveling with the procession, and what formations they would use. The problem she was having right now was thinking of what kind of emergency situations they might run into. There was a rumor going around that the Sons of Liberty had been spotted within Academy Island, and while she didn't believe in rumors that had no evidence to support them, there was a very real possibility that someone would try to do something.

"Lucretia?" a voice suddenly asked.

Looking up from her work, Lucretia glanced at the second desk she had purloined for her use. Sitting behind it was her time clone. It looked exactly like her right down to the lolita outfit she was wearing. At that moment, her clone had a pensive frown on her face.

"What's wrong?" asked Lucretia.

"I've been going over several reports regarding the allocation of equipment and troops, and it looks like there's some unusual activity that has me concerned."

"Oh?"

Lucretia hopped off the chair and made her way to her clone's desk. Like most desks, this one came up to her chest. She felt a flash of irritation. Why couldn't people make desks shorter for smaller individuals like her? With a sigh, Lucretia shoved aside the anger in her heart and looked at the report on her time clone's holographic monitor.

She frowned.

"Who ordered so many weapons?" she asked herself. "We don't normally order that many weapons, do we?"

"We do not," her clone confirmed. "I checked our previous records, and it looks like we're spending fifty percent more on weapons this month than we ever have before. However, our record does not show us owning two times more weapons than normal. Also, it seems as if someone has been messing with patrol routes and pulling members from their duties. Several of our soldiers have been disappearing at times when they should have been on duty."

The frown on Secilia's face grew as her chest tightened. She felt something unsettling build within her gut.

The fact that they were spending twice as much on weapons that didn't appear in their records was disturbing enough, but now members were being pulled from active duty and disappearing? That was a completely different level of terrifying.

Only a few people should have the authority to pull members of the Academy Island Private Security Forces from active duty like this, and she was one of them. The only other people who could do such a thing were the two commanders above her and members of the Board of Directors.

Tapping her wristwatch, Lucretia opened a holographic screen, pulled up a caller ID, and tapped on it.

"Captain Dennison, I need you to run a check on all of our equipment. Gather a squadron and do a complete count of how much equipment we currently have, what kind of equipment it is, and whether or not it's been bought within the last month. If possible, create a list of all the new equipment that came in with our last shipment. Also, do not just pull up a list from our records. It's important that your group counts every piece of equipment that arrived with our last shipment."

"I understand, ma'am. I'll get right on that," Captain Dennison's voice entered her mind rather than her ears.

"Good. Report back to me when you are finished."

"Ma'am."

Lucretia went back to her seat, but she no longer worked on creating contingency plans in case the peace conference went south. She leaned back in her chair and closed her eyes.

She didn't know how long she waited. It could have been minutes. However, it felt like hours. Eventually, Captain Dennison opened a line of telepathic communication with her and reported his findings.

"We've checked all of the equipment and the amount matches what's on our records, ma'am."

"I see. Thank you."

Lucretia didn't let any emotions slip into her voice, but her blood had run cold. She disconnected the telepathic communication and placed her hands on the desk as she churned this issue over in her mind. Their records and the amount of equipment they had matched. However, they had spent two times more than normal. Not even the price of their equipment increasing due to inflation could accommodate this kind of abrupt change. To be sure, she pulled up information on the latest prices for their equipment and cross-referenced them with the prices from several months ago.

The prices had risen, but not by much.

Certainly not enough to explain why they had paid so much more this time.

Something was wrong. Very wrong.

Hopping down from her chair, Lucretia began walking toward the door.

"Keep working," she said to her time clone. "I'm going to pay MiliTech a visit."

"Okay," her time clone said as the door opened to let Lucretia exit.

***

As the days passed, more and more important figures began showing up on Academy Island. The news would always report on which important person had appeared. There were kings, presidents, prime ministers, and various aristocrats from the many independent nations scattered across the European Federation and Asia. Academy Island had never played host to so many powerful personages before.

At the moment, Anthony was at the airport with Brianna, Marianne, and Secilia. They were sitting in a set of chairs. Anthony was in the middle of Brianna and Secilia. Marianne sat on Secilia's left, her eyes never once leaving the door that led into a currently unused boarding ramp. Her left foot bounced up and down at a constant but frantic pace. He wondered if she knew that she looked like someone with ADHD on a sugar high.

"You need to calm down," he said to her. "Being anxious isn't going to make your mom arrive any earlier."

"I-I know that," Marianne mumbled in embarrassment. "But it… it has been so long since I saw her. This is the longest time I have ever been away from Mother, so of course, I'm anxious to see her again."

"It sounds like you have a good relationship with your mother," Brianna said.

"Mother and I have always been close," Marianne confided. "I do not have a father. Mother told me he died a few years after I was born, so she had to raise me herself. Of course, I have maids and servants, but even though Mother was busy ruling a nation and trying to convince the other warring factions to sue for peace, she refused to let them raise me."

"Sounds nice," Brianna said with a melancholy smile.

Anthony was currently the only one who knew that Brianna did not have any parents. She had been an orphan when Custodes Daemonium found her and brought her to their headquarters to be trained as a War Maiden. While Brianna never expressed dissatisfaction toward her life circumstances, no one in this world did not truly care about where they came from. Any orphan who grew up never knowing their family would long to discover where they came from and why they had been abandoned. It was the natural consequence of being raised by people who were not your family and realizing how abnormal that was.

"It looks like your mother's plane is coming," Secilia said before anyone could say something else.

Marianne's head snapped toward the window and finally spotted the airplane coming toward the boarding ramp. It was a sleek craft more reminiscent of a space shuttle—airplanes these days did ascend into space to allow for faster travel, so the design made sense. Her eyes lit up as the plane stopped. The boarding ramp extended toward the plane, locking it in place. Marianne stood up and looked ready to bolt over to the exit, but Secilia placed a hand on her shoulder.

"Slow down and wait. Be patient."

"Right. Right. Patience. I've got to be patient."

Marianne took several deep breaths to center herself, then sat back down and waited. Her wait was fortunately not long. The exit door soon opened and allowed several people into the terminal.

The first among them was a gorgeous woman who looked like Marianne's older sister. Silver hair that appeared to have been spun from silk threads glittered in the sunlight and overhead lamps. It was wavy and descended to her lower back. Bangs framed a beautifully pale face with features so exquisite, Anthony thought he was staring at a fairy. She looked so much like Marianne it was startling. However, this woman possessed a maturity and elegance that Marianne lacked.

There was another big difference between Marianne and her mother.

Her breasts.

Marianne was the possessor of very small bosoms. She wasn't completely flat, but her boobs were no bigger than a handful at most. On the other hand, her mother's chest was on par with Brianna's. They strained against the confines of her dress, an elegant piece with a cleavage-revealing front and no back. Simple strings along the back kept the dress from falling off her buxom frame. Even her sides were revealed in all their splendor. Anthony could actually see hints of sideboob peeking out as she walked over to them.

"Mother!"

Marianne could no longer withstand her desire and raced over to the woman, who smiled as she spread open her arms and accepted the young vampire into her embrace.

"My daughter, I'm so glad you are okay. I have missed you terribly."

"I missed you too, Mother. I missed you so much."

The reunion between mother and daughter was certainly touching, but Anthony's attention was forced away from the pair and onto the men and women behind them. Several of them were dressed as maids and butlers. There were about twelve in total. While he would have normally reeled at someone who needed so many people to attend them, he could tell from how they carried themselves that they were all extensively trained in combat.

They were bodyguards disguised as servants.

There were two other people present, but they looked completely out of place as they stood directly on either side of Elizabeth Tepes.

On the left was a woman in her late forties or maybe her early fifties. Her hair was a mixture of black and gray, her eyes were brown, and despite being older, she carried herself like a woman in her twenties. She wore a black unitard with blue lines glowing across it, a cloak that went down to her ankles, and was carrying a case that no doubt contained her weapon.

To Elizabeth's right was a young man with blond hair, blue eyes, and a masculine face. He had a sort of prince charming appearance. He looked very much like those princes people often read about in fairy tales. His chest and shoulders were broad. Adorning his body was a unitard similar to the one worn by the woman, but it was designed for men instead. Like the woman beside him, he also carried a case.

"Instructor Noel!" Brianna exclaimed in surprise, and then her eyes widened even more when she saw the young man. "Calencio?!"

"Brianna."

The young man's eyes lit up as he took one step forward, then another. It looked like he was going to walk right past Elizabeth and make his way toward her, but then Instructor Noel stuck out her arm, stopping him.

"You are on duty right now," Instructor Noel chided. "You know it is against protocol to act out of personal interest while on duty."

"Oh. Right." The young man known as Calencio rubbed the back of his neck and offered the older woman a sheepish smile.

Instructor Noel sighed, but then she turned to Brianna and smiled. "I see you are doing well, Brianna."

"I am doing very well, thank you," Brianna said.

Instructor Noel nodded before looking at Anthony, who stood right next to Brianna. She studied him with her scrutinizing eyes that looked like they could see right through to his core. While he wouldn't say he was used to such a look, Anthony did his best to put up with it.

"It looks like you have gotten stronger since the last time I saw you, Anthony," she said.

"I've been working hard," Anthony responded with a shrug.

"I bet, but that is not what I meant."

Anthony did not know what this woman meant by that, but before he could ask, a flash of killing intent caused his body to stall. He recovered and tried to find the killing intent. He would never get the chance, however, as the moment Noel had said his name, Elizabeth Tepes had discovered his existence.

"Anthony Amasius, it is a pleasure to finally see you again," the woman said as she walked over to stand before him. Her words caused everyone except Anthony to feel a burst of confusion.

"I'm surprised you remember me," Anthony said.

"Hmph. You say that, but it would be very hard not to remember you after Lilith spent nearly an hour showing you off to me." Elizabeth paused, then released a sigh as her eyes turned pitying. "Please let me express my sympathy toward you for your loss. Lilith was more than just a friend to me. She was also one of the few people who shared my desire for peace between the races. Her loss has made the entire world a much darker place."

"Thank you for your condolences," Anthony said, keeping his voice diplomatic.

While Elizabeth spoke with Anthony, everyone else, including Marianne, looked at the two of them in surprise. It was clear they didn't know that Anthony and Elizabeth were acquainted with each other. No one asked about it thankfully. Now was not really the time since they were in the middle of an airport terminal.

Elizabeth took a step back and clapped her hands as she gently smiled at everyone.

"I would like to spend more time with my daughter. Since you and your bondmates are here, why don't you three come with us? I'm sure Marianne would feel a lot safer if you were there as well."

The suggestion caught everyone by surprise, but the moment she said those words, Marianne's eyes lit up. She clearly enjoyed the idea. On the other hand, Secilia, who had yet to say anything since Elizabeth and her group exited the boarding ramp, looked a lot more uncertain.

"Are you sure that's okay? I mean, you're kind of a big deal and stuff. Meanwhile, we're just..."

Elizabeth's smile caused Secilia to trail off. "I understand why you might think this way, but you have to understand that Anthony is actually a bigger deal than you might think. Everyone who is in a position of power knows about him by now. I would honestly not be surprised if he receives several dinner invitations within the next few days before the peace conference."

"Are you serious?" asked a shocked Secilia.

"Of course." Elizabeth wore a serious expression. "That is how powerful the presence of an incubus is. Many people are going to try and rope him into their schemes and power plays. I thought it might be a good idea if I spoke with him first because of this."

Secilia had nothing she could say to that, and Anthony thought having dinner with Elizabeth was a good idea. His reasons weren't just because of what she said, however. Since Anthony wanted her daughter to become his bondmate, he believed it was imperative that he speak with her and receive permission to... court? Was he courting Marianne? He didn't know if that was the proper term for their situation, but he felt it was important to have Elizabeth's permission to court, or date, or whatever he was doing with her daughter.

"I will gladly accept your invitation," Anthony said. He placed his left hand at his waist, right hand lowered toward the ground, and bowed in the manner of a European Federation noble. "Thank you."

"It is no trouble at all." Elizabeth waved her hand as though what she had done was not worthy of his thanks. "I have been wanting to speak with you for a while now anyway. Lilith never let you spend much time with me... or anyone else for that matter, so this will be a good opportunity to become more acquainted with each other. Now, let us be off."

Elizabeth's words were essentially law. The moment she spoke, everyone formed up and began moving down the airport terminal. Their large procession received a lot of attention from everyone. Of course, when several strikingly beautiful women were in the same place along with an army of butlers and maids, it was bound to attract attention. Anthony ignored the stares like he did when people glared at him.

What he could not ignore was the burst of killing intent at his back.

He turned around and tried to find the source of the intent, but the killing intent once more disappeared from his senses, making him wonder if he might have been mistaken.

"Is something wrong?" Brianna asked as she stopped next to him.

"No." He shook his head and slowly turned back toward the group. "There's nothing wrong."

Reaching out to take Brianna's hand, Anthony ignored the palpitations in his heart and followed behind Elizabeth and Marianne Tepes.

CHAPTER 5

ELIZABETH TEPES WAS STAYING AT THE OMNI CHARLESTON. It was a hotel located in the very heart of Academy Island.

The hotel was not a towering building that spanned several dozen stories, but a complex of private houses that people could rent, if they could afford the ridiculously high price. Each house was about the size of two luxury suites belonging to a five-star resort.

The limousine they were riding in took them through the complex, which was gated and could only be opened if you were registered as a guest, and Anthony was finally able to see what true indulgence looked like.

While the road was paved the same as any other, either side of the street was filled with beautiful gardens. The sheer variety of flowers was something he couldn't even fathom. Soft green grass complemented by a cacophony of colorful blossoms spread across a hilly landscape. Mixed within this scenery were several parks, forests with various paths to walk, and a few houses.

The houses were not spaced close together. Each one looked like it was a world unto itself, an isolated paradise which nobody could intrude upon. Not all of the houses were the same either. Some were only one-story tall, some were two, some were designed to look like a castle, while others appeared more modern. They even passed one that looked like it had been carved from a single crystal.

"I've heard about this place, but I never imagined I would actually get to visit at some point," Secilia muttered as she also watched the passing scenery.

"It is pretty nice," Anthony said.

Secilia snorted. "What kind of understatement is that? Don't tell me you've seen something more ridiculously opulent than this. The Omni Charleston is literally the most expensive resort in all of Academy Island. There's not a single place you can go that will be more expensive than this, or more luxurious."

"Are you forgetting who I was bound to?" asked Anthony, a grin tugging at his mouth. "Lilith was the most powerful succubus in the entire world. She had more money than she knew what to do with, so of course, everywhere we stayed was about as good as this. I've also visited numerous beautiful mansions like Elizabeth's seaside resort."

"You have?!" That was not Secilia who spoke, but an incredibly surprised Marianne, who gawked at him with wide eyes and a dropped jaw. "W-when was this? Why did I not know you had come to visit?"

"That would be my fault." Elizabeth thrust herself into the conversation. "I did not want you to meet Lilith. She was a dear friend, and someone I respected a lot. However, she was also very... um, indelicate."

"You mean she was lewd," Anthony deadpanned. "It's okay, to be honest. Lilith was an incredibly horny woman who had sex at least six or seven times a day. I'm certain your mother did not want you seeing that and did her best to keep you away."

Marianne looked at Elizabeth, who seemed to have become quite fond of the scenery. Anthony was then the witness to the extraordinary sight of his new roommate pouting. Her cheeks swelled like a chipmunk with too many acorns in its mouth and her cheeks turned red. When combined with her narrowed eyes, he could not help but think she looked utterly adorable.

He was sure that wasn't what she was going for.

"Mother, I am twenty-one years old! That's more than old enough to know about... that kind of stuff." Though she started off strong, Marianne puttered out at the end. He was surprised she hadn't decided to speak to her mom with that second persona of hers. He guessed it was probably something she reserved for other people, or when she needed to be strong.

"Back then you were only nineteen," Elizabeth said. "I didn't want you seeing how much sex that woman had. And I didn't want you accidentally stumbling upon them while they were having it."

"That..."

Marianne looked like her face might explode with blood as she trailed off. She placed her hands between her thighs and squirmed as if imagining what it would be like to walk in on someone having sex. Anthony almost sighed. If she was embarrassed by that, how would she feel about actually having sex? Yet the moment this thought crossed his mind, Marianne looked up, her gaze locking with his... and then she smiled.

Time seemed to stand still for a moment as her smile, complete with seductively upturned lips and slightly narrowed eyes, appeared within his vision. It seemed she was, in fact, still relying on her public face to deal with her mother, but she was being a lot more subtle about it.

"If you wanted your daughter to stay away from that kind of thing, why did you task her with finding me?" asked Anthony, trying to ignore the dangerous look in Marianne's eyes. He could already see her ears turning red, so it would be best to pretend he saw nothing.

"Because I need someone who can protect her," Elizabeth confessed. "Being who I am, my life is an incredibly dangerous one, and the people I am close to are also in constant danger. When I heard you had become an incubus, I thought sending my daughter to your side would keep her safe. I never expected she'd be attacked before she even arrived."

That made a bit of sense. Just a bit.

It was true that Elizabeth was always in danger from attacks by various factions. Humans hated her because they thought all vampires were evil, and demons hated her because she wanted to make peace instead of war. While she did have her allies and was able to push the Demonic Covenant through after years of bitter struggling, that did not mean everyone accepted it. The only reason the Demonic Covenant even existed was that the countless wars between humans and demons had exhausted too many resources. There were still plenty of people who wanted to see the war begin anew. These people were not above kidnapping or killing her daughter to force her into compliance.

Now that she had brought this up, however, he really had to wonder about something: was the reason Elizabeth pushed Marianne into finding him because she had already faced such dangers before? Had something happened that made her decide to send her only daughter to him?

He didn't ask despite wanting to know.

"It looks like we're coming up on another house," Brianna said.

"That should be the one I am staying at," Elizabeth told them.

Anthony looked out the window again to find the house they were both talking about. It wasn't hard. The mansion was massive, easily four or five times bigger than his apartment. Made from what appeared to be white marble or some other shiny substance, it looked like something that had come straight out of a fantasy, with gorgeously decorated columns, several spires, and stained-glass windows. He was vaguely reminded of a cathedral, but there were enough modern aesthetics to ruin the theme.

The limousine parked itself outside on a donut-shaped driveway, and the door on the far side of the limo opened, allowing the five people to exit.

They had arrived in two separate cars. Anthony, Secilia, Brianna, Marianne, and Elizabeth were in one car, while Noel and Calencio were in another car with Elizabeth's on-hand butlers and maids (aka, her personal bodyguards).

"Are the other people attending this conference living in these houses?" asked Secilia.

"I doubt it," Elizabeth answered. "I had to rent this house because I do not own my own place on Academy Island. However,
many of the other people who will be at the re-signing of the Demonic
Covenant own their own property here."

"I had no idea," Secilia muttered.

"It isn't very well-known, but Academy Island would have
never gotten off the ground if it wasn't for their backers," Elizabeth
explained as she walked up a set of steps that led to a gate. "Many
powerful countries and individuals poured hundreds of billions of dol-
lars into this city, which is how it became the technological marvel
that it is today. Many of the companies and labs are funded not
through the Academy Island's Board of Directors, but through private
investors. The technology these people fund is also shared with Academy Island itself, which is how the city can flourish as it does. Of
course, these backers have their own property here."

Elizabeth's many maids and butlers preceded the woman as they
rushed to open the gate. Anthony glanced at the three women by his
side before they followed Elizabeth and bypassed the gate, which led
into what looked like a courtyard. Behind them came Noel and Calencio. Anthony could feel the other man's eyes piercing his back.

Was that jealousy he sensed?

Anthony tried to ignore the person glaring holes into his back as
he followed Elizabeth into the mansion.

Just like the outside, the inside was lavish and decorated with
furnishing so expensive even Professor Incanscino might have
dropped her jaw. Expensive oil paintings lined the walls. The tiles on
the floor looked like they were inlaid with diamonds. He'd never seen

such a decadent expression of opulence even when visiting all the expensive resorts and casinos when he was still a member of Lilith's harem.

"Why don't we adjourn to the sitting room?" Elizabeth suggested as she turned to her army of butlers and maids. "Please prepare us some tea and snacks."

"At once, My Lady," the army shouted in unison. They were well-trained, it seemed.

The sitting room was just one of many of the rooms inside this mansion, and it looked like a mostly empty space with a sunroof. There were a few crystal tables, which glittered in the light pouring in from above, and each table was surrounded by chairs. The chairs were not made of crystal. However, they still looked like something the average family wouldn't be able to afford even if they saved up for a year.

Elizabeth bade them all sit down. Of course, by "them all," she meant him, Brianna, Secilia, and Marianne. Noel and Calencio stood behind Elizabeth as though to protect her from an enemy attack.

As he sat down, Anthony felt uncomfortable. He worried about what might happen if they broke these chairs. How much did they cost anyway? He imagined it was somewhere in the hundreds of thousands if not the millions. No way he could afford to pay for a replacement.

Not long after they sat down, a fragrant scent wafted into the room, followed by a maid and a butler. The maid was carrying a tray with an expensive tea set on top. The butler was pushing a trolley with a multi-tiered display stand filled with baked goods. There were

Danishes, donuts, croissants, eclairs, bite-sized slices of key lime pie, and cheesecake.

While the butler set the display stand in the table's center, the maid set the teacups in front of each person sitting. Then she took the teapot and began pouring their tea. The fragrant scent that had filled Anthony's nose became much stronger. He could detect a hint of plums in this tea, but it was mixed with several other smells that he didn't recognize.

"Thank you," Elizabeth said to her maid and butler as she took the teacup in front of her and brought it to her lips. She took a slow and elegant sip. Anthony could not help but think she looked like a queen with the way she did everything. "This tea is delicious. It's lavender with a hint of plum."

"You always did love tea," Marianne mumbled as she took a slow sip from her cup. Anthony thought she was every bit as elegant as her mother, but there was an immaturity to her actions that he found endearing. "I sometimes feel like you love tea more than you love me."

"Now that isn't true at all. You know you are the greatest treasure of my life." Elizabeth gave her daughter a tender smile, though it disappeared as she turned to Anthony. "Now then, Anthony, I have a question for you, if you don't mind."

"Ask away," Anthony said.

"Then please excuse me, but can I ask how you are still alive and how you became an incubus?"

Elizabeth's unexpected question sent a jolt racing down his spine. He was not the only one either. Both Brianna and Secilia suddenly looked hostile, and even Marianne had covered her mouth with her hands. The two Custodes Daemonium members behind her tensed. Elizabeth either didn't notice or didn't care about the looks she was receiving as she clasped her hands on the table, leaned over, and pinned him with a stare.

"My understanding is that bondmates are tied to a succubus's life. When the succubus dies, the bondmates die with them, and yet you are still alive—and an incubus to boot. Just how did that happen?"

Anthony calmed down as he realized what she was asking and why. This woman wasn't trying to be rude. Her question just came across as blunt because of its straightforward nature.

"Honestly… I have no idea." Anthony sighed as he raised his cup to his lips and took a slow sip, biding his time. He set the cup back down. "During the battle with Cane, many of my brothers were killed. In desperation, Lilith used the spell she gained from me. It was her greatest trump card, a spell that tore apart space and created that black hole that's now floating above what had once been a massive city called New York."

While he was talking, Secilia had begun piling Danishes, eclairs, and cheesecake bites onto her plate. Marianne was also nibbling on a croissant. Brianna was not eating and merely sipping her tea, though she stopped when Anthony finished talking.

"Wait. That power she was able to use came from you?" asked Brianna.

"Surprising, right?" Anthony chuckled, though he trailed off and shook his head soon after. "The power Lilith got from me was Spatial Manipulation. She could control the laws of space, bending them to her will to create all manner of attacks. It also allowed her to transport herself to any location in the entire world by ripping apart the fabric of space to create a wormhole. During the battle against Cane, her Spatial Manipulation ability was her greatest asset."

As she listened to Anthony speak, Elizabeth released a weary sound like she was tired. "Cane always did covet Lilith. I remember they met at the first peace conference fifteen years ago. He had seen her dancing with Dominique and became smitten. It was the first time any of us had ever seen the strongest Vampire Warlord act like a lovestruck fool." She had a smile on her face while she was speaking, but the smile disappeared the longer she talked until it was replaced with a frown. "We never could have imagined that his infatuation with Lilith would be so strong he would attack her and kill her bondmates out of spite and jealousy."

Silence elapsed between them, heavy to the point of being stifling. Marianne looked back and forth between Elizabeth and Anthony. Brianna was staring at Anthony with a look he couldn't place. The only one who seemed unaffected was Secilia, but even she was paying close attention to everything they said.

Noel and Calencio were also staring at Anthony. While Noel looked like she was seeing him in a new light after learning the power he granted Lilith was Spatial Manipulation, Calencio merely looked like he was trying to burn a hole through Anthony's heart.

"I am sorry. The topic I chose was far too heavy for simple tea and snacks," Elizabeth said with a conciliatory smile.

"It's fine," Anthony said, shrugging. "I don't mind answering your question. The battle between Cane and Lilith happened over a year ago. Anyway, you asked how I survived. The truth is... I don't really know. I had been on the verge of death back then. I was bleeding out, I couldn't feel my body, and I was certainly going to die, but then Lilith appeared before me. She kissed me and said I had to live. I passed out after that and woke up in the Academy Island Hospital for Magical Catastrophes, alive, whole, and no longer human." He paused. "I believe Lilith passed on her powers to me, which is how I became an incubus, but I have no evidence to prove my theory."

"Hmm. I do not believe you have to confirm your theory," Elizabeth said after a moment of silence. "I actually believe you are correct. There is still so little we know about your kind, but I do know that every incubus in recorded history was, at one point, the bondmate to a succubus." She grabbed a Danish and took a small bite before setting the remainder on her plate. "Do you wish to hear my theory?"

"If you don't mind," Anthony gestured for her to continue.

"I believe that when a succubus forms the last bond she needs to unlock her full potential, she gains the ability to turn one of her bondmates into an incubus through a self-sacrificing ritual." Elizabeth finished her tea, and the maid came back up and poured her a new glass. As she stirred some milk into her tea, the woman continued talking in an almost absentminded voice. "This self-sacrificing ritual is one where the succubus gives all of her powers, mana, and even her soul to her bondmate. As you know, succubi are creatures who cannot live without mana. When she transferred her mana to you, it killed her."

Anthony's right hand twitched at the words "it killed her." He stared at his twitching hand, eyes narrowing as he willed it to stop.

Even though he did manage to stop his hand from spasming, it did not stop the pain that filled his heart, the pain that made it hard for him to breathe.

"Well, that's just the theory I have," Elizabeth admitted. "I've done some studies on incubi before, but none of the ancient texts I have discovered tell me anything about incubi beyond hearsay. Even Custodes Daemonium's text on incubus tells us nothing about how one is created."

Elizabeth turned her head to glance at Noel, but all the woman she stared at could do was shrug.

After spending several hours talking, Elizabeth told Anthony and his group that she wanted to spend more time with her daughter and invited them all to spend the night at her residence. They had no reason to refuse.

Each one of them was given their own room. Elizabeth had asked them if they wanted to share a room, but Brianna and Secilia did not enjoy sleeping in the same bed. It was a little disappointing. Anthony would not lie and say he hadn't thought about what it would be like to sleep with both Brianna and Secilia at the same time.

The night was late; the bright moon hung over the sky, spreading a soft luminescence upon the land like a quilted blanket. A few clouds were hovering in the velvety darkness of heaven's canvas. They blotted out some of the stars. Orion's Belt was currently invisible, hidden behind the thick clouds.

Anthony knew he should have been asleep, but his thoughts were in disarray. They had been ever since Elizabeth posed her question. Instead of sleeping like he should have been doing, Anthony stood before the window and stared at the moon, dressed in only light pajama bottoms.

Lilith sacrificed herself to make me an incubus.

It wasn't a pleasant feeling, knowing his lover had killed herself to turn him into something not human. He would have much rather been the one to sacrifice his life. Even though he knew it was far too late for regrets, he still felt it keenly like someone stabbing his chest.

A knock at the door drew his attention away from the moon. The doors were not the automatic sliding doors found in almost every building. Like Professor Incanscino's home, these doors were made from varnished wood.

"Anthony? You awake?" It was Secilia.

Walking over to the door and opening it revealed the girl in question, her body clad in a simple white nightgown that complemented her milky complexion. Her hair was let down. It billowed around her head like a gentle wave. The nightgown stretched against her chest, showing off the large swells of her breasts and even revealing her nipples as they poked through the fabric.

"What's wrong?" asked Anthony. "Can't sleep?"

Secilia gave him an aggrieved look. "Don't you think I should be the one asking that? Ever since Elizabeth—erm, ever since Lady Elizabeth asked you about Lilith, you've been in a complete daze. I bet you didn't even hear the rest of our conversation."

"Guilty as charged." Anthony shrugged and confessed since there was no use hiding it. "I'm always sensitive when it comes to Lilith, so of course I can't stop thinking about it now that it's been brought up."

"Hmm…"

Secilia walked into his room. Anthony shut the door behind her and turned to the woman as she plopped down onto his bed, placed her hands behind her, and leaned back. The act caused her chest to jut out. Since she was not wearing a bra, they jiggled within the confines of her nightgown.

Anthony moved over and sat beside her, so close their thigh and shoulder were touching. He didn't say anything at first. Secilia had obviously come here for a reason.

"Do you… regret what happened back then?"

"Every day of my life," he admitted. "There has not been a single moment where I haven't regretted what happened. Even now, I can still remember that battle, remember how fiercely Lilith fought against Cane, how much pain she felt when one of us was killed. I remember Cane's laughter as he killed us, his words to Lilith, and how deeply they cut into her. If I could go back and change history, I would have made it so Cane never existed."

Even now he still sometimes had nightmares about what happened, though they occurred with less frequency than before. Brianna's and Secilia's presence helped. However, they were also reminders of what he had lost.

"This will probably sound callous of me… no, this will definitely sound callous, but I'm glad all that happened." Anthony's head snapped up to stare at Secilia as she spoke, his eyes widening. Secilia lifted her feet off the ground and kicked them up and down as she continued talking, heedless of his reaction. "If you hadn't fought Cane, if none of that had happened, you wouldn't have come to

Academy Island. I would have never met you, fallen in love, and become your bondmate. I know what happened is the greatest source of pain for you, but it was the greatest blessing for me."

"Secilia... I..."

Anthony didn't know what to say. Her words could definitely be construed as cruel in some ways. She was telling him that the single moment of his life which brought him the greatest pain was something she was grateful for. At the same time, while her words were, indeed, quite callous, they caused a small warmth to spread through his chest. She wasn't saying she wanted him to feel heartache, but that she was glad to have met him. Even he knew they would have never met if not for that battle.

Secilia leaned into his shoulder and closed her eyes. "I would have never been able to fall in love with you if you had remained Lilith's bondmate. You can think I'm a cruel and evil person for taking pleasure in your pain, but I would not want what happened to you to change."

"I don't think you're cruel or evil," Anthony whispered as he raised his arm and placed it around Secilia's shoulder, drawing the woman close.

They remained like that for several long seconds. Secilia eventually shifted, turning as she swung a leg around his body and straddled his thighs. Now face to face, their noses almost touching, Anthony could see the gentle expression in Secilia's eyes, the soft smile on her face.

Her scent filled his nose, a delicate smell that was unique to her. It filled his mind with an odd calm.

"Hey, Anthony. Do you think these rooms are soundproofed?" asked Secilia, a slight smile on her face.

Anthony could feel his own lips twitching into a smile. "There's only one way to find out."

Their kiss started off slow, but it wasn't long before Secilia had pushed her tongue past his lips and teeth to reach the wet interior of his mouth. She stirred up the saliva between them, caressing his tongue, exploring his depths. An electric sensation like chain lightning traveled from his mouth to his brain.

Anthony placed his hands on Secilia's hips as he kissed her back. Without anything to support him, he fell onto the bed as Secilia pushed him down, their lips never leaving each other. Nasally gasps escaped them as they continued their current course of action. Whenever they needed to breathe, they would simply do so through their noses and continue kissing. Neither of them was willing to stop.

By this point, Anthony was harder than steel. It felt like there was a dagger trying to poke a hole through his pajamas.

Secilia felt it too. She moved her hips, grinding her asscheeks against his stiff erection through their clothes.

"Look at you," she gasped as she finally let go of his mouth. "You're already so big and hard." She reached down and wrapped her fingers around him through his clothes. The pajamas were thin, so he could feel the heat from her palm and fingers. Her grin widened. "Your cock is throbbing so much. That must be painful for you. Do you want me to relieve it?"

"Do you know how to relieve it? I'm assuming you have an idea?" Anthony asked, playing along.

"I do," Secilia confirmed with a nod. "We just need to get these off."

Secilia climbed off him, grabbed his pajamas, and slid them down his hips. His dick sprang free with a wild bounce. It was engorged, thicker than one of Secilia's wrists, and had an impressive length. Once his pajamas were gone, Secilia stared at his soldier before wrapping her hands around it and moving it back and forth.

Anthony groaned.

"This thing reminds me of those old-school joysticks. You remember the ones, right?"

"I... I have no idea... what you're talking about."

"Hmm... maybe you have never played old-school console games before." Secilia continued handling his meat like it was one of those "joysticks" she mentioned as she spoke. "Mom used to be a huge gaming nut. Back when I was younger, she had all manner of old-school arcade games, which she and I would play. She was actually the reason I got into gaming. Anyway, most of those games were fighting games where two people would compete against each other. To control the characters, you had to move the joystick around while pressing buttons to make the characters punch and kick."

"Haaaah... and these... joysticks... they looked like... my dick?"

"Well, not exactly. They were a lot thinner and not as long, but still, seeing your meat stick made me think of them."

"I'm not sure how I feel... about that..."

"Heheh."

Secilia didn't say anything to ease his worries, but Anthony's concerns flew out the window when Secilia slid her nightgown off her shoulders. His throat went dry when her breasts became exposed. They were not the biggest he'd ever seen. Certainly, Brianna was much bigger than her, but they had a great shape and were still quite large. He loved the way they curved to form something of a crescent.

Putting her hands underneath her breasts, Secilia lifted them up and moved forward, sandwiching Anthony's cock between them. Anthony took a deep breath as the warmth and softness of her skin engulfed him. It felt like he'd been sandwiched between two marshmallows. Secilia was not done, however. Leaning over his dick, she opened her mouth and allowed her drool to leak onto him. The coolness of her saliva contrasted with the warmth of her tits, making him twitch like mad.

"For lubrication," she said when she noticed him staring.

Anthony didn't need to ask what she meant.

Once she had coated his dick in her saliva, Secilia began moving. Up. Down. Up. Down. A pleasant thrum ran through his body as she used her tits to stimulate him. It felt like a current was flowing through his dick, traveling up his spine, and shooting into his brain. The saliva she'd coated him in allowed her to move more vigorously without rubbing their skin raw.

As if this action wasn't enough, Secilia leaned down and took his head into her mouth. She swirled her tongue around the mushroom-shaped tip even as she continued with her current actions. Anthony was unable to speak as she pleased him both orally and with her breasts. He leaned back and gripped the bedsheets as a powerful pressure made his balls contract.

"Secilia! I'm—" was about as far as he got before he came.

"Ah!"

Secilia jerked her head back as he shot several loads into her mouth. Even after she let go, he continued spurting cum out. The long threads of white liquid splashed against Secilia's face and chest, covering her milky skin in another layer of white.

"Haaah… Haaaah… Haaaaaah…"

As Anthony took several deep, raspy breaths, Secilia reached up and began rubbing his cum into her skin. She inhaled deeply, eyes going half-lidded, a strange smile appearing on her face.

"I've noticed this before, but why is the scent of your cum so intoxicating?" she asked as she took another deep breath, still rubbing her skin.

Anthony's dick twitched as he saw his cum dripping over her chest, covering her nipples. The knowledge that she was now coated with his scent turned him on more than he thought it would.

"It's because I'm an incubus," he answered after regaining his breath. "An incubus's cum contains powerful pheromones that enhance its taste, smell, and causes an aphrodisiac effect to whoever smells it."

"So that's how it is." Secilia nodded as her cheeks became increasingly redder. "I had always wondered why drinking your cum made me so fucking horny. Now I know. It's all your fault. I hope you plan to take responsibility."

"Aren't you the one who should take responsibility for me? You are coming into my room and seducing me with your body, not the other way around."

"Semantics. The man is always supposed to take responsibility."

"Such infallible logic you have. How could I possibly argue?"

Anthony didn't give Secilia time to retort as he grabbed her hand and pulled her onto the bed. Secilia squawked as she flew before landing on her back. He was sure she would have said something about how he should be gentler, but Anthony did not give her even a second to retort as he dove underneath her nightgown.

Secilia was wearing black panties with lace. They didn't have much volume. In fact, they only barely covered what should be covered, and he could see the outline of her pussy through the fabric.

He reached out and placed his hand against her cooch, noting that she was already wet. That was from the aphrodisiac effect. He rubbed her pussy through her underwear, going from the bottom, all the way to the top. When he reached the top, he found her clit. It was already engorged and stiff. His cum certainly did work wonders. As he pressed his finger against it, Secilia cried out.

"It seems I'm not the only one who's horny," he said.

"That's…"

Secilia tried to say something, but Anthony pushed her panties aside and leaned forward. Another cry escaped his bondmate's lips as he sucked on her clit. He didn't stop there either. Anthony pressed two fingers against her cunt and pushed them inside, relishing in the sensation of her pussy spreading apart from his fingers.

Her hips bucking as he continued his actions, Secilia was no longer able to speak, but she could still produce sounds, and Anthony did his best to make them escape her honeyed lips. He flicked his tongue against her clit and pumped his fingers into her pussy, caressing her rigid walls, finding that sweet spot inside of her. Secilia lifted her hips from the bed, her feet pressed against the mattress, toes curling to clutch the sheets until she finally came. Her nether lips twitched and released a flood of juices.

He decided not to stop at just one orgasm and continued pleasuring her until she came two more times. Only after he was thoroughly satisfied did he remove his tongue and fingers. His face was drenched in her nectar.

Sitting back up, Anthony studied Secilia as she lay on the bed. Her body was covered in sweat. She glistened in the moonlight as she took several deep breaths, which caused her breasts to heave. Her flat stomach twitched as if she was experiencing aftershocks. She was still covered in his cum, but that only made him hornier.

Anthony leaned back over and slid his dick inside of her. Secilia released a low moan as he bottomed out. She tried to wrap her legs around his waist, but Anthony stopped her by placing his hands underneath her thighs and pushing them forward until her knees were pressed against her chest. Perhaps it was this new position, but he felt like he was hitting her in a different way than usual. He also felt a fierce spike of ecstasy from the bond he shared with her. She must have been feeling it too.

Her feet bounced in front of him as he thrust his hips from this new position. He had to flex his abdominals to generate the right amount of force, but it wasn't long before the sound of his balls slapping against her butt cheeks echoed around the room, though they were overpowered by the loud moans and delighted squeals Secilia produced.

"Ahn! Ah! Ah! Haaan! Hyk! Aaaah!"

Anthony had no idea how long this went on, but he felt his balls contract seconds before he shot his load inside of her. Despite having cum, he didn't stop—couldn't stop. His dick was still harder than diamonds. He continued thrusting himself forward like the pistons of an old car engine, churning her insides and causing their mixed juices to leak from her and onto the bed.

"Haa… haaa… ahn… ah… hrrnnn! Ooooh!"

As he fucked her like this, Anthony found himself oddly attracted to her feet. He noticed it before, but whenever she was close to cumming, her toes would clench up. He was paying such careful attention to the way her toes were squirming that he was almost taken by surprise when her pussy suddenly spasmed around his cock as she orgasmed once again. Despite this, he didn't stop.

"A-Anthony…" Secilia moaned. "If you… haaan… haaa… if you keep this up… I'm gonna—ahn! Gonna break! Fuck! You're gonna snap me in half!"

Anthony was surprised she could speak, but that just meant he wasn't working hard enough. While he didn't increase his pace, he did change positions, pushing Secilia until she was lying on her side, lifting her leg, and thrusting himself inside of her that way. Their new position made Secilia's eyes widen as her mouth opened, drool leaking from her lips.

"Ahn! Han! Ahn! Ah! Hnnn! Hn! Haaa!"

With gritted teeth, Anthony struggled against his next impending orgasm, wanting to enjoy this moment for as long as possible. He increased the pace of his thrusts. The sounds of his hips smacking against Secilia's was drowned out by the delighted screams his bondmate was producing. Her leg muscles were spasming, and her toes were clenched tightly. She was close. And so was he. Anthony bared his teeth as he increased the power of his thrusts, which caused Secilia's pussy to begin erratically twitching before, like a wave suddenly crashing over a coastal city, they came together.

"Haaaah… haaaah… haaaah…"

Anthony struggled to regain his breathing as he stood at the edge of the bed, his now flaccid cock still buried inside of Secilia. He was capped out on mana. Speaking of, his bondmate was twitching and shuddering from the aftereffects of her orgasm. Even her nether lips were spasming like she was being stimulated by an electric current.

With a sigh, he pulled out of her sopping cunt with a wet plop. Ignoring the liquid spilling from her snatch, Anthony fell onto the bed, wrapped an arm around her stomach, and pulled Secilia into his embrace. They didn't bother moving any further and fell asleep like that.

***

Lucretia stood in front of a computer terminal inside of MiliTech's main headquarters and supply depot. Several men and women were standing around her. However, all of them were frozen as if they had become blocks of ice. They didn't move, didn't make a sound, didn't even breathe. It was like they had been frozen in time.

Even Lucretia with all her powers could not freeze time for long. It not only required vast amounts of mana, but it also took a good portion of her concentration. She'd even been required to relinquish her time clone still working at the Academy Island Private Security Force's HQ to do this.

The computer terminal was a bit old-school. It didn't feature a holographic screen. It was just a simple monitor with a keyboard, but Lucretia had been alive long enough to remember when this kind of equipment was the new standard. She even remembered when they didn't have computers at all.

She had already used a decoder—courtesy of Secilia—to hack into the main server, and now she was perusing their files for anything that looked out of place. What she wanted to find was evidence that they were building and shipping off more equipment than what they were sending to the Academy Island Private Security Forces, which would be in violation of the contract they had.

It took her a while, but she eventually found what she was looking for.

She contacted Captain Dennison.

"I'm at MiliTech. It looks like several orders of explosives, attack helicopters, and tesla tanks have been created and delivered to an unknown third party. All of the equipment was paid for out of our pockets. I'm sending you the files now. Have your men dig through them. If possible, try and find out where all this extra equipment was sent."

"Yes, ma'am. We'll get right on it."

Lucretia frowned as she downloaded everything on the MiliTech server, sent the file to Captain Dennison, then sent another file to her terminal both at her home and the Academy Island Private Security Force's HQ. She trusted the captain to get the job done. However, it never hurts to be cautious.

Once she was done sending off the files, Lucretia turned around and left the room. The moment the door closed behind her, the people who had been frozen in time suddenly began moving as if they had never stopped, and noise once more filled the headquarters.

It was like Lucretia had never been there in the first place.

CHAPTER 6

SEVERAL DAYS PASSED SINCE ELIZABETH HAD SHOWN UP. Marianne spent a good deal of time with her mother, though she refused to live in the same residence. Anthony wasn't sure why she hadn't opted to live with her mom in that opulent mansion, but he wasn't going to tell her what she could and couldn't do.

It was early in the morning and Anthony was taking a shower, though he hadn't bothered getting clean yet. The hot water poured down from above and drizzled his head. It matted his hair to his face and lightly pelted his back. This warmth was something he enjoyed very much, though he liked sharing it with Brianna and Secilia more.

Several minutes passed like this. Anthony frowned for a moment as he looked toward the entrance. When he realized no one was coming, he sighed and began washing off, grabbing a bar of soap and using it to lather up.

Taking showers wasn't the only way to clean off anymore. There were radiation baths now, which were cubicles a person could stand in and get sprayed with a special form of radiation that killed bacteria. Hospitals used them to help clean patients who couldn't clean themselves. However, those sorts of devices were expensive and not something he could afford. Of course, Anthony also liked taking showers. There was something nice about standing underneath the hot water.

There was also the fact that you couldn't have sex in a radiation bath.

It didn't take long for Anthony to clean up. When he was done, he turned off the shower, wrapped a towel around his waist, and walked over to the door. As the door opened to admit him, he stepped through—and then paused when he realized someone else was already standing in the changing room and halfway undressed.

The person who was in the process of removing her clothes was neither Secilia nor Brianna.

It was Marianne.

She had removed her shirt and bra, so most of her pale skin was now visible. Skin purer than freshly fallen snow covered every inch of her body, unblemished and perfect, smoother than anything he had ever seen. The long dark hair descending from her head created a stark contrast with her skin. Her small breasts were on full display. He had never seen her chest before, but her breasts were like a pair of small bumps, not even full hills. Her light pink nipples were also tiny and cute.

When Anthony stepped out of the shower, Marianne had become frozen like someone had just hit her with ice magic, though her cheeks had also grown a startling shade of red, proving that ice magic hadn't been used.

Anthony thought fast as he tried to figure out what he should say here. Marianne looked like she was on the verge of panicking. It was the first time she had ever looked like that in his presence, making him for once regret leaving the shower unlocked. He had been hoping Brianna or Secilia would recognize the invitation, but it looked like his plan had backfired.

"Uh... sorry," Anthony apologized. "I should have locked the door."

Marianne glanced from him to the door, though she didn't say anything right away. Her eyes looked like a scared animal's. At least, they did at first. As the seconds ticked by, she took a deep breath as though centering herself, then her eyes went back to normal, her posture relaxed, and her lips were tugged into a slight smile that made her look a lot sexier than before.

"Do you leave the door unlocked so Brianna and Secilia can come in while you're taking a shower?" It was a simple question, but the way Marianne smirked as she said it made Anthony shift on his feet. She was obviously using her public persona to shield herself from embarrassment. That... made him feel kind of guilty actually.

"Yes," he answered.

Her smile widened. "You have sex with those two a lot, I noticed. I regret to inform you that both of them are currently asleep. Brianna passed out on the bed not long after returning from your training, and Secilia fell asleep on the couch. They won't be sneaking into the shower with you for a while."

"Ah. I see."

Anthony winced, understanding the implications of her words. While incubi did not steal a woman's life force as the old legends suggested, that didn't mean the women who had sex with one didn't exhaust themselves. The myth that incubi stole women's vitality had been perpetuated specifically because of an incubus's ability to have sex nonstop for days on end. No mortal woman could keep up with that.

This was the real reason an incubus like Anthony needed to gather more bondmates. It was a problem Anthony was currently trying to deal with.

Anthony needed seven bondmates, but he only had Brianna and Secilia, which meant they were sharing the brunt of an incubus's lust between each other. But human women only had so much stamina, to begin with. They could not compete with an incubus when it came to endurance in the bed, and that was being proven right now. Both of his bondmates were being exhausted of their stamina thanks to him.

I wish I could find more bondmates, but it's not like I can just choose any passing woman I see on the streets. They need to be someone I can love. And they need to be someone I trust. Marianne and Professor Incanscino are the only ones who fit that mold right now, but Marianne gets embarrassed too easily for me to approach her and Professor Incanscino is... well, she's my teacher. I can't go around bedding my teacher, can I?

Marianne turned around to fully face him, her hair swishing through the air before falling around her body like silk curtains. A few strands fell down her front, hiding her nipples from view, though it was a little late since he'd already seen them.

She walked toward him, her hips moving with a hypnotic sway that could have mesmerized any man. Anthony was no different. However, most of his attention was focused on her face. While she was doing her best to put on a seductress act, the redness of her cheeks told him she was not comfortable doing this. Not even her carefully crafted public face, which she had created for the sole purpose of dealing with situations beyond her ability to naturally fix, could help her completely get rid of her embarrassment.

"Since Brianna and Secilia are not here, shall I... um... take their place?" asked Marianne as she stopped in front of him. While her words started off confident, it was obvious from the slight hesitation toward the end that she wasn't nearly as sure of herself as she pretended to be.

"That depends." He eyed the woman with both seriousness and lust. "Do you want to take their place? You already know how I feel about you."

Several days ago, Anthony had confessed his feelings to Marianne while they were shopping for groceries. He hadn't pushed her after that. It had been his hope that she would eventually respond to his confession with an answer, but she hadn't said anything about what happened that day to him, making him wonder if maybe he had come on too strong and scared her off. He didn't think that was the case since she was still living with him, but he also couldn't think of anything else.

"I..." Marianne hesitated as the persona she had made to protect herself while in public cracked a little. "I do not know. I have not been able to figure out what I want from you, or what I want our relationship to be. I'm not going to lie and say I'm not attracted to you. I've even mast—er, in any case, the truth is I do find you attractive, and I *do* like you, but becoming your bondmate isn't a choice I can make within a couple of days." She looked down at her bare feet. "I hope... you aren't mad at me?"

"Why would I be mad? I understand." Anthony sighed as he scratched his head. "I'm sorry if I feel like I'm pressuring you to give me an answer sooner than you're comfortable with."

"No. No. You don't have to feel that way. I've never felt pressured into giving you an answer. You've been very patient with me, more patient than I think anyone else would have been in if they were in your position." She smiled at him, and this time, it was genuine. "I like that about you. I appreciate how, even though I know you want to have sex with me, you have held yourself back for my sake. Please rest assured, I... will do my best to give you an answer in a few days."

There wasn't much Anthony could say to this, so he just sighed a little before giving her what he hoped was an accommodating smile.

"Okay. I'll wait."

"Thank you."

They stood there in awkward silence for a moment, neither of them knowing what exactly to say. However, Anthony eventually decided that he should probably just leave. The reason Marianne was here, removing her clothes, was obviously because she wanted to take a shower.

"Well, I'll see you in—waaaa!"

Unfortunately for Anthony, he had completely forgotten that he'd been standing in one place while soaking wet. A large puddle had spread beneath his feet. There was essentially no friction restricting his movements.

Anthony squawked as he windmilled his arms to try and keep from falling, but not only did this result in him not maintaining his balance, he accidentally latched onto Marianne and pulled her down with him. He crashed to the ground. His head smacked against the tiles, causing him to see stars, and the oxygen was expelled from his lungs in a loud whoosh. However, he didn't have time to regain the breath he had lost.

Marianne was above him.

The vampire girl was straddling his waist, her hands on either side of his head and her face so close he could feel her breath washing over him. She had closed her eyes when she'd fallen. However, now they were wide open and staring into his eyes with a shock that couldn't be masked, even by her fake personality. She stared into his eyes, then inexplicably retracted her gaze and looked down. He also looked down.

His towel was gone.

With the towel no longer around his waist, the long, hard, thick object situated between his legs was visible for them both. It was resting against her stomach, looking almost like a raging beast with its throbbing veins and large head.

This wasn't the first time she had seen it. She had actually played with it once. However, perhaps the shock of the situation was too much for even her persona to handle because Marianne's face had gone bright red.

"Uh… let's try not to panic now," he said.

Unfortunately, those were the wrong words to say.

Marianne's scream ended up waking both Brianna and Secilia...
and probably the rest of their apartment complex.

***

"Looks like you two had some fun in the bathroom this morning.
Did you enjoy your time together?"

Anthony and Marianne were both blushing as Secilia teased
them, a knowing grin plastered on her face as she looked at the pair.
Beside her, Brianna just sighed and pressed a hand against her face as
though she couldn't believe what had just happened really happened.

After Marianne's scream, Brianna and Secilia had been startled
awake and rushed into the bathing room, thinking something bad had
happened. They had been rather shocked to find Anthony and Marianne in such a compromising position. Of course, Secilia being Secilia, she was not one to let such prime teasing material go to waste.

"I always knew you could be bold, Mari, but I didn't realize you
were bold enough to push Anthony onto the ground like that."

"Th-th-that isn't what happened," Marianne mumbled as she
covered her face with her hands.

"Oh-ho? Then what *did* happen, pray tell?"

Secilia's words only caused Marianne's face to turn several
shades darker.

They were sitting at the dinner table and having breakfast. Because of what happened this morning, Marianne hadn't prepared anything extravagant. It was just simple bacon and eggs. That said, it

was definitely more delicious than anything he could make and was certainly better than the pre-packaged meals he used to buy.

"Stop teasing them already," Brianna said right before a loud yawn made her stop talking.

"Hmph. I'll tease them however and whenever I want." Secilia crossed her arms. "It's their fault we're so tired anyway. If they just fucked, you and I wouldn't be this exhausted all the time. They deserve this."

I want to say she can't blame us for that... but I really can't deny that she's right. Anthony thought with a sigh.

Marianne looked down at the table, seemingly ashamed by her inability to decide whether or not she wanted to have sex with him. Anthony could feel the conflict she had. He was pretty sure she did want to be with him, but she was afraid of committing herself to such a permanent relationship, which was completely understandable. Mating with an incubus was the most permanent thing a woman could do.

"All right," he said. "I think that's enough teasing for now. We should hurry up and eat breakfast. You and I have classes to attend, and Brianna has school."

"Fine. Fine. I guess I'll leave things at this," Secilia sighed.

Everyone began eating breakfast, though the affair was much more silent than usual. Now that he was looking at them, Brianna and Secilia really did appear much more tired than normal. Their postures were slumped, and they yawned periodically. That made him feel guilty, made him wonder if maybe he should put more effort into finding women to bond with. He still needed five—four if he was willing to count Marianne as his.

And yet I wouldn't even know where to begin looking...

The biggest issue with finding bondmates was that Anthony was extremely particular about who he wanted to bond with. It was a big decision. Whoever bonded with him would be bound to him for life, so he wanted to make sure each person he bonded with was someone he didn't mind spending eternity with.

While he was eating, his wristwatch began buzzing. He glanced at it and noticed he had a call. Once he swallowed his food, he excused himself, stood up, and walked further into the living as he accepted the call.

"Hello?" His voice did not transmit through the air but telepathically.

"Hello, Anthony."

The voice on the other end was familiar. He recognized the mature and soft quality from having spoken to her barely two days ago.

"Lady Elizabeth, I think this is the first time you've ever called me."

He had given Elizabeth Tepes his telechat ID so she could contact him whenever she needed to, but she had not used it before now. He wondered what she wanted from him.

"I am not one to make house calls for no reason. In either event, the reason I am calling you today is because there will be a ball held two days from now for all the attending members of the peace conference. I would like it if you and my daughter could make an appearance. Of course, your two bondmates are welcome to come as well."

"A ball? Well, I don't mind attending, but I don't have anything to wear?"

Anthony had been to balls before as a member of Lilith's harem, so he wasn't as unfamiliar with balls as the average person. They were extravagant affairs where nobles and dignitaries across the globe attended to bump elbows, make nice, and gather intelligence on their rivals and frenemies.

"You don't need to worry about that. I have already sent you the appropriate attire. It should be arriving at any moment."

As if her words were magical, the doorbell rang, causing Anthony to turn around.

"I'll get it," Brianna said as she stood up and walked over to the door. She pressed a button and the door slid open. On the other side was a man with a large parcel in his arms.

"I have a special delivery for Anthony Amasius," a voice that Anthony did not recognize said.

"Anthony is not available right now. I can accept the package on his behalf."

"Very well. Sign here, please."

Brianna signed a small tablet with her name, accepted the package, and closed the door. She wandered back into the living room, a box far larger than he expected in her hands. It was longer than it was wide by at least two feet and probably about six or seven inches thick. Anthony was not the only one who noticed the package in her hand.

"What's in the box?" asked Secilia.

"Don't know."

Brianna shrugged as she went into the living room and set the box on the floor. She took several steps back and studied the box as though looking at it from this angle would somehow reveal the contents to her. When it became clear that she wouldn't learn anything by standing there, Brianna knelt on the floor and opened the box.

"These are… dresses?!" Brianna muttered in shock.

There were, indeed, three dresses located inside of the box. Each one was gorgeous and probably cost more than he could ever afford. The one Brianna lifted out of the box and held up was a strapless black gown featuring a sweetheart neckline, expensive jewels along the bodice, and a floor-length skirt with a slit going up the front.

"They're gorgeous," Marianna said. Secilia just whistled.

Now that they knew what the box contained, Marianne and Secilia joined Brianna on the floor and began studying the outfits. The way their eyes sparkled as they pulled out the remaining gowns reminded him that all of three of these women were, well, women. It didn't matter that one was a vampire, another belonged to an organization that killed demons, and the last was an expert hacker and magical engineer. Women, no matter their profession, would always love to dress up.

At least, most of them.

"Hey, it looks like there is also a suit in here," Secilia said, holding up the white suit for them to see. "Looks like this one is in Anthony's size too."

"I wonder who sent these?" Brianna murmured.

"Your guess is as good as mine." Secilia shrugged.

"It looks like your outfits just arrived," Anthony said via telepathy.

"Oh, good. I was worried they wouldn't arrive on time. You and the girls should be sure to try them on before the ball. I'm confident they will fit, but it is always good to be sure. I'll have one of my butlers come to pick you four up at around four in the evening in two days' time."

Before Anthony could say anything, Elizabeth ceased the telepathic communication. He ran a hand through his hair. It looked like that woman wasn't going to give him a chance to decline. Well, he supposed he owed it to her to at least make an appearance. After all, he was trying to take her daughter away.

Wandering over to the girls, Anthony explained who these outfits were from and what they were for.

Needless to say, the girls were all rather excited, even Brianna.

***

It had been a very long time since Anthony had worn a suit, but it was nice to know he still looked good in one.

He stood before the window leading onto the balcony, staring at his reflection in the glass, making sure nothing was out of place. The dark blue jacket and slacks bordered on black and contained sharp creases. Notched lapels, basted sleeves, chest welt pockets, and a double-vented back lent the suit a refined air. It fit him well, being tight enough to show off his physique, but loose enough that it wasn't uncomfortable to wear. The fabric was soft and didn't roughen up his skin. He also wore black shoes that had been polished to a shine, finishing off the outfit.

"Sorry for the wait," a voice called from behind him.

Anthony turned around and opened his mouth to speak, but his jaw ended up dropping to the floor.

Brianna, Marianne, and Secilia were dressed in the gowns that had come with his suit.

They looked stunning.

Brianna's outfit was an off-the-shoulder gown that displayed her silky collarbone and shoulders. It was a deep burgundy color that complemented her hair. Applique lace designs around the bust brought attention to her large chest. Her hair had also been done up into an intricate bun near the back, meaning her graceful neck was also being showcased. It was a beautiful gown, but the one wearing it was even more beautiful. As always, she was carrying her music case.

Marianne was wearing a strapless gown. It looked magnificent on her. The jewels embedded into the bodice glittered as the light hit them. The dress was tight and showed off her slender body. While she did not have a full figure like Brianna or Secilia, that hardly mattered, and in fact, he would say this dress suited her more because of her smaller stature and petite frame.

Standing beside Brianna was Secilia, adorned in a pleated dress made from silk. Below the rounded neckline was a front cutout that went from her neck to her stomach, where it disappeared into a tight sash. He could see her cleavage, but couldn't see more than a hint, offering a tantalizing glimpse that was even more exotic than if she had been completely bare-chested. The short sleeves of the gown meant he could also see her slender arms, which were fairly muscular thanks to all of her engineering work. The way the dress revealed her curvaceous figure left him speechless.

"Have you been rendered dumb by our incredible beauty?" asked Secilia, snickering. While the other two women seemed a little embarrassed to be seen by him, she had no trouble. The smirk on her face was as mesmerizing as the clothes she wore.

"A little. Yeah," Anthony admitted.

Secilia seemed shocked by his admittance, but she recovered quickly. "Hmph. At least you can admit it. That said, don't think you're going to get away with not complimenting us properly. It was hard to put these dresses on, you know. The least you can do is tell us we look good."

"You three look incredible," Anthony said honestly. "I imagine the moment you arrive at the ball, all the other women are going to burn with rage and jealousy at how beautiful you three look."

"And the men will burn with rage and jealousy because you have three gorgeous women on your arms."

"That goes without saying."

While Anthony and Secilia flirted, Brianna gathered her courage and stepped forward. Her cheeks were red.

"I've never... worn something like this before," she confessed.

"I can tell, but you don't have to be so embarrassed," Anthony said. "You look great."

"Th-thank you."

"And... what about me?" Marianne asked, clasping her hands behind her back and smiling. It looked like her more confident persona was already in place. "Do I look good as well?" "That goes without saying." Anthony smiled in reply. "You look more elegant and refined than any princess I've ever seen... and I've met several," he added after a slight pause.

Marianne looked away. Her cheeks were red. Even her ears were blushing.

It was already nearing the designated time when Elizabeth's butler would come to pick them up, so the group traveled downstairs. There were several people in the lobby when they arrived. All of them gawked at the group of gorgeous women traveling toward the exit, trailing after them with their eyes. Anthony and the others tried to ignore the stares as they rushed out of the building.

They emerged from the building and onto the crowded street, where even more people stared at them, but they, fortunately, didn't have to be stared at for too long. An expensive black limo came flying in and stopped in front of them. The door into the limo opened automatically, an obvious invitation, and one none of them dared ignore.

Like the one they had been in when riding with Elizabeth, this one had a spacious interior. The leather seat traveled around the outside to form a U-shape. Not only was there the door, but this place also had a small bar, and it served alcohol. None of them partook, however, as they were much too nervous about the upcoming ball to even consider drinking.

"It's been far too long since I've attended a ball," Anthony said as he tapped his foot against the floor. He was seated between Brianna and Marianne. Secilia sat on Brianna's other side.

"At least you have been to one," Secilia retorted. "I've never even seen the inside of a ballroom."

"Well, you're gonna get your chance now."

"Oh, goodie."

While Secilia replied to Anthony's comment with sarcasm, Marianne looked past him to gaze at Brianna.

"Have you ever been to a ball before?" she asked.

Brianna nodded. "I have been to a few, but they were always as a bodyguard rather than as an attendee. I would sometimes go to these balls alongside Instructor Noel, who was often called upon for such assignments."

"Then you never wore a dress?" asked Marianne.

Brianna hesitated. "I did... but they were never like the kind I am wearing now. They were more breathable, easier to move around in, and definitely cheaper than this." She gestured toward her gown. "I'm really hoping nothing happens at this ball. I won't be able to fight like this."

"I wouldn't worry about that," Anthony said. "Don't forget who is going to be at this ball. All of the world's most powerful individuals are attending, and I don't just mean people who wield political power. The Beast King, the Vampire Warlords, and the Succubus Queens will all be in attendance. They aren't the kind of people you can attack on a whim."

"You bring up a good point." Brianna could only nod at his statement.

Now that they had a steady stream of conversation going, the tension and nervousness all four of them felt slowly evaporated. Smiles appeared on their faces as they began discussing the ball. Anthony gave them some insider information on the Succubus Queens, Brianna told them about her experiences with the Vampire Warlord known as Vlad Dracul, and Marianne informed them about the kind of man the Beast King was. Secilia didn't have any information to give, but she was listening intently.

Before they knew it, they had arrived at the resort where the ball was being held.

***

The resort hotel where the ball was taking place appeared to be a mixture of modern and ancient Mediterranean architecture. Its main building was a simple skyscraper, albeit one that curved like a corkscrew as it went further up. Most of the building was made of steel and glass. However, surrounding the main building were several other buildings with arched windows and doors, white stucco walls, and numerous gardens.

The surrounding buildings also featured ornamental details like stone carvings and elegantly fabricated iron detailing in the door work, gateways, and windows. Meanwhile, the main building retained its modern aesthetic, but it also had numerous balconies upon which a more Mediterranean style appeared. Standing before the front floor, Anthony could see hanging gardens high above his head on multiple balconies.

Anthony headed inside with Brianna, Marianne, and Secilia. Of the four of them, the most nervous was, surprisingly, Secilia. She'd been acting calm and trading jokes with them all throughout the drive here, but once they arrived, she clammed up and was now holding his arm in a vice grip.

It was actually kind of painful.

"Relax," Anthony said. "There's nothing to be afraid of here."

"Speak for yourself," Secilia snapped. "You at least have some experience dealing with bigwigs thanks to Lilith. Do you know how much experience I have in entertaining super-rich, super-powerful individuals? None. The most I've ever done for someone powerful was create a decoding program that let him hack into several security cameras installed in the women's changing room of a high-class resort."

"..."

"..."

"..."

"W-what?! Don't look at me like that, you three! It was good money!"

Secilia was met with three deadpan stares from Anthony, Brianna, and Marianne upon explaining the one thing she had done for a noble. And it was apparently one of the most ignoble things a person could do. Even Anthony was shocked that she had the gall to create a device that let someone hack into security cameras in a women's changing room.

There was a porter at the front door with a tablet in hand. They were required to give him their names. Apparently, everyone invited to attend this ball was listed on the registry. Anthony worried that maybe their names were not on there, since none of them were powerful or noteworthy individuals, but his fears became unfounded when the man let them through.

They soon entered the ballroom, an expansive space of marble tiles, large columns, and a ceiling painted to look like the Sistine Chapel. Numerous people were already present. Vampires, humans, therianthropes, succubi, and even sirens could be seen mingling together. Tables had been set up near one portion of the wall. It looked like they had a wide array of finger foods. A small orchestra was located unobtrusively in the corner, playing a gentle tune to accompany the conversation.

It didn't surprise Anthony because these people were nobles, but the scent from a myriad of perfumes soon wafted through his nose. He wanted to gag. Maybe on their own, these many scents would be delightful, but when combined, they created a pungent odor that even a pig would stay away from. How these people could deal with it was beyond him.

Secilia didn't like it either. "Ugh… What the hell is this smell? It's like someone smeared on different types of shit, decided to wear month-old dirty socks, and hasn't taken a shower in two years."

"That was an awfully specific insult," Anthony noted.

"Nobles love their perfume." Marianne shrugged. "You get used to it after a while."

Since there was no point in remaining by the entrance, Anthony moved in with his group of women—and immediately noticed that more than half the people around him had stopped talking. The stares began soon after. Secilia gripped his arm tighter, and even Marianne leaned in close. Only Brianna didn't seem bothered. She stared straight ahead with her shoulders squared like she was getting ready to battle against an overwhelmingly powerful enemy...

Okay. Maybe she was a little nervous, but at least her poker face was good.

"Who are those four?"

"Don't know. I've never seen them before in my life."

"One man surrounded by many beautiful flowers. I'm quite jealous."

"That man must be a powerful individual to have so many gorgeous women surrounding him. I wonder why I've never met him before?"

The conversations had switched from whatever these people were talking about originally to him and the three women in his company. He wasn't completely surprised, but he still couldn't quite believe these people were just as enamored with the women in his group as normal people were. This also made him uncomfortable. Not only did he not appreciate their lustful stares at his women, but he didn't want to be the center of attention.

"Anthony? Is that you?"

When a familiar voice appeared behind him, Anthony's entire body grew stiff. It felt like a tub of ice water had been dumped on his head. He turned around, slowly, alongside Brianna, Marianne, and Secilia, and looked at the woman who had called his name.

She was gorgeous. Decked out in a skimpy gown that rode so far up her legs he was surprised her ass wasn't hanging out, and with a cleavage exposing front, the woman before him possessed the body of a goddess. Her large bust, narrow waist, and wide hips were so anatomically perfect that everyone who saw them was unable to stop themselves from drawing their eyes up the lines of her body. Her skin was the color of dusk, her curly hair a dark brown, and her eyes a vibrant yellow. There was a seductive smile on her lips that caused every man present to gulp.

Standing behind her were six men, all handsome, all dressed in tuxedos that made them look like her servants.

Anthony knew who this was.

"Naamah… it's been quite some time."

"So it is you!" Naamah clapped her hands together as she strode up to him. "When I first saw you, I thought for sure that my eyes were deceiving me. After all, your mistress is dead, and everyone knows a bondmate dies when their mistress dies, and yet here you are." She leaned in close, and the scent from her body tickled Anthony's nose. He was fortunately unaffected by the fragrance, but it still made him uncomfortable. "Tell me, how are you still alive? I thought for sure you'd have… eh?"

Naamah was forced to take a step back when Brianna stood in front of Anthony, as though she was a protective shield to block him from this woman's wicked machinations. Her eyes were hard.

"Lady Naamah, I understand that you are curious about what happened to Anthony back then. I'm sure you also wish to know about what happened, but this is a ball. Please keep your emotions in check."

While the men behind Naamah bristled at Brianna's words, the woman herself did not appear to be affected. She stared at Brianna, then at Marianne, Secilia, and finally, her eyes locked onto Anthony again. A flash appeared in her eyes. It was like she had experienced an epiphany. Following that, a dangerous smile curled at the edges of her lips.

"Now I understand," she said, her smile growing wide. "Lilith passed down all of her powers to you, didn't she? Yes, yes. It all makes sense. You are the new incubus that everyone has been talking about. What's more, you're already in the process of gathering your harem. I'm impressed, Anthony. It only took one year, but you already have three beautiful women bound to you—and one of them is a vampire to boot. I didn't even know that was possible."

"There is a lot you probably don't know," Anthony said, keeping himself calm on the outside, though he was swearing up a storm on the inside.

For the past year, Anthony had done his best to keep a low profile. Nobody knew what he was, and Professor Incanscino had told him to keep it this way, but in the span of one second, Naamah had announced to the entire world that he was an incubus. So much for keeping a low profile.

"Oh, my. So that *is* Anthony," another voice said, and Anthony almost groaned.

He turned around to find another woman striding toward him. There were seven men behind her.

This woman, like Naamah, was so flawless that she appeared to have been sculpted by the gods themselves as they sought to create something that embodied perfection. Her wide hips swayed back and forth with an alluring swing, accentuated by the dress she wore. Her red gown had slits running up either side of her legs, all the way to her hips. There was no cleavage-revealing gap in the front. However, this gown was backless and showed off not only her flawless jade back, but it also revealed a portion of sideboob. Unlike Naamah, the woman before him had short blonde hair, dark blue eyes, and a pleasant smile.

Eisheth Zenunim.

He tried not to sigh. So many familiar faces.

"Eisheth, it has been a while. You look like you're doing well," he said with a polite smile.

"As well as can be expected. It is good to see that you are alive. At least this way, Lilith's legacy will continue to live on." Eisheth smiled at him before eyeing the women surrounding him. "Are you going to introduce me to your harem?"

His hand twitched several times as he resisted the urge to rub his neck. He had known these women would be here, but he had really been hoping not to meet them. Anthony should have known better.

"Of course. This is Brianna, Secilia, and Marianne." Anthony gestured to each of them in turn. "Brianna is a War Maiden of Custodes Daemonium, Secilia attends college with me as a magical engineer, and Marianne is the daughter of Elizabeth Tepes."

"That is quite the distinguished lineup." Eisheth placed a hand on her cheeks. "I have, of course, heard of Brianna and Marianne."

"You know who I am?" Brianna blinked.

"Of course. Sarah Fortis Noel is a well-known figure with a lot of connections, so naturally, her disciple is well-known. Still..." Eisheth turned to Marianne, who gulped lightly before her expression returned to being a pleasant mask. "I had no idea you could bond with non-humans. I wonder if this is an ability unique to incubi?"

"Your guess is as good as mine," Anthony said, sighing in relief. It looked like none of them could tell he hadn't bonded to Marianne yet. He didn't know why, but this knowledge made it feel like a weight had been lifted from his chest.

"Eisheth," Naamah said with a disgruntled expression. "I'm guessing Agrat isn't attending?"

Eisheth still wore her polite smile, though now it seemed a tad fixed. "You know her. She hates attending parties since it takes time away from her nightly activities. She'll likely be at the peace conference though."

"She's a smart woman." Naamah crossed her arms. "If it wasn't for the rumor that the incubus would be here, I wouldn't have bothered attending." She cast her gaze at Anthony and grinned. "But it looks like coming here was definitely worth it."

"Marianne, Anthony, Brianna, Secilia," another voice finally broke into the conversation. "I am glad the four of you could make it."

The person who had arrived at this time was none other than Elizabeth Tepes, like a savior appearing at the last second. Dressed in a simple white gown with diamonds lining her off-the-shoulder neckline, the beautiful mother of Marianne cut a stunning figure, though Anthony felt her appearance was still a little lackluster when compared to the two Succubus Queens.

"Elizabeth Tepes, congratulations. It seems we will have another ten years of peace thanks to your efforts," Eisheth said with a polite nod.

"You are too kind," Elizabeth said, bowing her head.

"Should we also congratulate you on your daughter's successful bonding to Anthony?" asked a grinning Naamah.

"If you want," Elizabeth said that like she didn't care what Naamah did. She then turned to him and the three women with him. "I apologize for not arriving sooner. I had been engaged in a conversation with the Prime Minister of the Atlantic Federation. It is a small country located in the middle of the Atlantic Ocean, but it's very powerful because they control all the sea routes between the Americas and the European Federation. Anyway, please come with me. I'll introduce you to all the important figures."

Eager to get away from Naamah, whom Lilith had never gotten along with, Anthony offered the two Succubus Queens a polite nod and hurried to follow Elizabeth.

✳✳✳

Naamah and Eisheth watched Anthony go. While Eisheth was still wearing her ever-present smile, Naamah was scowling.

"Who would have thought that Anthony had survived the attack by Cane. Not only is he still alive, but he's an incubus to boot! I cannot believe there's another incubus again after over five hundred years."

"The coming of an incubus is always a harbinger of great change." Eisheth pressed a hand to her cheek. "Last time it was Yokumaru, and he rearranged the entirety of Japan, ridding it of eight Bijuu and putting Gitsune Hagaromo in place as their leader. He also nearly annihilated Custodes Daemonium after they kidnapped one of his bondmates. I wonder what happened to that little girl anyway…"

Having existed for over a thousand years, the Succubus Queens all knew more about world events in the past than most. Even the Vampire Warlord, Cane, the strongest among the Vampire Warlords, had not been in power when the Three Succubus Queens rose to prominence. As the oldest among them, Eisheth was not only the wisest but the one who knew the most about this world's past.

"I hear she's living somewhere on Academy Island," Naamah said.

"Is that so? You are well-informed, I see."

While Eisheth knew a lot about the past, she was not as knowledgeable about the present. Many people often called her the Archiver of Knowledge. It was her job to catalog all knowledge of the past. She had records dating back to several thousand years ago, records that her predecessors had made. The Eishethnese Library, where she kept all this knowledge, was the largest in the entire world.

"It's my job to be informed." Naamah's scowl grew deeper. "We succubi are more than just queens. It is our job to keep the balance. That is why we threw in our support with Elizabeth when she begged us to help establish peace between the races. I cannot help but feel like this boy is going to disrupt that peace."

"You don't know that." Eisheth's smile widened as she watched Elizabeth introduce Anthony to numerous powerful figures. "This young man will definitely make ground-shaking changes like his predecessors, but I have a feeling the changes he makes will be a lot more interesting than the ones they did."

Naamah raised an eyebrow. "Oh? Care to elaborate on why you think this way?"

"I do not care to elaborate. This is a party, so I would like to enjoy myself instead of speaking about matters of the past." Eisheth turned around and began walking away. Naamah stared after the woman as she and her harem disappeared into the crowd before clicking her tongue.

"Bitch," she muttered under her breath.

CHAPTER 7

WITH AN ENTOURAGE OF BEAUTIFUL WOMEN AROUND HIM, Anthony followed Elizabeth as she led him to a group of three people.

He recognized all three of them. However, two of them were people he'd only seen on television.

Among the three present, the one who commanded the most attention was the man, whose face more closely resembled a lion's than a human's. His face was covered in a thick layer of fur, a mane of shaggy golden hair surrounded his face, and he had furry ears sitting on either side of his head. The dude was jacked. He had more muscles than Anthony knew what to do with. Professional bodybuilders were not this buff. Not only was he ripped and wearing a military uniform that made him look like the villainous dictator from a certain fighting game, but he was tall, easily standing at seven or maybe even eight feet. He towered over the entire crowd.

The two with him were his wife and daughter.

Svetlana had short hair and more human features than her husband. Anthony guessed she preferred looking human.

Therianthropes *were* shapeshifters. Her skin reminded him of polished jade, pure and unblemished, but hidden beneath that skin were rippling muscles. Her white gown was sleeveless, meaning everyone could see the way her triceps flexed as she held a wine glass with one hand. The dress stretched across her toned body. On her feet were a simple pair of sandals, but that didn't diminish her appearance. This was a woman whose beauty and commanding presence did not lose out to her husband.

Alexandra was wearing the military uniform Anthony remembered seeing her wearing when he was watching the news. She had a strict and stern bearing—at least, it was that way until Marianne arrived.

"Mari!"

"Sasha!"

Marianne's eyes lit up as she rushed over to Alexandra, or Sasha, and clasped her hands in the other woman's. They looked like long-lost sisters finally being reunited after years of separation.

While Marianne became engaged in conversation with Sasha, Elizabeth led Anthony, Brianna, and a shaking-in-her-dress Secilia over to Ivan and Svetlana.

"Your Majesty Ivan, you look like you are doing well," Elizabeth said with the calm of a monarch. She didn't seem intimidated by this man's presence despite knowing he was the most powerful person in the room.

"As well as can be expected while being forced to attend such an event," Ivan said. His voice was gruff and deep, a baritone rumble that reminded Anthony of a roaring beast.

"Thank you for all your hard work," Svetlana said to Elizabeth. "I know how rough it has been for you all these years, but we want you to know how much we appreciate the effort you've put into ensuring a lasting peace."

"Thank you for your kind words," Elizabeth bowed her head slightly. "If you don't mind, there is someone I wanted to introduce you to. I'm not sure if you've heard of him. This is Anthony Amasius."

"The incubus, eh?"

Ivan turned to size up Anthony, who felt as if a mountain was pressing down on him. This man's gaze contained a pressure Anthony had never felt before in his entire life. It felt like he was being crushed by the weight of Ivan's stare.

However, Anthony had also dealt with Cane before. He had watched his brothers get slaughtered one by one, had his entire body stained in blood, and had witnessed Lilith sacrificing herself for him. Compared to that day, the day he lost everything, confronting the King of Beasts as he just stood there was not nearly as tough.

"It seems most people know I'm an incubus. Guess it's not a very well-kept secret," Anthony said as he stepped forward.

"Secrets like this can never be kept for long." Ivan eyed him for a moment, then glanced at the two women by his side. "And these must be your bondmates. I've heard incubi are like succubi in that regard, but they bond with women instead of men."

"You heard right," Anthony said with a shrug. "This is Brianna and Secilia. Brianna is a member of Custodes Daemonium, while Secilia is an expert magical engineer who attends college with me."

Brianna and Secilia were silent as they spoke, which made him hope they were okay. Was the pressure of this man's presence too much? Were they being polite and giving him time in the spotlight? Well, Secilia had been pretty pale when Ivan looked at them, so maybe she wasn't doing so well, but what about Brianna?

"Hmph!" Ivan snorted, bringing Anthony out of his reverie. "I once heard that incubi were terrifyingly strong, but you don't seem all that special to me."

Svetlana and Elizabeth both shot him a reproving look, but he ignored them to glare at Anthony, and the pressure of his gaze increased. What had once felt like a mountain suddenly turned into an ocean. It was like Anthony had suddenly found himself drowning in the Mariette Trench.

Anthony smiled at him, but it was not a nice smile. "You shouldn't judge someone by their appearance. Doing so might get you into trouble."

While Anthony had never considered himself the confrontational type, he also wasn't the kind of person who'd lie down and take other people's crap. He squared his shoulders and stared at Ivan with a look that dared him to try something.

The many conversations that had been happening around them settled and a quiet tension filled the air. Anthony tried to ignore the stares they were receiving, but he could see people out of the corner of his eyes, whispering as they pointed at him and Ivan.

Ivan laughed. The loud sound reverberated throughout the ballroom, causing the many guests who had been staring to shudder. A quick glance around the room by Ivan caused those who'd been watching this confrontation to turn and renew whatever conversations they had been engaged in. As his laughter calmed down, Ivan grinned at him.

"It seems you have some courage. That is good. You still don't look very strong, but at least having courage can help a person gain strength."

"Anthony has more than just courage," Brianna finally chimed in. "He's already faced numerous dangers. Just recently, he fought against a gang of vampires and killed every single one of them."

"Oh?" Ivan narrowed his eyes at her.

"Was this when you rescued my daughter?" asked Elizabeth.

"It was," Brianna confirmed. "Back then, Mari had been kidnapped by Blue Blood, a gang located in the Americas. We tracked them down, found out where Marianne was being held, and defeated all the vampires during the rescue operation. Despite not having much formal combat training, Anthony was able to destroy several dozen vampires with nothing but his fists." She paused. "He is also bulletproof."

Ivan snorted and crossed his arms. "Perhaps you have strength. We shall see eventually whether you have what it takes to gain true strength."

Anthony had no idea what this man meant by "true strength," and he would not get the chance to ask about it. At that moment, Marianne and Sasha had finished greeting each other and came over, one grinning and the other wearing her smiling public face like a second skin.

"We meet again, Lover," Sasha said with a wicked grin. "I didn't expect to see you here."

Her words caused Ivan to choke on his wine. It was unknown whether the word "lover" had startled him, or if he had somehow misconstrued what she meant. Anthony was certain Sasha had done that on purpose.

"I didn't expect to be here either, to be honest," Anthony said.

"You look a lot different in a military uniform than when you wear casual clothes," Secilia said, finally talking for the first time since they entered the ballroom.

Sasha shrugged. "You ever heard that old saying about how the clothes make the woman? I'm the living embodiment of that."

"I can tell."

Having finally recovered from his coughing fit, Ivan gazed at Anthony and his daughter for several seconds. His countenance seemed a little stormy. Dark emotions flashed through his eyes like storm clouds billowing in from the sea.

"Excuse me, Daughter, but what did you call this man?" asked Ivan, his voice even deeper than before.

"What? You mean 'Lover'?" Sasha tilted her head as if she couldn't understand why her father was swaying on his feet like he had been struck by a dizzy spell. "I call him that because he and Marianne are lovers, obviously."

"He and Marianne?"

Ivan finally paused to look back and forth between Anthony and Marianne. In response to the man's inquisitive gaze, Anthony acted on impulse and grabbed the vampire girl's hand. Marianne stiffened up like an icicle. Fortunately for her, her expression didn't change.

"I see," he said at last. "So you were not talking about yourself, but your friend. That makes sense. Ha-ha-ha! There's no way you'd ever be interested in a scrawny guy like this!"

Anthony bristled at being called "scrawny," but when compared to Ivan and his hulking muscles, he was certainly scrawny by comparison. He couldn't deny it. But it still annoyed him.

"Oh, I don't know about that," Sasha said with a contemplative glance at Anthony. "I think he's rather hunky myself. Truth be told, I'm kind of curious to know what kind of heat he must be packing under that suit to catch Mari's interest."

Ivan began choking on his drink again.

"I'll never allow that... that... that manwhore to touch you!" At those words, the temperature seemed to drop several degrees—not that Ivan was paying attention. "Look at that man! He already has several lovers! If you became his lover, you'd just be one of many! You'd be pushed to the wayside and quickly forgotten! I'll never allow that to happen!" He paused, heaving for breath, then added, "Besides, you're not marrying until you're at least forty."

"You don't get to decide that!" Sasha snapped.

"I'm your father! Your entire future is decided by me!"

"Like hell it is!"

What had at once been a man raving about how Anthony wasn't worthy of his daughter soon became a squabble between father and daughter... with Anthony trapped in the middle. He wondered what he had done to deserve this.

What the hell is with these two? Is this how they always act?
They do realize they're in public, right?

Anthony didn't know what to do, Svetlana, fortunately, stepped between the pair and smiled at them both.

"Now, now, you two. Is this any way to behave at a ball?" she asked.

The two looked like they were about to say something, but their mouths abruptly snapped closed and their faces paled when the atmosphere around Svetlana darkened. The lights overhead flickered several times. Black miasma wafted from the woman's body as she sent the two a terrifying smile that froze the blood and stilled the heart. Even Anthony could not help but shiver, and he wasn't even the recipient of that look. He couldn't imagine how these two felt.

"Yes, dear," Ivan said as he looked away. "You are... correct. I forgot myself."

"I'm glad you recognize your fault." Svetlana was still smiling her creepy smile as she turned to her daughter. "And you?"

"It was wrong of me to act so belligerently," Sasha mumbled, scuffing her boot against the floor.

"Good. It's good that you can recognize your mistakes." Svetlana seemed satisfied... at least at first. "However, I'm not the one you should be apologizing to."

Father and daughter froze when they heard these words, but both of them reluctantly turned toward Anthony, who had been caught in the middle of their argument. Sasha appeared genuinely contrite as she looked at him. On the other hand, Ivan was truly defiant and was glaring down at him like all this was his fault.

"We're sorry," they said at the same time.

"It's fine," Anthony muttered. "No harm done."

Even as he accepted their apologies, he glanced at Svetlana out of the corner of his eye. She had somehow managed to suppress Ivan, a man who was hailed as the strongest demon in the entire world, someone even Cane would not dare to fight. He didn't know there was a single person who could do that.

What a terrifying woman.

***

The party continued. Marianne and Brianna ended up being dragged along by Sasha, who seemed to have taken a liking to the War Maiden due to her strength and combat experience. Last Anthony saw of that group, Sasha had been asking Brianna all kinds of questions regarding various battle tactics and combat forms. Poor Marianne had never looked like she wanted to leave more than she did now.

Secilia stuck to Anthony like glue, her arms locked around one of his as Elizabeth led them around the ballroom and introduced them to various officials and people in power. He met with the Prime Minister of the Atlantic Federation. His name was Alcard Atlas. He was a man with auburn hair, blue eyes, and a pale complexion. He seemed to be a gentle and soft-spoken man and carried an air of sorrow around him.

"I never thought there'd come a day when I'd get to meet an incubus. I have a feeling you will become a force to be reckoned with.

You need to make sure you are careful, though. Many people will do their best to squash you before you can rise to power," the man had said. He didn't know if this was a warning spoken out of concern, or just the man stating facts. But he didn't think he was being threatened.

Anthony had promised to keep his advice in mind before Elizabeth had them moving on to meet with other prime ministers, kings, and various important political figures. All of them had expressed great surprise upon learning he was the fabled incubus. Some of them heaped praises on him, some looked like they wanted to kill him, and some remained ambivalent. During the many conversations, Anthony made sure to keep his powers on a tight leash. It would not do if his pheromones leaked out here.

He didn't see Instructor Noel and Calencio at first, but then he spotted them once or twice while Elizabeth was taking him in a circuit around the ballroom. It looked like they were acting as security. The few times Anthony caught sight of them, he found Calencio glaring at him.

"I apologize for introducing you to so many people. You must be feeling overwhelmed," Elizabeth said after Anthony met with the nth important person. Anthony couldn't even remember his name. Jester… or something.

"It's fine. I understand why you are doing this," Anthony said with a wave of his free hand. Secilia had a tight hold on his other hand as she sipped some wine she had nabbed from a passing waiter.

"You do?" asked Elizabeth.

Anthony didn't answer her at first as he observed the ballroom. Most of the people present were talking amongst themselves, some were laughing, but a good deal of the ones close by were looking at him and Elizabeth.

"Incubi are a rather odd species," he said at last. "We're so rare that the last one to show up was around five hundred years ago. However, every time an incubus appears, they bring about an unprecedented catastrophe. Their strength is considered overwhelming. The last one nearly brought Custodes Daemonium, one of the most powerful organizations in the entire world, to its knees. It makes sense for you to try and borrow that power to quell any dissenters who might not approve of the peace conference. That is also why you have been making it a point to mention how close I am with your daughter."

"You are quite smart," Elizabeth said. Her eyes went a little distant as she looked into the crowd of people. "Many of these people may be acting amiable right now, but that's all a front. There are only a few people here who truly desire peace." She paused and pursed her lips. "Truth be told, were it not for people like Ivan, Lilith, Gitsune, and a few others, my dream of creating a lasting peace between humans and demons would be nothing more than that. Speaking of, I don't believe I've introduced you to Gitsune Hagaromo yet."

With those words, Elizabeth once more had him and Secilia wading through the crowd of people. He didn't know where they were being led, but before they could reach their destination, two people appeared before them.

"Lord Vlad, it is a pleasure to see you again," Elizabeth said. Anthony felt like he'd been shot in the face.

Vlad Dracul looked like a corpse. His face was pale and gaunt, his body was gangly and long, all thin limbs and little to no muscle.

He looked like a stiff breeze would blow him over. There were bags under his eyes. And yet, for how haggard he looked, Adam felt an indomitable strength emanating from him.

It was the strength of a Vampire Warlord.

The person with Vlad was a young boy of maybe fourteen or fifteen years old. He looked a lot like a younger and male version of Selene. He was very pretty for a boy. His features were androgynous, so if someone didn't notice the Adam's apple, it would be easy to mistake him for a girl.

"Elizabeth, I see you are as spritely as ever. This ball of yours is quite... ostentatious," Vlad said, eyes never leaving Anthony.

"I see you're curious about the company I keep. Allow me to introduce you two," Elizabeth said when she noticed where he was looking. "This is Anthony Amasius."

"I know who he is. Tell me, boy, have you seen my daughter?"

Adam sensed something unsettling in his words, but he shrugged. "Not for a while. The last time I saw her was several days ago."

"Hmph. I see that girl is causing trouble again as always. Do forgive me if she caused you any problems. That child is incredibly unruly. I'll be sure to discipline her when I see her again."

Something about the way Vlad said that set Anthony on edge, but he couldn't figure out why. Vlad and the child, who had not been introduced, left soon after. Elizabeth watched them, sighed, and turned to him.

"I had not intended to let you meet that man. The young boy with him is Vlad's youngest son. I am told that he and Selene share the same mother."

"I see," Adam said, mostly because he didn't know what else to say.

Elizabeth continued leading him and Secilia after that until they reached two women who were standing by the food tables.

Well, one of them was a woman. The other looked more like a young girl.

The woman was a beauty with hair so long it traveled down to her butt. It was blacker than anything he'd ever seen before, so deep and dark it made him think of the quantum black holes Secilia had once created with a device she had built. The blackness of her hair contrasted with her skin, which was so white it looked translucent. One might have mistaken this woman for a ghost.

Perhaps owing to the feminine charms kitsune were said to have, this woman was the possessor of a figure that could compete on even grounds with the Succubus Queens. Her hourglass figure was perfectly proportionate. She had large breasts, a small waist that he could probably wrap both hands around, and wide hips. She wasn't very tall. That was typical of a Japanese person. She was also dressed in a kimono with voluminous sleeves and made with bright pastel colors. Floral prints adorned the front and swirled up the sides of her right sleeve.

Nine beautiful, black fox tails were visible behind her.

The girl next to her couldn't have been older than ten or twelve. She was incredibly pretty for such a young child, but Anthony thought it was because she looked similar to the woman next to her. This young girl dressed in a pink kimono with the imprint of a nine-tailed fox was undoubtedly Gitsune's daughter.

"Gitsune Hagaromo-sama," Elizabeth said, addressing the woman with the respectful Japanese suffix for a person.

"Elizabeth-dono." Gitsune smiled. Her voice was husky and deep. Hearing it sent a shiver down Anthony's spine. "It has been some time since we last saw each other. You have not changed at all. You look just as beautiful now as you always have."

"Thank you for your kind words, but I fear I'm no match for you," Elizabeth said with a smile.

"Ahahaha, that isn't true at all." Gitsune laughed before her eyes landed on Anthony and Secilia. "Ara? Ara, ara? Who is this handsome young man?"

While Secilia gripped his arm tighter, Anthony took a short step forward as Elizabeth gestured to him.

"Gitsune Hagaromo-sama, I would like to introduce you to Anthony Amasius."

"Ara, ara. So you are the young incubus who has been making waves recently. My, it's a pleasure to meet the successor of Yokumaru-dono."

Anthony and even Secilia perked up when they heard her words. It was obvious to anyone what she meant.

"I heard you knew the previous incubus," Anthony said.

"Indeed." Gitsune Hagaromo smiled at them both. "You could say that your predecessor was my benefactor. Back then, the nine great Bijuu were at war with each other, fighting for control over

Japan. Because I was the strongest of the nine, the other eight decided to team up so they could defeat me. I would have died had Yokumaru-dono not come to my rescue. He helped me defeat the other eight Bi-juu, which allowed me to establish myself as the ruler of Japan."

Anthony was stunned to hear about what his predecessor had done back then. The incubus who came before him sounded like an amazing man, strong, compassionate, and able to change the political landscape with his power and presence. Compared to that, Anthony was pretty pathetic.

"As I recall, the incubus before only had three bondmates, but he was quite powerful," Hagaromo said.

"What kind of powers did he have?" asked Anthony.

"Hmm... let me think. Most of his powers were magic-based. He could control the five major elements, wielded the power of gravity, and could even control time."

"Time?"

Anthony felt like someone had shot him in the spine. He also knew someone who had control over time: Professor Incanscino.

"Hmm. His control over time was his most powerful ability. With it, he could turn back the clock on even the most powerful yokai, wade through time, and even see into the future and observe the past. It was that ability of his that eventually led to his downfall, however. The ability to manipulate time to such an extent was simply too powerful and frightened Custodes Daemonium into kidnapping one of his bondmates."

The fact that Custodes Daemonium was able to kidnap his bondmate was shocking, given the man's control over time, but this was perhaps a lesson Anthony should take to heart. No amount of magical power and ability could prevent every disaster a person came across. If it could, then Yokumaru would not have allowed his bondmate to be kidnapped.

"I see now. So that's how Custodes Daemonium nearly met its end," Anthony murmured.

"Indeed." Gitsune nodded, then changed topics. "By the way, this is my daughter, Tamamo. She is quite young right now, but she'll eventually grow up into a fine beauty. If, after several years have passed, you still have not found all of your bondmates, I would be more than happy if you could marry my daughter."

At those words, a slightly blushing Tamamo stepped forward, clasped her hands in front of her, and bowed.

"I'm Tamamo. It's nice to meet you."

"Er… it's nice to meet you as well," Anthony replied absently before turning to the mother. "Let me sleep on that suggestion and get back to you."

"Ara, ara. Very well. I understand this might seem a little sudden, but please do remember my words. My daughter will grow into a lovely young woman in a few years. I'm sure she won't disappoint you."

"… Right."

***

Gitsune Hagaromo appeared to be the last person Elizabeth wanted to introduce him to, for she finally let him go. Anthony used that moment to slip out of the ballroom and onto the balcony. The cool breeze buffeted his hair and rustled his clothes as he placed his hands on the balustrade, leaning forward and closing his eyes. Secilia was standing beside him, leaning against it as well.

"I really hate being here," she said at last.

"You too, huh?" Anthony sighed. "I'm not too fond of this ball myself."

"It's just a bunch of snobby rulers and nobles greasing elbows and talking politics while secretly planning how to backstab each other later. It's detestable."

Anthony completely agreed with her. "There's nothing more disgusting than a politician's double-speak. They're all snakes."

"There are a few good ones," Secilia admitted. "That Elizabeth seems nice enough, and Ivan doesn't seem like a bad guy despite how scary he is. Gitsune is okay too, though I think her trying to pawn her daughter off on you is a little skeezy."

"You mean really skeezy. Her daughter is, what... ten? Twelve? I might be an incubus, but I do have a strike zone, and that's so far below it, it's not even funny."

"I didn't realize incubi had a strike zone."

"Now you're being mean."

Anthony and Secilia shared a good chuckle as they joked in a relaxed manner. They hadn't been able to do this while inside; Secilia was too nervous and Anthony was too busy being introduced to various political figures. Being able to travel outside like this and just talk with someone he was close to helped Anthony relax.

"I wonder how long we're going to stay here," Secilia said after a few moments of silence had passed.

"Hopefully, it won't be for too long," Anthony muttered. "I want to go home and—"

"Have sex."

"Get some sleep." Anthony glared at the woman by his side, but Secilia just stuck out her tongue. "After putting up with all these people, I'm not really in the mood for sex. And don't give me that look. Just because I'm an incubus, that doesn't mean sex is all I think about."

"Really? Could have fooled me."

"Oh, put a sock in it."

"What's that? Did you just say, 'Put a cock in it'? I would love to, but we can't. We're in public."

As Secilia continued teasing him, Anthony looked up at the night sky and sighed. He really did want to go home and get some sleep.

***

Anthony opened his bleary eyes and found himself staring at a familiar pair of breasts. He realized he was lying on his side. The breasts belonged to Secilia, whom he had fallen asleep with that night.

The light of the moon filtered in through the window, illuminating the bedroom with a soft glow. Anthony briefly thought about taking one of Secilia's nipples into his mouth but didn't commit to such an action. He had already exhausted her. When he looked up, he saw that her eyes were closed, her mouth was parted, and a little drool was leaking from between her lips.

He was thirsty.

Because he didn't want to wake her, Anthony was careful when extricating himself from the woman's embrace. He moved slowly, climbed out of bed, slid on a pair of pajama pants, and made for the door. He gave one last look at Secilia before exiting.

As he left his room, he noticed there was light coming from the living room. He wandered in and found the holographic TV was on. Sitting before the TV was Marianne. The vampire girl was sitting with her feet on the couch, knees tucked into her chest, and her arms wrapped around her knees. The show she was watching appeared to be a cooking class that was teaching how to make Beef Wellington.

"Can't sleep?" he asked.

Marianne squealed when she heard his voice. She almost fell off the couch as she turned to him. When she noticed who it was, however, she placed a hand on her chest and took a deep breath.

"Anthony, you startled me."

"I'm sorry." He gave her an apologetic smile. "I didn't mean to."

"It's fine." Marianne calmed down, then remembered his previous question. "Yeah, I couldn't sleep. I have too much on my mind."

"Wanna talk about it?"

Marianne bit her lip, hesitating, then nodded. "Maybe I should. It has to do with you, so you should hear it."

Anthony nodded as he wandered into the kitchen, grabbed two glasses, filled both with water from the tap, and came back into the living room. He set one glass in front of Marianne and drank from the other. The cool liquid quenched his parched throat, which was sore from all that moaning and grunting he had done earlier that night.

"So, what's this problem that has to do with me?" he asked.

"It… I wouldn't call it a problem per se," Marianne said as she picked up her glass and took delicate sips. When she placed her lips on the glass, her fangs became visible. "Sasha was asking me all kinds of questions like what it was like being your bondmate and whether the… the s-sex was as good as the legends say." Her cheeks turned red, but then she switched personas, becoming a little more confident. "It got me thinking about how despite living with you and being with you every day, I haven't really done anything for you."

"That isn't really true," Anthony said before pointing out the flaw in her words. "You've been cooking and cleaning for us. That's something none of us are able to do. Brianna and I aren't messy, but we have no talent for cleaning, and Secilia is a complete slob. Without you, I can only imagine how bad off we would be."

Marianne smiled but shook her head. "Thank you for saying so, but I still feel like I haven't done enough. Not only did you save my life, but you took me in without a second thought. Compared to that, I haven't done much. Also… you confessed to me, but I still haven't given you a clear answer."

"No one is expecting you to answer right away." Anthony shrugged as if it wasn't a big deal. "You can take your time and think things over before answering me."

"That's just it. I already have my answer. I was just debating how I should go about giving it to you. Do I act like my true self, or should I use this fake personality I crafted for when I'm in the public's eye? I actually felt like… I should be my true self when answering you, to express my sincerity, but the more I thought about it, the more nervous I became, until I was unable to say anything. What's more, we've been so busy that there hasn't been a good chance for me to speak with you."

Anthony scratched his head as he listened to Marianne talk. "Well… it is true that we have been busy, but at least we're speaking now, right?"

"Yes. You are right." Marianne shifted on the couch, setting her right foot on the floor as she turned to face him. "And I suppose now is as good a time as ever to let you know my answer. Just… please give me a second."

"All right."

Marianne placed a hand against her chest and took several deep breaths. She was wearing a set of pink pajamas, which Anthony had bought for her a while back after she spent all the money he had given her to buy clothes on food. The sleeves were short and her bottoms, likewise, did not extend past the middle of her thighs. Anthony gazed briefly at her milky legs before looking back at her face.

"The truth is, I… um… hold on. Give me another second please." Marianne blushed a bit, closed her eyes, and then opened them. The moment her eyes opened, a strong gleam appeared within them. It was a little different from her public persona. The determination shining brightly within her eyes was the kind that came only from a person's genuine feelings. "Anthony, I've thought about this for the past several days... and I've decided that I want to become yours. I want you to make me yours."

Anthony wondered if Marianne had shifted to her public persona, but he immediately discarded the idea. This was different. She wasn't acting like the shy young girl who blushed a lot, true, but he was well-acquainted with her by this point to be able to distinguish between her two personalities. He wondered how much courage she had used up to be able to say all that while still being true to herself.

Anthony studied the young woman as she gazed at him with strong eyes, lips pursed with determination. Her cheeks were still a little red, showing she wasn't quite as confident as she appeared, but her actions were a testament to the strength she was gaining.

"This is what you really want?" Anthony asked. "I'm going to give you one more warning. If you do this, you cannot take it back. Once you become mine, I'm never letting you go. Is that what you want?"

"Yes. That is what I want." Marianne nodded.

Anthony sighed in relief, then scooted closer to Marianne, until their thighs were touching.

"I'm glad you've finally made a decision. Now I don't need to hold back."

With that, Anthony leaned forward and pressed their lips together. Marianne's eyes widened, a blush grew on her cheeks, and her body went stiff, but then it relaxed as she closed her eyes. She leaned into the kiss and moaned softly when Anthony began nibbling on her lower lip. Her hands went around his neck as she pulled him closer as if seeking to deepen their kiss.

Marianne's lips were impeccably soft and pliant. They had a springiness that he found himself enjoying. He liked the way her lips gave when he nibbled on them, and from the way she was moaning and squirming, Marianne enjoyed his actions too.

It wasn't long before simple kissing was not enough. He wanted more. With one hand on the couch, Anthony cupped her crotch through her clothing with his other hand and began rubbing her. The fabric was thin, so he could feel the outline of her lips and pressed his finger until the fabric folded between her outer labia. A small bump near the top emerged. He rubbed it as well.

Marianne squirmed as a louder moan echoed inside of his mouth. Her breathing grew heavy as a damp spot appeared on her pajamas. While her cheeks lit up in a blush, she did not try to stop him, and instead spread her legs a little wider to grant him better access.

Anthony removed his hands from her crotch, but that was only so he could slip his hand down her pajamas and panties. Now cupping her warm, moist lips directly, he could feel how hot she was; it was like a furnace.

Her lower lips were as pliant and soft as the ones on her mouth. As Anthony rubbed his fingers along her outer labia, he admired their springy sensation. He dragged his finger along her lips, then began rubbing her clit. The small bump like a little pearl twitched under his ministrations.

The more he rubbed, the wetter Marianne became, the juices flowing out of her and onto his hands and her inner thighs.

Perhaps it was because he was playing with her, but Marianne broke their kiss and, gasping for breath, she looked at him and said, "Um… can I… touch you too?"

"Of course you can. In fact, why don't we remove these annoying clothes."

In less than a second, Anthony had removed his pajamas, then slid Marianne's bottoms off her thin legs. Her crotch was soaked. The underwear she had been wearing clung to her as he pulled it off.

Now that both of them were exposed, Anthony went back to kissing her. He cupped her warm and wet pussy, slowly inserted a single finger, and used his thumb to stimulate her clit. Marianne's hips bucked as he toyed with her. Her stomach muscles tightened as she unconsciously ground her moist lips against his hand.

She was tight. He honestly wasn't sure he would be able to fit inside of her, but Anthony did his best to make her body lubricated so she was ready for him.

Marianne was not the only one receiving pleasure in this exchange. She had already placed her hands around his thick shaft and was slowly stroking him with her hands. Her movements were erratic and clumsy. However, her clumsiness was endearing and served to further increase his arousal.

Anthony ceased kissing Marianne's lips and instead began roughly kissing her neck. She tilted her head and looked up. Her sightless eyes were staring at the ceiling yet not at the same time. Her vision was blurry, eyes filled with lust and passion.

"An-Anthony… I-I'm about to cum! Haaaah… aaaahh… why did it happen so fast? I… ahnnnn!"

Marianne's body shuddered as she orgasmed. The walls of her vagina constricted around his finger, her stomach muscles tightened, and her thighs quivered. After a moment, the strength in her body seemed to have fled as she fell forward, into his chest.

"Haaaah... haaaaah... that was... f-far more intense... than when I do this on my own..."

"So you enjoyed it?"

"Mmm. Yes."

"Heheh, I'm glad, but you realize we're not done yet, right?"

Marianne blushed bright red, but she nodded nonetheless.

Since it was her first time, Anthony had Marianne lie on her back. He lifted her left leg into the air and slowly slid the head of his shaft into her tight entrance. He sucked in a deep breath as her walls clamped down around him and struggled to push forward. Her pussy was so tight it felt like he was trying to shove his dick inside a hole in a wall that was too small for him to fit.

"Anthony..." Marianne whined. "It hurts."

"I'm sorry." Anthony leaned down and pressed their foreheads together. "I didn't think it would be so hard. Do you want to stop?"

Marianne shook her head. "Please, don't stop."

"Mmm. Okay. Mari, why don't you bite me? That should help a little."

Marianne didn't say anything and instead leaned forward and clamped her mouth down on his shoulder. Her teeth broke skin. Blood welled up inside of her mouth. It stung, but Anthony ignored that as he pushed his way inside, breaking her hymen and moving all the way in until their hips were connected.

"Haaah… haaaah…" Anthony took several deep breaths as he struggled against the desire to cum. Brianna was tight, but Marianne's pussy felt like it was several sizes too small for him to fit. Every time she breathed, her muscles seemed to contract, which sent electric waves of pleasure and a bit of pain racing through him.

"We're… we're connected," Marianne muttered in awe. Her mouth was stained with blood. He thought something must be wrong with him for finding that cute, but it could also be due to the establishment of their bond. There was now a space inside of him where he could feel Marianne's presence.

"We are at that." He smiled before stroking her cheek with his free hand. His other hand was still holding up her leg. "Are you ready?"

"M-mm. Please be gentle."

"Don't worry. I will."

With her permission, Anthony began moving. He rocked his hips back and forth. His slow actions meant he could feel every inch of Marianne's pussy rubbing against him, which made him wish he could move faster, but she had asked him to be gentle.

Despite the slowness of his actions, sweat began forming on their skin. Marianne was still wearing a shirt, so the moisture building around her chest and stomach caused the fabric to cling to her. It was, fortunately, a button-up shirt. Anthony undid the buttons one by one, revealing more and more skin. Just as he expected, she was around a B-cup. Her small breasts were charming. There was something about them that made him want to kiss them.

He didn't resist the impulse.

"Ahn! A-Anthony! If you do that! If you kiss them like that! I feel like I'm gonna—ahn! Haaa! Oooh! Ahn!"

Anthony had already begun kissing and licking Marianne's chest before she spoke. He kissed her breasts, the valley between them, suckled on her nipples, and licked the sweat off her skin. His actions caused Marianne to squirm and thrash. She covered her face with her arms as if to hide her embarrassment, yet he could see her mouth, which was open wide, tongue hanging out, and drool leaking from the sides.

Once he had his fill of her chest, Anthony placed his mouth against her now open mouth. He pushed his tongue into her mouth and swirled it around. Marianne tried her best to respond, but her actions were clumsy and uncoordinated, showing her inexperience. Even that had its own charm though.

As he continued making love to her, Anthony felt another area inside of him unlock, like a key being inserted into a chest and opening. Emotions, thoughts, and images that did not belong to him flooded into his mind. He could feel himself inside of Marianne. He could feel the way her body felt as he slowly pushed and pulled his dick in and out of her tight passage. The extra stimulation this brought caused him to lose control. He came inside of the woman, who threw her head back and released a cry as her entire body spasmed from her own orgasm.

"Haaaah… haaaaaaaah…"

Marianne's breathing was heavier than it had ever been as she came down from her post-orgasmic bliss. Her eyes were a little glassy, but there was a satisfied smile on her blushing face.

"Anthony... that felt... so good... is this how Brianna and Secilia always feel when they are with you?"

"Probably."

"I like this feeling."

"Then do you want to go again?"

Marianne paused at his question, then bushed fiercely enough to
start a forest fire. She turned her head. The redness of her cheeks descended past her neck. However, she still answered his question.

"Yes, please."

That night, Anthony made love to his new bondmate until she
fell asleep from exhaustion.

CHAPTER 8

"IT'S JUST AS YOU SAID, Commander. Large amounts of equipment and ammunition were paid for by us, but they never arrived at any of our depots."

Lucretia listened to Captain Dennison give his report as she sat at her desk. Because she was so short, her legs did not reach the ground, and the desk came up to her chest, but the captain did not say a single thing about her height. He was a smart man.

There were bags under Lucretia's eyes. She hadn't slept well in the last few days. Most of her time had been spent digging around for information. There was only a day left before the peace conference, and with the recent knowledge that someone was using the Academy Island Private Security Force's funds to purloin equipment, she had good reason to believe they were planning to do something to disrupt the peace conference.

"Were you able to track where the equipment was sent to?" asked Lucretia.

"We were."

Captain Dennison placed a tablet on her desk, face-up, and activated the holographic function. A mana projection appeared in thin air, displaying a map of Academy Island. There was a large marker several miles away from Academy Island's main city, in a remote region near the southern coast.

"After discovering that our equipment had been commandeered by an unknown third party, we looked through our satellite feed and discovered that several hover tanks were sent to this location. Their point of origin was MiliTech's main supply depot, leading us to believe our stolen equipment was sent here."

"Not stolen," Lucretia mumbled.

"Excuse me?" Captain Dennison said in surprise.

"I said it wasn't stolen… at least, not in the way you are thinking," Lucretia amended.

Captain Dennison scratched his head. "I'm afraid I don't understand."

"Don't worry about it." Lucretia hopped off her chair and walked around her desk. "Prepare a hovercar for me. I'm heading out."

"Uh, yes, Commander," Captain Dennison said, turning around to watch the small woman's retreating back. "If you don't mind my asking, where are you going?"

Lucretia reached the door, which slid open to allow her out, but she didn't leave right away. Turning, she looked at the captain who stared back at her with a perplexed expression. There was a daring smirk plastered on her face.

"I'm going to pay our esteemed sponsor Felton a visit," she said before leaving.

***

"... And that's how I met the Beast King," Anthony finished telling his story to his younger brother, who lay comatose on the bed. "But I've got to admit, he wasn't nearly as frightening as the rumors say. I mean, he does have that overbearing sense of presence, but the man's a total tool who lets his wife control his thoughts and actions. Plus, he's one of those really overprotective father types. He and Sasha kept butting heads most of the night."

The morning sun lit the hospital room, which was filled with numerous gadgets. The bed that his brother slept on was one such device. It looked like a cryotank—a giant, cylindrical object meant to keep someone in stasis—and resting beside it was a device that displayed Calvin's vital functions. It also served to provide him with nourishment since he obviously couldn't feed himself.

"I wish you could see all this with me," Anthony said after a moment of silence. He leaned back in his chair, his lips trembling as he smiled. His eyes stung but no tears were shed as he continued talking. "So many things are happening right now. Marianne became my bondmate, the peace conference is coming up, and Elizabeth has asked me to take part in it. My role isn't going to be very big. I'm just part of the guests who are attending. Even so, only nobles and rulers are allowed to attend, so this is a pretty big deal."

The sound of the door sliding open reached Anthony's ears, though he didn't move and continued to talk. Footsteps approached from behind, light, feminine, and graceful like a warrior's. They stopped just behind him. Then a hand landed on his shoulder.

"Anthony." Brianna's voice, soft, gentle, compassionate. "I'm sorry to interrupt your time with Calvin, but it's time to head out. The peace conference will begin in less than an hour. Our ride is waiting downstairs."

"Right. Thanks for giving me as much time as possible."

Anthony stood up as Brianna removed her hand from his shoulder, turned around to face the redhead, and smiled as he reached out and grabbed her hand. Brianna's cheeks turned a little red, but she squeezed his hand back. Together, they left the room and headed down to the lobby on the first floor.

Brianna did not ask him how his brother was doing. He did not tell her either.

When they emerged from the double sliding doors of the hospital and walked onto the busy street, Anthony immediately spotted the limo hovering about a foot above the ground. It was hard to miss since it was right in front of him. As he and Brianna walked up to it, the door slid open, admitting the pair.

"Hey, Anthony," Secilia greeted as she leaned against the leather seating, a bottle of beer in her hand. "Did you know these limos come with all kinds of drinks? They've got beer, wine, vodka, soda, jack, rum… this cabinet uses spatial magic to increase its size, so it can carry two times its normal carrying capacity."

"I did know these limos had their own bar." He gestured toward the very obvious bar on the other side of the limo. "However, I was not aware it used spatial magic. That's pretty impressive. Spatial magic is one of the most difficult to master magics alongside time and dimension."

"Right? Whoever built this thing is a super genius."

While Secilia looked like she was in high spirits, with flushed cheeks and a wide grin (she was clearly feeling a good buzz), Marianne was much more subdued as she smiled at Anthony. Unlike the other woman, who'd clearly been drinking booze, she had a bottle of tomato juice in her hands.

"How was your brother?" she asked.

"Same as always, I'm afraid," Anthony muttered.

"O-oh. I'm sorry. I guess... that was a dumb question." Marianne tilted her head toward the floor.

"No such thing as dumb questions," Secilia said. "Just dumb people—owch! Why did you hit me?!"

Brianna lowered the arm she had used to swat the back of Secilia's head, giving the woman a reproachful glare. "Because you are being dumb right now. I had not realized that getting mildly drunk would make your lips so loose."

"I'm also loose with my mouth... except when I'm sucking." Secilia gave Anthony a wink, but that just made him and Brianna groan in synchronicity.

In an attempt to get Marianne's mind off her unintentionally faux pas, Anthony reached out and placed his hand over hers. The woman jumped, startled. However, he merely smiled softly like any man would when faced with his disheartened lover.

"Don't worry about it. I know you were not trying to make me feel bad. Since this is your first offense, I'll forgive you if you give me a kiss." Marianne looked at him blankly like she couldn't figure out what he meant, but then her eyes lit up—until he added, "Without the persona you use in public."

"Th-that's cruel…" Marianne muttered with heavily flushed cheeks. "You know it's… harder for me to express these emotions when I'm not using my public face."

"I know, but this will show your sincerity."

"F-fine…"

After she released a long-suffering sigh, Marianne gave him a shy smile as she moved a strand of hair behind her ears, leaned over, and pressed their lips together. Her ears were bright red. She, like Anthony, could no doubt feel the two sets of eyes on them. Unlike Anthony, who completely ignored Brianna and Secilia as they watched, she could not.

"Th-there," she mumbled, pulling her lips away. "Are you happy now?"

"Not really."

"W-why not?!"

"Because I want to kiss you some more."

"… You are being very mean to me right now."

Only two days had passed since Anthony and Marianne had consummated their bond, but she had already cemented her place within his life. It likely had something to do with him being an incubus. Once the bond was complete, a connection formed between them, which allowed for a flow of emotions to pass through. This bond not only helped him understand Marianne better, but it also caused the feelings he had toward her to grow.

It was almost like drinking a love potion.

Once Anthony and Brianna were seated, the limo began moving. Like all hovercrafts, while this one did have someone sitting in the driver's seat, it was automatically piloted. The driver was only there in case the limo's AI malfunctioned. All hovercraft, from limos like this to normal hovercars, could have their AIs turned off so someone could pilot them manually. This function only activated during emergencies, however.

There were a lot of hovercars on the road that day. It seemed traffic was backed up thanks to the peace conference. Their own vehicle was stopped several times, and this happened more frequently the closer they got to the city's center.

"I hear they've sectioned off parts of the city to keep traffic away from the peace conference," Brianna said as she gazed out of the window. There was quite a big line ahead of them. This was no doubt due to the city being sectioned off like she had said. "It might take a little longer to reach the peace conference than I thought it would."

Like always, Brianna had her music case on hand. Given everything that happened to them, he didn't blame her. He had also brought his truncheons. Even Secilia was carrying her sniper case, though she had somehow managed to make it even smaller than before. Instead of being over a yard long, it now appeared to be a little over a foot long.

"I guess… we should have left earlier, huh?" Anthony scratched the back of his neck. It felt a tad itchy now, though no matter how much he scratched, the feeling didn't dissipate. "I'm sorry about that."

"Don't be." Brianna's red hair swayed with every shake of her head. The soft smile that lit her face was warm and compassionate as she gazed at him. "We all know how important Calvin is to you, and this is the first time you've been able to talk to him for a while. I'd rather miss the peace conference than have you miss talking to your younger brother."

While her words were heartwarming, Anthony believed they were misplaced. The peace conference was a once-in-a-lifetime event, something that probably wouldn't happen on Academy Island again for another fifty or so years.

He looked out the window and wondered just how big this event was going to be. How many people were attending? Would newscasters be broadcasting this live? Who among the world leaders was signing? Anthony couldn't wait to find out.

Several dozen miles away from the city proper, deep within an area surrounded by flora, and far beneath the surface existed an intricate underground operation center—a base.

While this base had become relatively empty, that did not mean it had no one guarding it. This was still an important center of operation for their forces. Numerous guards were wandering the hallways,

guarding doors that led into secure rooms only those with proper au-
thorization could enter, and keeping themselves on high alert.

"Hey! Pay attention, Marcus! We're supposed to be guarding
this entrance!"

Marcus Carcass sighed as he cast a weary glance at his partner,
an older man with graying sideburns, square jowls, and some wrinkles
around his eyes and mouth. He wore the standard attire of an Academy Island Private Security Forces member. The sole difference between regular PSF attire and theirs was the armband on their right
arm. Printed on the surface was the image of a falcon killing a snake—
the image of the Sons of Liberty.

"I am paying as much attention as I need to." Marcus yawned as
a few tired tears sprang to his eyes. "Why do we need to guard this
base anyway? The operation is already underway. It's not like anyone's going to come here."

"You don't know that," the man snapped. "It's important to remain vigilant because you never know what might happen in the future. Didn't you learn that in your classes?"

"I never paid attention in class."

His partner sent him a fierce glare, but Marcus was too tired to
pay attention to the man's annoyance. He'd been up late last night
because the operation was getting underway. All of them had been up
late, actually, including the old man next to him, but unlike this old
codger who was strict and by the book, Marcus was simply not the
kind of guy who could run on so little sleep.

He let his mind wander as he stood there. Their attack on the
peace conference would begin soon. Would it succeed? He honestly

didn't care whether it succeeded or not. He was only working here because they paid well. Once he had served his time, Marcus planned on retiring and getting a home in Muraca.

Perhaps it was because he wasn't paying any attention that Marcus was unable to do anything when something suddenly wrapped around his throat. He gagged reflexively and brought his hand up to the object constricting his ability to breathe. It was a whip. There did not appear to be anything weird about this object, but the moment he touched it, his hands became withered and wrinkled.

"Marcus!" a shocked scream came from his side. It was his partner, whose eyes had bulged in their sockets as he watched what was happening.

"H… help… me…" Marcus muttered.

It would be the last thing he said before all the fluids in his body dried out and he died.

✵✵✵

Lucretia Incanscino appeared within the underground passage and stared at the corpse of the person she had killed. She didn't know his name, didn't know his goals, and didn't know what kind of person he had been in life. It was better that way. The more you cared about your enemies, the harder it became to kill them when the time came.

"You… who… Commander Lucretia?!"

The other guard had lifted his rifle and aimed it at her, but he hadn't fired yet. The older man was far too shocked.

Lucretia turned her head to stare at the man.

Then she vanished.

"What the—?!"

Before he could even finish his sentence, Lucretia was behind him, slashing her whip down with a casual swing of her arm. The whip glowed with a golden light as it struck the man. In most cases, such a strike would not have done any damage. This man was wearing impressive armor that nullified many different types of magic. However, the moment her whip touched him, the clothes around his body rotted and fell away, though it happened so fast it looked like they had been sliced off, and then her weapon struck the man's chest.

Rotting blood spilled from the now gaping wound in his chest. Her attack had sliced through his skin, muscle, and bones, but more than that, she had manipulated the time around her whip to accelerate the time of anything it touched. That allowed her whip to appear as if it was cutting through any object it came into contact with, though in truth, it was just rotting away whatever it touched at an accelerated rate of a thousand years per second.

With both guards now dead, Lucretia moved on, walking down the hallway as though she was the commanding officer of this base.

"There's an intruder!"

"Everyone! Open fire!"

"Shit! It's Lucretia Incansino!"

"Fire! Fire!"

Her intrusion did not go unnoticed. Of course, there were several cameras located all throughout this base, including the hallway she was traveling down and the entrance she had used to get inside. A group of men and women wearing the same uniforms as the Academy

Island Private Security Forces appeared from around a corner and took up firing positions.

Mana welled up inside of Lucretia, and before any of the soldiers could open fire, several magic circles appeared beneath their feet. Every soldier present froze in place. Their expressions, their bodies, not a single muscle moved. The magic circles began spinning, quite suddenly, and the men and women who were trapped within them started to wither. Their skin became ashen and wrinkled, their bodies became thin and frail, and before long, the dozens of people who had come to attack her turned into dried-up husks.

This was the power of the Time Witch.

Lucretia continued strolling through the base. Several soldiers tried to stop her, but they, like the rest, became dried husks after she used her time magic to accelerate their time. It was impossible for a body to remain intact after she had accelerated their time to the point where they aged one hundred years in a single second.

She walked through everyone, traveling deeper and deeper into the base.

This base had multiple levels. She had already gone down three, but it seemed to have even more. Each level contained anywhere between ten to one hundred rooms, depending on what the level was used for, and no single elevator went all the way to the bottom. It was annoying because she had to travel through each level and kill all the guards, who were quite persistent in guarding this place—she almost had to admire them. This base had probably been designed that way to make it harder for people to reach the bottom.

Lucretia frowned as she finally stopped walking. This method was not getting her anywhere, or rather, it was getting her to where she wanted to go far too slowly.

With a sigh, she let her mana flow through her again, and a magic circle appeared underneath her feet. The circle spun rapidly before rising up from the floor to engulf her body, encasing it in a golden glow.

She didn't feel any different. Nothing seemed out of place. However, that was only internally. When she looked around, she could see that everything had slowed down to the crawl of a snail. Of course, that wasn't truly it either. It wasn't the world that had slowed down; it was Lucretia's time that had sped up. In most cases, accelerating one's time was dangerous because it meant one would age quicker.

Fortunately, time was something she had in abundance.

With her time accelerated, Lucretia made her way down multiple levels in what must have seemed like the blink of an eye to many people. The guards who'd stood in her way were slaughtered without pause. Because her time was accelerated, she could slice through their bodies with complete ease, though nothing appeared to happen at first. Once she decelerated her time, their bodies would explode into splatters of flesh and gore.

Finally, after an unknown amount of time, Lucretia made it to the last chamber. Her body abruptly stopped glowing as she canceled Self-Acceleration, a spell she had invented herself that sped up her time and perceptions of time relative to the amount of mana she pumped into the spell. It was a dangerous spell that consumed a vast amount of mana. That was why she rarely used it except in emergencies.

She didn't hear the bodies of the guards she had slain as they hit the floor with wet thumps, but she knew the trip back up would not be pleasant. That hardly mattered right now. With bold strides, Lucretia entered what she recognized as a command chamber. She glanced around at the control panels with their flickering lights and holographic projectors. In the very center of the room was a large table with a holographic map of Academy Island.

No one was present in this command chamber, which caused her to frown, but she strode over to the holographic map and studied it with eyes keenly narrowed in focus. She could feel gravity tugging her lips. Her heart palpated. This map was not displaying the standard Academy Island, but the underground network, which was a series of tunnels that expanded beneath the entire city. Not only were the tunnels visible on the map, but there were a large number of armed forces moving through them.

An unsettling feeling grew in her stomach.

Turning away from the map, Lucretia wandered over to a command console and used a device Secilia had created to hack into the console. A holographic screen appeared before her. She quickly manipulated it to display information on the formation of tanks within the underground network. She needed to know what these people were doing.

"Oh, no…"

Lucretia's eyes widened as she finally discovered the information she was looking for. She had already suspected it would be bad, but the information was even worse than she had expected. To make matters more complicated, she was too far away to make it in time to stop what was about to happen. She simply didn't have enough mana to manipulate time on such a large scale.

In short, there was only one person who could help her right now.

She needed to get in touch with Anthony.

***

The peace conference where the signing of the Demonic Covenant would take place was the Academy Island Convention Center. It was not the tallest building around. In fact, it was only ten stories. Compared to the several hundred-story buildings surrounding it, this building seemed rather small, but that was only when considering it from a perspective of height. With over 1,000,000 square feet of space, the Academy Island Convention Center covered more mass than any one building within Academy Island.

Anthony had been to the convention center a few times. They hosted a lot of events, including a medical convention where all the best medical minds gathered to host lectures, unveil the latest in medical technology, and discuss any and all matters concerning medical procedures and related news. He attended every year since coming here.

"Check out all these people," Secilia muttered in shock. "I knew this place was going to be crowded, but holy shit, I didn't expect it to be this bad."

"The signing of the Demonic Covenant is a massive historical event," Brianna said. "It's only natural there would be so many people attending."

Marianne nodded. "Most of them are foreign dignitaries who've come to witness the signing take place. I'm positive only a few people from Academy Island are even going to be in attendance."

"The Board of Directors will probably be here," Anthony said. "They are in charge of Academy Island. Aside from them, maybe Professor Incanscino will be in attendance since she's so important to the city."

"Speaking of," Secilia began, "I haven't seen or heard from her in a while. What do you suppose she's doing?"

"I haven't the foggiest idea," Anthony muttered as worry flashed through his mind. "She hasn't been attending classes. The 'Professor Incanscino' who has been showing up is one of those Time Clones. I wonder what's going on?"

No one questioned Anthony on how he recognized the real Lucretia Incanscino from her Time Clone. He ignored their knowing smirks.

"She might be busy helping with the peace conference," Brianna said. "Since so many people are attending, security has to be tightened, extra patrol routes need to be established, and guards need to be assigned to protect the various politicians who will be in attendance. I'm sure she's swamped with work right now."

"Yeah… that's probably it," Anthony agreed.

Anthony grabbed Marianne's and Brianna's hands since they were closer to him. Marianne latched onto Secilia's hand. Since there were so many people present, it was important to have that physical contact so they didn't get separated.

As they waded through the sea of people, numerous sights, sounds, and smells assaulted them from all sides. A pair of vampires in expensive suits flitted past Anthony's eyes. The scent of someone's perfume tickled his nose. So many people were talking that it was hard for him to hear what any one person was talking about.

Getting into the convention center proved to be a task in and of itself. They first had to stand in a large line and wait until they reached the security checkpoint, at which point they would be required to undergo a scan to ensure they were not carrying anything dangerous into the convention center. Their cases would also normally be checked, but Anthony waved his hand to open a holographic display, which showed they had special permission from Elizabeth Tepes to bring their cases inside without requiring a check.

"You four can go on through," the security guard said, waving them through the checkpoint. "Hurry up, please."

"What a pleasant fellow," Secilia murmured as they walked into the convention center.

"He's just doing his job." Anthony shrugged.

"He could be nicer while doing his job."

"Why don't you try taking his place and see if you can be nice while dealing with several tens of thousands of pushy people?"

"No, thanks. I think I'll stick to unjustly complaining about the poor attitude of the security guards."

As Anthony and Secilia bantered, Brianna cast her gaze around the convention center. Aside from the tens of thousands of people coming to attend the peace conference, there were also a large number of security guards. All of them were carrying anti-magic assault rifles and wore flak jackets installed with shield generators. Their helmets did not have visors on them, so she could see their faces. Unlike most militaries, the Academy Island Private Security Force had members from every race.

"We should find our seats," Marianne said. "I believe they are in the B-block."

"So we're close to the front," Secilia said.

"Um, I guess. I don't know where B-block is."

"I know where it is," Anthony said. "I've been here several times before."

"Me too. Just follow us," said Secilia.

They kept their hands tightly clasped together as they waded through the sea of people. Since there were so many people present, no one paid them much attention, though a few of the people they passed did give them a second glance.

B-block was located close to the very front of the stadium. They passed through a large archway and into a seating area with only a few chairs. These chairs were much bigger than standard seating and padded with leather so they were more comfortable than what you'd get in the other seats.

The Academy Island Convention Center acted as both a center for conferences and a stadium. One section was the stadium itself, while the rest was dedicated to a variety of rooms meant for smaller conferences. The stadium took up about a third of the convention space and was where sports games, large-scale events, and performances were held.

"Ahhhhh! This is so nice!" Secilia moaned in satisfaction as she plopped down in a leather seat. "I've never had the chance to sit here before. I feel like one of those rich frat boys who rely on their daddy's money to pay their way through university and get whatever they want."

"Just don't start drinking and fucking every woman you see," Anthony said as he sat beside her.

"Hmph. I think you're the one I should be saying that to."

Brianna and Marianne also took their own chairs. B-block only had five seats available, meaning there was just one left.

Once they were all sitting, Anthony glanced at the stadium field, which was covered in white cement. A stage sat in the very center of the field. Several dignitaries were already sitting on the stage at two long tables situated at diagonal angles so they formed an arrow shape when pressed together. Anthony could see Elizabeth sitting at the head of one table and the Prime Minister of Britannia at the other. Instructor Noel and Calencio were behind Elizabeth. Both looked tense.

"It looks like the tables have been separated between humans and demons," Brianna observed with a keen eye.

"That's because this Demonic Covenant was signed because of the war between humans and demons," Marianne said. "We have to remember that humans and demons were enemies at one point. Even though we achieved peace a few years ago, old wounds are still hard to ignore. I'm sure people from both sides are still bitter about the war ending without a real resolution."

Anthony didn't say anything, though he did agree.

He looked around the stadium and saw the seats were filling up. Somewhere within these many seats were the Board of Directors. They probably had a conference room instead of actual seats. There were several box rooms near the top. While they wouldn't be able to see the signing up close, the glass panels were actually screens that allowed them to zoom in and watch what was happening as though they were standing right on stage.

"What time is the signing supposed to begin?" asked Secilia.

"It will begin in about fifteen minutes," Brianna said.

Secilia sank into her chair with a tired sigh. "And here I thought we were going to be late."

"We almost were late. Fifteen minutes isn't a lot of time, you know."

"It's more than enough time for me."

"That's because you're the type of person who likes to show up at the very last second." Anthony cut into their conversation with a wry grin.

"I don't want to hear another word out of you." Secilia mock glared at him.

Before he could offer a witty retort, his wristwatch began beeping. He swiped his hand to activate a holographic screen. His eyes widened when he saw who was calling him.

"It's Professor Incanscino," he murmured, standing up. "I'll be back in just a second. I need to take this."

"We won't be going anywhere," Secilia said with a wave of her hand.

Anthony stepped out of the box for a moment and leaned against the wall as he accepted the communication. He could feel the mental connection being established between him and his teacher. These wristwatches were connected to their minds and bodies, so they were able to directly access the neural pathways that dealt with communication to allow for telepathy.

"Professor? I'm surprised you're calling me at a time like this. Is everything okay?"

"*No. Everything is not okay. We don't have much time and there's a lot I need to tell you, so listen carefully and don't say a single word until I am done. Understand?*" Anthony did not even get a chance to let her know he understood before she was going again. "*I just learned that the Sons of Liberty plan to attack the peace conference. They have planted several bombs in the underground network beneath the convention center and are going to set them off during the signing. I'm too far away to get there in time. Anthony, you're the only person I can rely on. You have to stop that from happening!*"

CHAPTER 9

ANTHONY FELT AS IF HIS BLOOD HAD FROZEN OVER. A terrorist organization had planted bombs in the underground network beneath the Academy Island Convention Center? Was this for real? The very thought seemed unfathomable, but this was Professor Lucretia Incanscino he was talking to. She wasn't the kind of woman who would lie. She especially wouldn't lie about something like this.

"Why… are you telling me? Shouldn't you inform the Academy Island Private Security Forces?"

"I can't. There's a good chance the Private Security Forces have been infiltrated. At present, I do not know who among them I can trust." The voice inside of his head stopped talking for a moment before beginning once more in a much softer voice. *"I know I'm asking for a lot this time, but you're the only one I can depend on right now. The only one this island can depend on. Even if I use Time Manipulation to speed up my own time, I won't arrive before the bombs go off."*

Anthony understood her predicament, and he knew he had to make a choice right now. This situation was not something he could sleep on. That being the case...

"All right. You can leave this to me."

"Thank you. I'm hurrying over to the peace conference, but I'm on the edge of Academy Island. It's going to take a long time for me to get there. I need you and your harem to journey into the underground network, dismantle the bombs, and take care of anyone who gets in your way. I'm sending a map to your wristwatch. The location of each bomb is marked on the map."

"I understand. You can count on us."

Anthony shut off his communication with Professor Incanscino, then ran a hand through his messy locks and sighed. This was the worst possible thing that could have happened. However, now that things had come to this, Anthony had no choice but to deal with it.

He returned to his seat. His grim expression must have startled the girls because they immediately stiffened the moment they laid eyes on him.

"Something happened, didn't it? What's wrong?" asked Brianna.

Anthony shook his head and gave her a strained smile. "We have a situation on our hands."

Because they were short on time and needed to act fast, Anthony summed up the situation within as few words as possible. The Sons of Liberty had planted bombs in the underground network and were going to set them off during the re-signing of the Demonic Covenant.

While Secilia and Marianne paled at the knowledge, Brianna's expression grew hard and stern.

"It sounds like we shouldn't waste any time here," Brianna said.

"You are right. We need to hurry." Anthony looked at Marianne. "Can you send a telepathic communication to your mother? Let her know about the bombs, but tell her to act as if nothing is happening. Should the worst happen and we fail, it will be good to have someone here who knows what's happening so they can respond."

"I can do that right now," Marianne said.

She closed her eyes, brows furrowing as she concentrated. Vampires were naturally powerful mages, though the magic they could use was limited to those dealing with the darkness element. Fortunately, telepathy was actually classified as dark magic since it dealt with manipulating the mind. As beings who were capable of enslaving others to their will, vampires had strong telepathic powers.

And Marianne's powers were above even those of vampire nobles.

"I've done it." Marianne opened her eyes and gazed at him, her expression no longer shy and demure but serious. This situation was not one where she could let her true nature take hold. "She knows the situation and promised to be on alert. She also plans on letting Ivan know."

"That's good. He can definitely help out." Anthony nodded. "In that case, we should leave now."

No one disagreed.

They grabbed their equipment and walked out of the seating booth, through the short archway, the main lobby, and out the doors.

A bright sun greeted them. The warm and humid air felt stifling after being inside the air-conditioned convention center. Anthony ignored the sweat forming on his brow as he opened his map application and used the information Professor Incanscino had sent him to find the nearest underground entrance.

"It looks like the nearest entrance is at the crossroads of Lowrie Avenue and San Mateo Avenue," he muttered. "That's ten miles from here."

"Then we should hurry," Brianna said.

"Marianne can fly, but Secilia, you don't have any Physical Enhancement abilities, right?" asked Anthony.

"Of course not. The only power I have is Farsight," Secilia answered.

"I thought as much." Anthony turned his back to her and hunched down. "In that case, get on. I'll carry you piggyback—and before you ask, no, I won't be princess carrying you. It will be easier for me to run like this."

"I-I wasn't gonna say anything," Secilia muttered.

"I'm sure you weren't."

"What kind of response is that?! Don't think I can't see you rolling your eyes at me!"

"Actually, I think Secilia and I should remain here," Marianne said suddenly, causing Secilia to pause when she was halfway on his back. Before he could ask for an explanation, Marianne spoke again. "I think we should keep an eye on the situation here. Secilia's talent lies in her sniping and while I'm not weak, I'm more fit for protection detail than actual combat. You and Brianna are the only ones who can really be counted as frontline fighters. Having us would just slow you down, and I believe mine and Secilia's unique abilities would be of better use here. We can also inform you of any unexpected changes in the situation."

Anthony and Brianna glanced at each other, then back at Marianne, whose serious expression was a far cry from her normal ones. It was different from the confident public face she so often donned. He actually wondered if maybe she hadn't created several personas to deal with any given situation.

"You bring up a good point," he said after a moment. "We'll leave the situation at the convention center to you and Secilia."

Marianne smiled in relief. "Thank you."

While he didn't say anything, Anthony believed another reason Marianne wanted to remain in the convention center was to help her mother if trouble arrived. There was a good chance the bombs weren't the only part of the Sons of Liberty's plans. If the bombs failed to go off, they might try something even more drastic like attacking the peace conference.

Since they didn't have time to waste, Anthony and Brianna activated Physical Enhancement and took off down the street. The world around them turned into blurring streaks of color. Wind pushed against their bodies, but they cut through it with ease, increasing the speed they traveled to over sixty miles per hour. They could easily keep up with the hovercars traveling through the streets.

It didn't take more than a few minutes to reach the underground network entrance. It was located in an alley off the main street. The old-school steel door was marked by an old-fashioned access panel.

To enter the door, he needed to type in the access code his teacher had given him, but once that was done, the access panel beeped and the door unlocked with a click.

Anthony opened the door and peered inside. Darkness entered his field of vision, making it hard to see more than ten feet in front of him, but he could at least make out the staircase that led down. He turned to Brianna.

"You ready?" he asked.

Brianna already had her Geminius Sword out and at the ready. She gripped it tightly with one hand and nodded at him.

"I am."

"Then let's go."

Anthony entered first, followed by Brianna, and they descended the stairs together. The staircase led to another door, but this one was for an elevator, which they used to descend all the way to the underground network.

"Can you tell me anything about the underground network?" asked Brianna.

"I can tell you what I know at least," Anthony said. "The underground network was established during the creation of Academy Island. It was originally used as a means of transporting supplies across the island without having to deal with traffic and other obstructions. After Academy Island was finished, the underground network remained and is now used to help with repairs to the city. I hear it's not used very often these days."

"So it's mostly abandoned," Brianna said with a nod. "We can probably expect to run into heavy resistance down here."

"Probably."

The elevator stopped moving and the door opened. Anthony and Brianna emerged from the elevator to discover they were standing inside of a large hallway made primarily from metal and cement. The hall was wide enough to fit large construction vehicles through. The floor was also made of blacktop like the streets above ground.

"Let's get moving," Brianna said. "Where is the nearest bomb?"

Anthony activated his map again and checked their position relative to the position of all the bombs.

"It looks like the nearest one is half a mile south of here."

Anthony kept the map active as he pulled out his truncheon and proceeded through the tunnel. Brianna followed by his side, her vibrant eyes glowing like incandescent green orbs.

While they proceeded swiftly, they were also cautious. Both of them knew there were likely to be enemies down here. No one would be dumb enough to leave the bombs they planted unattended in case someone caught onto their plans. There were sure to be patrols.

Their caution paid off. They had just been about to turn a corner when the sound of grinding reached their ears. Anthony stopped and pressed himself against the wall before peering around the corner. What he found was several soldiers dressed as members of the Private Security Forces surrounding a large tank.

The tank was a tesla tank, which possessed a fully tracked chassis and two small yet advanced tesla coils mounted on the turret. It was also equipped with an electromagnetic disruptor, which could disable enemy vehicles.

Tesla tanks were interesting weapons in that they had very limited use. They could not be used against other tanks because tanks were faraday cages. If someone did hit an enemy tank using their fancy tesla coil guns, they would achieve nothing. The electricity generated by the tesla coils would go through the armor and the tracks into the ground. Tesla tanks were anti-infantry weapons because they could fry a human or demon from the inside out. However, that was really their only use outside of their EMP ability, which could disrupt enemy electronics.

"Given that those people are down here, it looks like there are terrorists who infiltrated the Academy Island Private Security Forces," Anthony said. "Seems Professor Incanscino was right. There are traitors among us."

"We should defeat them before they can sound off an alarm and alert their forces," Brianna added.

"Right. In that case, can I leave the tank to you? Your sword will be better suited to cutting through that thick armor."

"Yes. And I'll leave the soldiers to you."

Half a dozen soldiers were surrounding the tank in a diamond formation. Dealing with all of them would normally be difficult, but Anthony had some new abilities thanks to bonding with Marianne that would make this task much easier.

Kneeling, Anthony pressed his hands on the ground and concentrated. The cold concrete sent a chill through his fingertips. His mana surged within him, roiling around like a storm attempting to break free. He had a lot more mana now than he used to. It felt like his mana reserves had doubled ever since he bonded with Marianne.

Taking hold of his own mana with his will, Anthony pushed it into the ground—or more specifically, he pushed his mana into the shadows that lay across the ground. He enforced his will upon them. In return, the shadows writhed and swayed as though they were living creatures. He felt a connection between him and the shadows within his mind. It was like they had suddenly become extra limbs.

Once he was certain he could do it, Anthony manipulated the shadows. Screams echoed from around the corner.

Anthony had not shown mercy. The shadows did not rise up and immobilize his enemies. They turned into stakes and skewered them, piercing through their Kevlar vests like they were made of paper. Of course, these Kevlar vests came equipped with an anti-magic barrier, but those only worked to a certain extent.

Anti-magic barriers worked by creating a barrier that absorbed the mana from spells, thereby rendering a spell useless. Such a device worked well against normal adversaries. However, it was possible to overload the barrier by channeling more mana into it than the barrier could withstand.

At that moment, Brianna burst into action, racing around the corner with magically enhanced speed. She ignored the bodies impaled on the shadows and charged at the tesla tank. Her speed was such that she appeared as a blur to everyone's perceptions. The tesla tank couldn't track her as she raced forward and swung the Geminius Sword, cutting through both tesla coils with ease.

She didn't stop there. Leaping onto the tesla tank, she thrust her sword into the driver's hatch, then yanked it out and leaped onto the hull. She drove the Geminius Sword down at approximately where the communication expert would be located and used her weapon's spatial severing ability to cut through the hull with ease.

A scream was abruptly cut off, letting her know she had succeeded in killing someone. She didn't stop there. After pulling out her weapon, she traveled to the access hatch and sliced it apart, leaped inside, and killed the remaining two members of the crew: the commander and the gunner. They couldn't even put up a proper defense as she sliced through their bodies and the tank with the same level of ease.

Anthony dropped the magic he'd been using. The shadows went back to being normal shadows, and the bodies dropped to the ground with wet thuds as they fell into the puddles of blood beneath them. He walked out from around the corner as Brianna hopped off the tank.

"That shadow magic is really something," Brianna said as she looked at the six dead soldiers. "Even a vampire noble would have trouble controlling shadows to this extent."

"Now isn't really the time to be impressed." Anthony gave a wry smile. "Let's keep moving. The bomb is just up ahead."

Brianna didn't dispute him. "You are right, of course. We need to hurry."

They continued traveling and eventually reached the area on the map where the first bomb was supposedly located. Upon arriving, however, neither of them found anything that remotely resembled a bomb.

"I should have guessed it would be hidden," Anthony complained.

"We should find a ventilation grate or a hatch of some kind," Brianna said.

They switched their search from a bomb to a place where the bomb might be hidden, and they eventually found a small hatch. Brianna used the Geminius Sword to cut the hatch away, revealing a control panel. This was likely an emergency control panel for people to use in the event something happened. The monitor displayed a grid showcasing the distribution of power in this section of the city. Anthony's guess was that this control panel could be used to turn the power of the city on and off in the event of an emergency.

The bomb was attached to this control panel.

It was not very big, about the size of his fist, and shaped like a square. It had been adhered to the control panel with some kind of sticky substance that resembled tar. There was no timer on the bomb, but he assumed it would be activated remotely.

"Now that we've found the bomb, we should disable it," Brianna said. "It's a good thing Secilia is so good at inventing and hacking. You'd better let her know we found it."

"I'm way ahead of you," Anthony said as he activated his wristwatch's communication function and contacted Secilia. "Hey, Secilia? We just found the first bomb."

***

"Hey, Secilia? We just found the first bomb."

The words echoed through her mind the moment she accepted Anthony's communication. Despite knowing that he was speaking to her telepathically, Secilia still felt self-conscious and peered around as though expecting someone to have overheard them. That was impossible, of course, since the only other person present was Marianne. Even so, she couldn't stop the nagging fear that someone else was listening in on their conversation.

She did her best to shove those fears to the back of her mind.

"It looks like they found the first bomb," she said to Marianne.

The vampire, who had been quietly wringing her hands together as she watched the signing, whirled on her. "Really?!"

"Yeah. I'm about to walk them through the disarming process now."

Marianne nodded and smiled in thanks, but rather than sit by her, she went back to observing the peace conference. At this moment, the conference had begun and the people involved were going through their speeches. It all seemed like pretty standard stuff about maintaining the peace they had at all costs and such. Secilia didn't pay it any mind as she began speaking to Anthony.

"Okay. I want you to see if the bomb has a port for you to plug in a cable. If it does, plug your wristwatch's cable into it. If it doesn't, then I want you to run a scan and send it to me."

"I'll get right on that."

Anthony went silent, and Secilia was left bouncing her left leg as she waited for him to finish. She was a nervous wreck the whole time. Sweat had already appeared on her forehead as her body became both hot and cold. She could practically feel the anxiety flowing through her, turning her into a jittery mess.

Secilia had been in numerous dangerous situations by this point. She'd been blackmailed by her former boss/enslaver, strangled, kidnapped, and shot at. One could say she was used to life-and-death situations.

But she had never experienced this kind of pressure before.

The pressure of knowing that the peace of the entire world was hanging on what she did next.

She felt sick.

"It looks like this doesn't have a port. I'm sending you the scan now."

The moment Anthony's voice came to her, Secilia opened a holographic screen and used her skills as a hacker to connect with Anthony's wristwatch. The scan of the bomb came to her seconds later. When she saw the bomb, Secilia's blood ran cold and her breathing had completely stopped.

"What the fuck?! Are those sons of bitches trying to annihilate this entire island?!"

"What? What is it?"

Anthony was not well-versed in technology, so he probably had no idea what kind of bomb this was, but Secilia was a tech-nut who lived for learning about new and innovative technological developments. This included military developments. That was why she knew about the Academy Island Private Security Force's stealth planes.

Of course, she also knew what this bomb was.

It was not a normal bomb.

It was an antimatter bomb.

Antimatter was defined as a material composed of the antiparticles of the corresponding particle of ordinary matter. It was the opposite of normal matter. To be more specific, the sub-atomic particles of antimatter had properties opposite those of normal matter. The electric charge of those particles was reversed.

Matter was made up of atoms, which were the basic units of chemical elements, such as hydrogen, helium, or oxygen. Each element had a certain number of atoms: Hydrogen had one atom; helium had two atoms; and so on.

At the heart of an atom, known as a nucleus, were protons and neutrons, which had a positive and negative charge respectively. Electrons, which generally had a negative charge, occupied orbits around the nucleus. The orbits could change depending on how "excited" the electrons were.

In the case of antimatter, the electric charge was reversed. Antielectrons known as positrons behaved like electrons but had a positive charge. Antiprotons were protons with a negative charge.

Because of the nature of antimatter, it was hard for people who never studied science to fathom it, but antimatter was neither hard to understand nor difficult to use as a weapon in this day and age. The Academy Island Private Security Forces even had antimatter knives as part of their standard equipment.

Antimatter weapons were incredibly powerful. With the level of technology they now possessed, an antimatter bomb such as the one Anthony had discovered was strong enough to level an entire city block. It would destroy the underground network and cause the city above to collapse inward, killing who knew how many people.

Several antimatter bombs were enough to destroy the entire island.

Academy Island was home to 60.5 million residents. The Sons of Liberty were attempting to commit genocide in the most complete way possible. There wouldn't be anything left of this island if those bombs went off.

When Secilia told Anthony this, he swore like she had never heard him swear before. She would have been impressed by his vocabulary if the situation weren't so dire.

A beep suddenly echoed from her watch.

"Okay. I've got the scan. I also hacked into your wristwatch."

"When did you do that?!"

"Never mind that! Just shut up and let me work. I'm going to use your wristwatch as a medium to hack into the bomb and disable it."

Wristwatches were a feature unique to Academy Island. They were a device that seconded as a person's identification, but they were also miniature computers in their own right. You could open lines of telepathic communication, check your email, access your accounts and profiles, browse the web, store information, read eBooks, and do any other number of functions depending on what apps you had available.

As an inventor and admittedly self-proclaimed genius hacker, Secilia had created several apps on her wristwatch that would get her thrown in jail. This included her hacking programs and decoding applications.

The holographic monitor displaying Anthony's wristwatch was already up. She didn't hesitate to upload her hacking and decoding apps into his wristwatch without his permission. She could always delete them later. Once that was done, she swiped her hand through the air and changed the screen to display the bomb.

Bombs of this nature were controlled via code-based algorithms, meaning she could hack into it using one of her programs.

Manipulating Anthony's wristwatch, Secilia established a link between the bomb, Anthony's wristwatch, and her wristwatch. Once the link was established, she hacked into the bomb and erased the program that would make it explode.

Beads of sweat formed on her brow and dripped off her chin. What she was doing sounded easy, but it was actually quite difficult to hack a bomb like this because they always came with a security program that would cause it to detonate when it detected a hacking attempt. This particular program was one that constantly evolved. Secilia was forced to use Farsight and manually access her program to bypass the security.

While the bomb's ability to activate was erased, she left the connection between the remote activation and the bomb untouched. She didn't want whoever was in control of the bomb to realize what was happening.

She sighed as though exhausted and wiped the sweat from her forehead. "Okay, the bomb has been deactivated. Move onto the next one—and hurry up! I have a feeling that whoever is plotting to disrupt the peace conference will act soon."

***

There were a total of ten bombs, and each one of them had been strategically placed around the convention center. Anthony had no idea what their plans were. He would have expected the Sons of Liberty to keep at least some of the dignitaries alive and use them as hostages, but Secilia said they were planning to annihilate Academy Island in its entirety. Whatever their plan was, it was so unfathomably horrible that he simply couldn't comprehend it.

Anthony traveled quickly through the tunnels with Brianna. They no longer bothered using stealth. Secilia had been right. Time was of the essence.

"There are intruders down here!"

"Calm down! It's just two of them! Open fire!"

"Th-their moving so fast! I can't track them!"

It was because they had foregone stealth that they were caught, but Anthony and Brianna did not mind. They would have had to deal with these people anyway.

Using his newfound Shadow Manipulation ability, Anthony slipped through the shadows and appeared directly behind one of the soldiers. With a swing of his truncheon, he slammed his weapon into the soldier's head, smashing it like it was an egg. Blood and brain matter splattered everywhere as the soldier went down, but Anthony was already on the move.

One of the soldiers took aim with his anti-magic rifle and fired at Anthony. He missed when Anthony darted toward the left and used another soldier as a shield. The anti-magic bullets tore through the man's protective shield and struck him in the chest, though they didn't penetrate his Kevlar vest—not that it mattered.

Anthony thrust his truncheon forward with magically enhanced strength, narrowing his eyes as the tip tore through the Kevlar vest, punched a hole through the man's back, and emerged out the other side. Choked gurgles echoed from the man's mouth as he released a dying rasp. Anthony jerked his weapon out and leaped backward.

As he landed back on the ground, Anthony tapped his foot against the hard blacktop. The shadows suddenly writhed as they came to life. His enemy, who had been getting ready to fire again, suddenly screamed in surprise and horror, though even his screams died as a stake made of shadows speared through his throat. With his eyes wide, the enemy combatant died. His corpse dropped to the floor after Anthony released his shadows.

While he killed two more soldiers, the other three took aim and fired at his back, which was left completely unguarded. The bullets should have penetrated his flesh and killed him instantly. That wasn't what happened.

Three sets of eyes widened when a black crack appeared in the space between them and Anthony. The bullets were sucked into the crack, disappearing from view, and then the crack sealed shut.

"What kind of magic is that?!"

"Did he just create a tear in space?!"

Anthony didn't answer the two shocked voices as he turned around and dashed forward, slamming his truncheon into the head of one soldier. His attack caused the person's head to break apart. Paying no attention to the now falling corpse, Anthony reversed his swing and struck another enemy across the face. That person's scream died the instant Anthony's weapon tore apart his face. Anthony then kicked him in the chest, snapping his ribs and sending him flying.

Only one person remained. Anthony turned to them. The man who looked like he had been about to attack with an antimatter knife froze when he locked eyes with Anthony. His entire body went into a series of full-body shudders.

"D-don't kill me... please... I... I don't want to die!"

Anthony's expression was cold as he stared at the man. "If you didn't want to die, you should have never joined the Sons of Liberty."

The man released a shrill shriek, turned around, and tried to run, but Anthony wouldn't let him. He was on the man before he could get away. A horrified scream pierced the air as Anthony used his inhuman strength to punch a hole through the man's Kevlar vest and back. The tip of his truncheon pierced the man's heart. The scream cut off as the man died instantly, and his body flopped to the floor when Anthony kicked him off his weapon.

While Anthony dealt with the soldiers, Brianna had dealt with another tank. This time she had completely dismantled the weapon. The treads were sliced to pieces. The tank lay in segments. It looked like she had chopped the tank apart similar to how someone might cut cheese into several cubes before serving it.

"We only have one more bomb left," Brianna said. "Let's hurry."

Anthony didn't say anything. His mouth was drawn into a thin line as he and Brianna moved to the location of the last bomb.

They found this bomb inside of a ventilation duct, and once again Anthony allowed Secilia to remote hack his wristwatch and use the connection to somehow disable the bomb. He had no idea how she did it. Anthony could use technology just fine, but that didn't mean he understood the inner workings of everything he used. All he could do was marvel at how fast Secilia worked.

"And that's the last of them," Anthony said with a sigh. "With this, our problems should be solved. Now all that's left to do is have Professor Incanscino arrest whoever is responsible for this."

"I don't know about that," Brianna muttered, looking uncertain.

"What's wrong?" asked Anthony.

"It's just… I can't see someone who planned to disrupt the peace conference giving up merely because we disabled the bombs they planned to use. No one would go through all this trouble just to stop because something went wrong." Brianna bit her lower lip, then continued in a slower, softer voice. "If it was me, I would have several contingency plans put in place in case the first one failed."

Anthony took her words into consideration, felt a chill run down his spine, and was about to suggest they return to the surface. Before he could even open his mouth, however, a loud rumbling sound echoed around them followed by the earth-shaking.

"W-what is this?! An earthquake?!" asked Brianna.

"No." Anthony glared up at the ceiling. "This is coming from above us, not below us."

Just then, Secilia's voice came through his mind. She sounded panicked.

"Anthony, you and Brianna need to get your asses up here right now!"

"Why? What's going on?" asked Anthony.

"The convention center is under attack! There are tanks and helicopters and troops pouring in from all over! The convention center has been sealed, but that isn't going to hold them back for long!"

Fear coursed through Anthony's body, causing him to shudder from his head to his toes. For a moment, he almost forgot to breathe, but he knew now wasn't the time to hesitate.

"Secilia, I want you and Marianne to hook up with Elizabeth! Do what you can to help fend off the attackers! Bri and I are coming back! We'll be there soon!"

"Just hurry up."

The telepathic communication went dead. Anthony turned to Brianna.

"Bri! Let's hurry!"

Brianna acknowledged his words with a nod, and together, the two of them rushed down the tunnel toward the nearest access hatch. Anthony could only pray he would make it in time.

CHAPTER 10

THE PEACE CONFERENCE was a gathering of nearly all the international leaders in the world. While there were a few diehard people who refused to even consider peace between demons and humans, the vast majority had, however reluctantly, accepted the Demonic Covenant, which imposed heavy restrictions on the harming of people, both humans and demons.

A part of the reason so many people accepted the Demonic Covenant was undoubtedly due to Ivan's support. The Beast King of Russia was known as the most powerful person in the entire world, bar none, and he had sided with Elizabeth Tepes, another great power who could influence the masses. With the strongest person in the world supporting peace, there were no doubts that peace would eventually reign.

Felton hated that.

He did not want peace.

Because he was part of the Board of Directors, Felton was sitting in one of several viewing booths, watching the proceedings on a large screen that granted him a perfect view of the stage. His nose wrinkled when he saw Ivan and Elizabeth sitting at the demon's side of the conference. He tried his best to hide it, but even he could not completely rid himself of this expression that made his disgust visible.

"Are you feeling well, Felton? You look a little sick."

Felton was startled, but he didn't let the person who spoke to him see that as he turned around, replacing the disgusted look with a grandfatherly smile.

"It is nothing. I am merely feeling a tad under the weather today. I was so excited by the prospect of seeing the peace conference today that it was hard to sleep the previous night."

"I understand what you mean. I was really nervous about today as well."

The person speaking to Felton was a younger man with blond hair and green eyes. Of course, he was only younger relative to Felton, who was in his sixties. Alexis Lawson, who was the Treasurer of the Board, was forty-something years old. Felton didn't know his exact age since he didn't care. The only thing that mattered to Felton was this man, like the others, was a supporter of demon rights. He advocated for the equality of demonkind, which of course meant he needed to die.

As Alexis blathered on about how excited he was to finally take part in the peace conference, Felton ignored him and watched as the seconds ticked by. The plan was for Felton to detonate the bombs just as the Demonic Covenant was being signed. That was part of the reason he maintained his vigilance and watched the peace conference despite how distasteful he found it.

The time eventually came. Elizabeth and Ivan were standing up to accept the document they would sign. He waited until Elizabeth was reaching out for it, then discreetly activated his wristwatch, opened the application to ignite the bomb, and pressed the button.

Nothing happened.

Elizabeth grabbed the document from the human man handing it off to her and went back toward Evan. The explosions he'd been expecting did not come. In fact, nothing happened that was out of the ordinary.

"W-what the heck is… going on?!"

"Is everything all right, Felton? What are you screaming about?"

Felton ignored Alexis even more as he tried to once again activate the bombs his men had strategically placed across the underground network. This explosion should have generated enough power that the floor underneath them collapsed, taking this entire damn conference center with him. Except that wasn't what happened. The building was still whole. There was no explosion.

Something was wrong.

Worry penetrated his gut as he activated a telepathic communication between him and the various members of the squadrons inside the underground network to ask what happened. A few of them responded, which caused him to nearly sigh in relief, but there were several that didn't. The relief he had felt just a few seconds ago changed once again into worry. He looked at the signing down below and noticed they were almost done. It was now or never.

Since it looked like something had happened to his bombs, Felton was left with no choice. He activated another communication app, but this one only contained a single voice recording message, which spread to every channel of his forces.

"Attack and annihilate everyone."

He sent the communication to his forces. They had come too far to stop down.

***

Secilia had hoped against hope that disabling the bombs would be all there was to resolving this matter, that after rendering them ineffective, the person who had orchestrated all this would be unable to do anything else. It was naive thinking. She understood that, but she had still dared to hope.

Her hopes were dashed before they could even fully form.

The first sign that they had been dashed was when something slammed into the convention center's barrier. Whatever had slammed into the shield exploded, not with light, but with sound. A powerful blue barrier lit up the sky as the earth rumbled and shook. The barrier was something that had been installed as a preventative measure in case someone was dumb enough to attack the peace conference. According to what she knew, that barrier was made from magic and should be capable of withstanding a nuclear explosion.

Several more objects slammed into the barrier, causing it to grow weaker and flicker. The people inside the convention center screamed and panic spread throughout.

The barrier protecting them was formed from a complex magic matrix and powered with a massive mana stone located in the basement of the convention center. It was an extremely powerful barrier that not even the Beast King would be able to break. However, the objects exploding against the shield were not regular missiles. Every time one of them was released, it would unleash thousands of tiny spheres about the size of a person's fist, which punched holes clean through the barrier.

Anti-magic missiles.

There were some materials in this world that had an innate resistance to magic. These materials were often used as cuffs meant to keep powerful demons or mages from using magic, but they could also be formed into weapons. The Academy Island Private Security Force's main method of attack was actually the use of anti-magic bullets. These missiles were just an upgraded version of those.

Several holes appeared in the barrier, and as more anti-magic missiles exploded against it, more holes began appearing while the previously made ones expanded. It wouldn't be long before the barrier disappeared entirely.

"Mari!" Secilia shouted as she grabbed her case in one hand and the girl's hand with her other. "Take us to the stage! Anthony said we should head to your mother and do whatever we can to help out!"

She had just gotten off the telepathic line with Anthony and now she was relaying what he had told her to Marianne. While the other girl looked so frightened even her confident persona couldn't fully mask it, the girl nodded and used her powers to fly them through the air. She pulled Secilia into the air with her as they flew toward the stage.

While none of the people on the stage looked like they were about to panic, there was a clear sense of shock permeating them. Even Ivan looked stumped.

"Mother!" Marianne shouted as she and Secilia dropped onto the stage. Instructor Noel and Calencio both stepped back as they landed on the platform.

"Marianne!" Elizabeth also shouted when she saw her daughter and rushed over. "What are you doing?! You should try to evacuate with the others!"

But Marianne shook her head, rejecting her mother's proposal. "Anthony told us to help."

"Anthony did…?" Elizabeth looked like someone had struck her with lightning, but she shook herself out of the daze threatening to consume. "Does Anthony know what's going on? Where is he?"

"Let me explain the situation," Secilia said as she stepped forward and began letting them know what she knew.

She started with how they learned explosives had been planted around the convention center in the underground network and then explained how they worked hard to disable the bombs. They succeeded, but then this happened, and now the convention center was under attack from outside.

"I cannot believe all this happened," Elizabeth murmured in shock. "Who would even dare to attack the peace conference like this?"

"There is one group who might do it," Ivan said as he walked up to them. He wasn't the only one. It seemed the other powerful dignitaries in charge of signing for their countries had followed him to form a circle around Elizabeth, Marianne, and Secilia. Even Vlad was present, though he did not look like he cared about what was happening.

"You are referring to the Sons of Liberty?" Elizabeth asked.

"None other." Ivan spread his arms as though to encompass what was happening. Several more holes had appeared on the barrier. "Who else do you know who could do this?"

"Does it even matter who is responsible?" asked a man with red hair and a goatee.

"I suppose who is responsible does not matter right now," Elizabeth said with a slow nod. "What we should be doing now is figuring out how to rescue everyone and get out of this." She turned to Noel. "I want you and Calencio to help with the evacuation."

"We normally shouldn't be leaving you alone," Noel said with a pensive frown. "But I guess the situation here means we can't follow protocol. Don't worry. We'll help evacuate the civilians."

Noel prodded Calencio into following her, and the two disappeared. The last Secilia saw of them, the pair was leaping onto the seating stands with magically enhanced strength.

"We need information," Ivan said, crossing his arms. "I want to know what the enemies' numbers are like and where they are attacking from."

"That'll be hard to acquire when we're stuck here," Elizabeth said.

It was at this moment that Secilia interrupted them. "I can get that information."

Everyone turned to her. Even Marianne looked surprised.

"You can?" asked Ivan.

Secilia was nervous in the presence of so many powerful individuals. She didn't think she'd ever been in a position where so many important figures would be looking at her, but she didn't have time to be frightened.

"I can," she said.

With a swipe of her hand, she activated her holographic screen and began typing away. She used a hacking program to hack into one of Academy Island's many satellites. Then she manipulated the satellite to zoom onto the convention center and the surrounding area. Ivan, Elizabeth, Marianne, and the other political bigwig gathered around her and watched in shock as the map appeared on her screen.

"This is a map of the convention center... and this—" she did something to her screen that caused several hundred red dots to suddenly appear all over the map "—are the enemy forces arrayed against us. It might be a little inaccurate. I'm using a code that turns every vehicular weapon and any human with a weapon into an enemy. Some of these might be guards, but I'm certain the numbers are at least relatively accurate... what? What are you all staring at me for?"

"You're a genius," Marianne murmured.

"Huh?"

"She's definitely smart," Elizabeth agreed.

"Urm..."

"I like you. Why don't you come with me to Russia? I'll let you join my army as the head of the intelligence division."

"Uh..."

Secilia had no idea how to deal with so many compliments pouring in—at least, not when those compliments came from such powerful people. Her cheeks turned hot and she averted her gaze.

"Th-thanks, but... I... um... I only want to help my bondmate so..."

She was trying to tell them she had no intention of working for any of them, but those hesitant and embarrassing words never fully left her mouth before the barrier suddenly broke apart. The sound was like shattering glass. Not only was it loud, but it caused the people currently panicking to scream louder as they panicked even more.

There was no longer any time to hesitate. Ivan, as the strongest among them, used his overpowering presence to calm everyone down and began ordering the people running through the seats to get back into the convention centers main lobby. The security guards who'd been ordered to protect them went as well. He also sent his daughter and wife with them since they were both powerful individuals in their own right and could help protect the civilians.

That still left one huge problem—namely, the barrier that was gone and the helicopters that were now bearing down on the stadium. Several released more missiles. It was hard for Secilia to tell what kind of missile they were, but since the barrier had gone down, she assumed they were regular missiles that would explode on contact.

Before they reach the stadium's interior, Ivan leaned backward, sucked in a deep breath, and released a roar. Secilia and Marianne screamed as they crouched low. Secilia could feel her ears rattling from the pressure of Ivan's roar, but the attack had its intended effect. Soundwaves spread from his mouth and slammed into the missile, which launched them off course and disabled their internal circuitry. The missiles, now useless, slammed into the stadium floor and shattered.

"Hmph." Ivan closed his mouth, crossed his arms, and glared up at the helicopters as they continued hovering above the stadium. "They are flying out of my reach. It seems whoever is attacking is well-aware of my one weakness."

"Then please leave these to me," Elizabeth said.

With that, Elizabeth did something all vampires were capable of: flight. She soared skyward at a speed that could have put rockets to shame. Darkness shrouded her body like a cloak, billowing behind her as she swerved through the sky to avoid a spray of anti-magic missiles, and then she raised her arms and swung them. What flew from her body was the black shroud. It was like miasma as it formed into a pair of giant arms that slammed into several helicopters, causing them to detonate in a brilliant flash of flame.

However, for as many helicopters as she destroyed, dozens more appeared to take their place. If something wasn't done soon, she would be overwhelmed.

"Let me help, Mother!"

Marianne did not fly into the air like her mother but instead remained on the ground as she swung her arm through the air like she was trying to slice apart the sky. Everyone looked at her like she was weird. Those looks, however, vanished when a black tear appeared in the space near several helicopters. Nothing seemed to happen at first, but then the tear suddenly fractured, becoming numerous cracks in the sky that resembled a mirror after someone smacked it with a bat.

The helicopters didn't stand a chance. They were torn apart, shattered into thousands of fragments that rained down from the sky. Several figures also fell out of the helicopters. Some of them were whole, but most of them looked like bloody chunks of meat.

"That's... Dimension Magic?!" Ivan shouted in surprise.

Secilia also looked at Marianne. "When did you learn Dimension Magic?"

"It's the ability I got from Anthony," Marianne admitted with a slight smile.

"That's kind of an overpowered ability. I'm jealous. All I got was Farsight."

"Farsight is a pretty powerful ability, too, if you know how to use it."

"But I can't destroy several dozen helicopters by swinging my arm."

"Well..."

Their banter was cut short by the appearance of even more helicopters. Marianne looked back up at the approaching attack vehicles and once more swung her arm out, creating the same dimensional cracks as before. Once more, the helicopters were destroyed. However, this time, Marianne was breathing heavily and had sweat pouring down her forehead. Her already pale face had become even paler.

"You're running low on mana," Ivan observed. "How many more of those attacks do you think you can do?"

Marianne shook her head. "S-sorry... but this is all I can do right now."

Two attacks. That was not a lot, but Dimension Magic was supposedly extremely power-consuming. The amount of mana consumed to release one attack with Dimension Magic was twice or even three times the amount needed for a spell using another element like fire or wind. That Marianne could even launch two attacks was a testament to her powerful reserves.

"I guess we can only rely on Elizabeth, Gitsune, and... where did Vlad go?"

When Ivan mentioned Vlad, everyone looked around, only to see that Vlad was not present among them. It only took a moment to realize that he had run off. Vlad was no coward, evidenced by his bloodthirsty history, but it seemed he had no desire to get caught up in this battle. He was one of those people who had only agreed to sign the Demonic Covenant because he'd been strong-armed into it.

"Dam him!" Ivan growled and clenched his hands into fists.

With Vlad no longer present, the only person they could rely on was Elizabeth and Gitsune Hagaromo, who could use her foxfire to take down the attack helicopters. No one else had their range. The other demons present were therianthropes with no ranged attacks or minimum range attacks like Ivan's soundwaves.

"I can help," Secilia said.

"How?" asked the red-haired human.

Secilia set down her case and opened the latches, revealing the sniper rifle she'd stored inside. It was currently in pieces, but Secilia was a practiced hand at putting it together, and the sniper was reassembled in less than five seconds. During that time, Gitsune and

Elizabeth held off the helicopters with blue waves of foxfire and dark magic.

"I did not realize Anthony's other bondmate was a skilled sniper," Ivan said.

"I'm skilled at a lot of things."

Secilia didn't look at Ivan as she responded with her typical sarcastic retort. She felt much better with a sniper in her hands. She'd also donned her gloves, which contained a powerful program to help her fire the rifle and enhance her strength, though it had nowhere near the strength of someone who could use Physical Enhancement.

Adopting a wide stance, Secilia looked down the sight of her scope. This one was different from her standard scope, which could only be used lying down, but the reticle and HUD display were the same. She lined up one helicopter with the help of her gloves and Farsight, then fired.

Bang! Bang! Bang! Bang!

Four bullets were fired in rapid succession as Secilia shifted her rifle from side to side. Each attack slammed into a helicopter's cockpit, blasting a hole clean through the pilot. With nobody left to steer, the helicopters listed to one side before crashing into other helicopters, resulting in both going up in flames. The result was that Secilia took care of two helicopters for every one shot fired.

"What the hell is with this girl?!"

"She's such an amazing shot!"

"Damn, I wish I had her in my army!"

The praises heaped upon Secilia made her blush, but she didn't lose focus as she continued sniping each one down. Seeing them being outdone by such a young girl, Elizabeth and Gitsune also began laying more suppressive fire. Large arcs of blue foxfire flew from Gitsune's nine tails, blasting apart helicopters with increasing frequency. Elizabeth's arms had become pitch black as the miasma from her dark magic gathered along them and created massive hands that she used to swat helicopters out of the sky.

The number of explosions increased. Because there were so many helicopters blowing up above them, the heat and displaced air struck those standing on the ground in the face, causing their hair to billow and sway. The humans expressed more discomfort. After all, they did not have any supernatural abilities to protect themselves.

Once all of the helicopters were shot from the sky, everyone thought they could breathe a sigh of relief.

They spoke too soon.

"Lord Ivan!" Someone rushed up to the group, a man dressed in the uniform of a soldier belonging to the Academy Island Private Security Forces. "We have a problem!"

"What is it now?" asked an annoyed Ivan.

"We've evacuated everyone to the main lobby, but the convention center is surrounded by tanks and infantry!"

"What?!"

Everyone shouted at the same time. It was one thing to be attacked by helicopters, but now it seemed as if their troubles were only just beginning.

"It gets worse," the man continued, taking a deep breath.

"How can it be worse?" asked Elizabeth.

"The people who have us surrounded are wearing the Academy Island Private Security Forces uniforms. We have been betrayed," he said, causing the blood of everyone present to run cold.

***

When Anthony and Brianna emerged from the underground network, it was to discover the streets had become filled with tanks—tanks and members of the Academy Island Private Security Forces. At first, Anthony thought this was a response force meant to fight off the terrorists. There were a few problems with this idea though. The first and most obvious was that it looked like they were fighting themselves. Gunshots and screams echoed all around the city as members dressed in the same uniform, wielding the same weapons, attacked each other. Anthony was obviously confused.

"What... the hell?"

"It looks like the real Academy Island Private Security Forces have decided to act," Brianna said. Unlike him, she was not confused. Her eyes were narrowed as she watched one man getting mowed down by gunfire, another being blown to bits by a tank round, and two more being fried by a tesla coil. "Look at the men with the armbands. I noticed those armbands on the people we fought in the underground network. I'm guessing they are the traitors and the ones fighting them are the people who are still part of the Private Security Forces."

Her guess was good enough. Anthony was certain she was right. In either event, they didn't have the time to stand there and debate this matter, so they moved soon after.

Anthony activated Physical Enhancement and dashed forward at a speed no human could hope to match. He reached a shadow, then slipped inside, appearing from within another shadow much closer to the enemy forces. Before his foes even knew what was happening, he swung his truncheon, breaking through a soldier's personal barrier, slamming into his body, and sending him flying. He would have been split in half, but the Kevlar vest protected him.

"What the—?!"

"Who is that?!"

"When did he get here?!"

"Never mind that! He's obviously an enemy! Shoot to— aaaaahhhhh!'"

Anthony pressed his hands against the ground as his mana swelled like the rising tide. The shadows underneath the men's feet sprang to life and turned into spikes that tried to impale them. Their magic barriers only held for a second before the overwhelming mana he'd used in his attack broke through. While the Kevlar vests were great at protecting against physical attacks, they were not so good at protecting against magic. The spikes impaled their foes through the chest, the legs, the shoulders, and even the face. Most of the traitors died before they even knew what hit them. Those who hadn't died screamed in agony before they were silenced by more spikes.

The men and women who hadn't betrayed the Private Security Forces stopped what they were doing to stare at Anthony in shock.

Before they could even figure out who this strange man wielding shadows was, Brianna had appeared on the scene.

Like Anthony, her body was covered in the glowing blue circuits of the spell Physical Enhancement, which boosted her physical abilities to well beyond human sensibilities. With her incredible strength and the power of the Geminius Sword, she demolished a tesla tank, slicing it into so many pieces that it no longer resembled a tank so much as building blocks. Once the tank was gone, she helped Anthony kill the remainder of the soldiers present.

It was only at this point that the soldiers recovered from their shock. However, rather than ask questions like "who are you?" or "what are you people doing here?" or something similar, they gazed at Brianna with shock in their eyes.

"Hey, aren't you the girl who accompanied us on our mission awhile back?" one of them asked. It was a vampire woman. Like the rest of her species, she had pure white skin, glowing red eyes, and sharp fangs. Her hair was blonde and tied into a bun behind her head.

"Ah!" Brianna put a hand to her mouth in shock. "You were the squad that helped me rescue Anthony back then?"

"That's right," the woman said. "I'm glad you remember."

"What's going on here?" asked Brianna.

The vampire sighed. "Long story short, we got a call from Commander Lucretia, who told us to get our butts out here."

The vampire woman, who neither Anthony nor Brianna actually knew the name of, explained that Commander Lucretia—Professor Incanscino—had sent them a message saying there were traitors in the Private Security Forces. She ordered those who were loyal to mobilize and head toward the convention center where the peace conference was still taking place. This woman along with her squad was among the loyal ones. They'd done as asked but ran into the traitors along the way. The battle had been fierce until just a few seconds ago when Anthon and Brianna had shown up.

"I hadn't realized you'd become so powerful." The woman shook her head. "You two took care of those traitors in a second."

"It seems there are more traitors among the Private Security Forces than any of us realized," Brianna murmured, turning to Anthony. They looked into each other's eyes and found that both were of like mind. Brianna turned back to the woman. "You guys should continue fighting against the forces around here. Anthony and I are heading to the convention center to help out."

The woman looked like she wanted to argue, but then she snapped her mouth shut. Given what she had just witnessed, telling them not to go was stupid. They were clearly stronger than her entire team. Both of them could probably take her team out with little help.

"Be careful," she said instead.

"We will," Brianna promised.

Anthony and Brianna took off with their magically enhanced speed, racing toward the convention center at the fastest pace possible. They ran afoul of numerous battles taking place throughout the city. It seemed the number of people who turned traitor was far higher than either of them could have assumed. The two forces looked almost evenly matched. Worse still, the traitorous forces had managed to prepare tesla tanks and a few mechs—two-legged, humanoid machines piloted by people.

The mechs were called Thanatos. They functioned primarily as heavy cavalry units and looked like two large barrels held aloft by triple-jointed legs. Their arms were not really arms but weapons. The right had a Gatling gun that fired thousands of rounds per second, while the left fired missiles. There were other weapons on this as well. The shoulders carried several more missile bays, which they did not hesitate to launch at anything designated an enemy.

This included Anthony and Brianna.

While Brianna prepared to dodge, Anthony narrowed his eyes as he channeled his mana and thrust out his truncheon. His bondmate looked at him like he was an idiot. That expression only lasted for a second before a black sphere appeared in front of them. It wasn't very big, about the size of a fist, but it soon swelled a mere second after it appeared, going from a fist to the size of a person. The missiles that the Thanatos had fired at them soon bent as though something was sucking them up. They moved inward, converging around the small black sphere, then disappeared entirely.

After getting rid of the missiles, Anthony took a deep breath and prepared to move again, but Brianna had overcome her shock this time and darted forward. Her first swing dismantled the mech's left leg. As it fell to the ground, she leaped into the air, swinging the Geminius Sword at its left arm, which was lopped off with the same ease as its leg. It fell to the ground with a loud crashing sound, then Brianna screamed a battle cry as she cleaved through the machine's middle. The spatial magic of her sword ensured the machine was split in half.

"Since when could you use Dimension Magic?" asked Brianna as she placed the tip of her sword against the ground and looked at Anthony.

"I learned to use it after bonding with Marianne," Anthony admitted. "However, I haven't had many chances to use it. This was only the second time I've tried it."

"I see. Still... you could have told me."

"I'm sorry."

"Haa... whatever, let's just keep going."

Anthony didn't argue.

They continued moving, mowing down any enemy who stood in their path, and eventually reached the convention center, which was surrounded by hundreds of tanks, mechs, and maybe even tens of thousands of soldiers.

***

Secilia and the others arrived in the main lobby and walked through the large mass of people. Many of them were shaking with nerves, a few were crying, and some had even begun praying to whatever god they worshipped. Quite a few people even appeared to have given up hope. Secilia saw one person crouched against the wall, arms hugging his knees as he rocked back and forth.

Ivan went up to the nearest guard. "What is the situation outside like?"

The guard snapped to attention, his expression stiff, face pale. "We're completely surrounded, Lord Ivan. I can't get an exact estimate of the forces surrounding us, but the enemy has thousands of infantry and dozens of tanks."

There was a scowl on Ivan's face as he listened to the man's words, but he didn't say anything right away. It was clear that he was considering this situation carefully.

He waded past the people crowding around the lobby and toward the entrance, which consisted of several sliding doors, and looked outside. Secilia and the others followed him since they didn't know what else to do. What they found outside was exactly what the guard described. There were thousands of soldiers and what must have been at least a few hundred tanks.

"What should we do?" asked Elizabeth.

Ivan crossed his arms as the scowl on his face grew even more frightening. "If it was just me, I would have already charged out there. However, many of these people do not know how to fight. If we leave them behind, these people could slip around us and use them as hostages. Even like this, protecting all of them will be hard."

The simple fact was there were too many enemy soldiers and not enough people present to both attack and defend against them.

"Mari!" As they were trying to figure out what they should do, Alexandra rushed over to the group and stopped in front of Marianne. "I'm glad you are okay."

"I am fine, but our situation is still tenuous," Marianne said with a gentle frown.

Elizabeth, Gitsune, Ivan, and Svetlana tried to discuss various options for dealing with the situation while Marianne, Alexandra, and Secilia stood together. Many plans were put on the table but all of them were rejected. They couldn't charge out and leave these people unprotected. Ivan argued that he could take these forces out on his own and offered to attack by himself, but his idea was also rejected. This army had tesla tanks. While Ivan was strong, therianthropes were all weak against weapons like that, which ignored the outer defense of a person and fried their insides.

Just as it looked like an argument was about to erupt, screams echoed from the other side of the lobby. The sound was followed by gunshots. Everyone whipped their heads around and found several people dressed in Private Security Force garb firing into the crowd. Several foreign dignitaries went down, blood bursting from their bodies and staining the ground red.

"Dammit! They found a way in through side passages!"

Ivan scowled when he realized how these people got in, but they didn't have time to lament. With a roar, he leaped over the people between him and his enemies, then came back down like an avenging angel. He slammed into the ground in the middle of the enemy forces. The punch he unleashed was so ferocious that a shockwave spread out from the center of impact and bowled numerous people over.

Elizabeth, Gitsune, Svetlana, and even Alexandra were also quick to react. More guards were pouring in through the corridors off to the side, so the group was forced to split up. Svetlana and Alexandra joined Ivan. Elizabeth and Gitsune took the other side.

The group consisting of Ivan, Svetlana, and Alexandra fought with a ferocity that made all those present pale. They were vicious and brutal. Punches blasted holes through bodies. Heads were twisted off. Limbs were sheared from powerful claw attacks. The amount of blood flying through the air made several of the humans present lose their lunch.

On the opposite side of the lobby, Gitsune and Elizabeth used their magic and some incredibly elegant hand-to-hand combat to fend off the attackers. Gitsune Hagaromo's nine tails were lit up with foxfire, which she flung at the opponents further away. Each burst of foxfire slammed into someone, exploded, and burnt them to cinders. Beside her, Elizabeth was attacking with fists, feet, and shadows. Shadows impaled enemies through their chests. Tendrils wrapped around people's bodies and flung them into walls. She was utilizing dark magic to the fullest.

They weren't alone. Noel and Calencio were quick to join up with Elizabeth and begin attacking the traitorous Private Security Forces. Noel was wielding a Geminius Sword just like Brianna, except she wielded it with even more grace. Calencio was swinging a pair of curved longswords that were attached together by a cord. He would sometimes throw one of his hands, impale someone from a distance, then pull the sword back.

"We should also help," Secilia said.

"You are right," Marianne agreed. "We can't let them fight on their own, but I don't have much mana left..."

"Is there a way to recharge your mana?" asked Secilia.

"It will naturally recharge with time, but I can also get more by drinking blood," Marianne admitted. "However, the situation right now won't allow for that."

"So, in other words, you can't do anything right now."

"... I'm sorry."

Secilia wanted to tell her this wasn't something she needed to apologize for. However, they were still dealing with a large crisis. Even with Ivan, Svetlana, Alexandra, Elizabeth, Gitsune, and the guards fighting, they were still in danger. For every person they killed, four or five more appeared to take their place. They were like waves crashing upon the shore. What's more, the group of demons was limited in how much power they could bring to bear since there were innocent people inside of the lobby with them.

"Let's try to find a higher vantage point," Secilia said at last. "If I can find a place where I can provide cover fire, you can just protect me. You still have a lot of physical strength as a vampire, so I think it wouldn't be asking for too much."

"I can at least do that much," Marianne agreed.

The convention center consisted of several levels. Secilia and Marianne went up to the second floor and found a walkway that gave them a view of the first-floor lobby. Secilia brought out her sniper once more and took a position on her stomach. She took careful aim and began firing. One. Two. Four. Eight. Sixteen shots were fired, resulting in sixteen enemy soldiers getting their brains blown out. Every shot Secilia made was a headshot thanks to a combination of Farsight and the technological marvel that was her sniper and the gloves she wore.

While Secilia was providing cover fire, Marianne protected her. Several soldiers came up to the second floor and tried to take her out, but they were defeated by Marianne. While vampires were not as physically strong as therianthropes, they were still a lot more powerful than normal humans. Marianne's punches launched people clean off their feet, shattered bones, and liquified internal organs. Since she was using purely physical attacks as well, the magical shield that made the Private Security Forces so formidable was completely useless.

No one knew how long they had been fighting for. Time seemed to have no meaning. However, Secilia eventually ran out of bullets. She only carried five hundred rounds on her since the idea that she'd need to fire more than five hundred times seemed utterly ridiculous—at least it had before now. Secilia was presently wishing she'd had more foresight and come with several thousand rounds.

Just when it looked like they might be overrun, the soldiers attacking them began to taper off, though no one could explain why. It was like they had run out of soldiers, which should have been impossible since there had been thousands of soldiers surrounding their base.

"What is going on?" wondered Marianne.

"I am not sure…" Secilia took apart her sniper and put it away. She no longer had any use for it since she didn't have any ammo left.

Marianne went over to the railing of the walkway and leaned over to look out the second-story window. Her eyes widened when she did.

"Secilia! Look!"

Standing up and grabbing her case, Secilia went over to the railing and looked at what Marianne was pointing to. Her eyes bulged when she did.

"Is that…?"

"It is! It's Anthony and Brianna!"

Anthony and Brianna were outside of the convention center, wading through the army of enemy soldiers—no. It was more like they were slaughtering their way through.

Wielding the truncheon she had made for him, Anthony was engaged in close combat with a number of soldiers, but none of them could do a thing as he swatted them aside like they were made of paper mâché. He didn't just stick with physical attacks either. Shadows rose from the ground and skewered the people who were too far for him to reach. Rips appeared in the air, forming black cracks that annihilated numerous tanks and mechs.

Brianna was right by his side. All of her attacks were purely physical, but the Geminius Sword she wielded allowed her to cut anything and everything that stood in her way. She protected Anthony's flank as he drove forward. Each swing of her blade severed something: an arm, a leg, a head. When she faced up against a tank or a mech, she showed no mercy and used her incredible strength to slice them apart. Lines would appear on her foes before they quite literally fell to pieces.

Already a huge gap had appeared in the enemy's formation, and it was growing larger as members of the Academy Island Private Security Force that hadn't turned traitor joined Anthony in his efforts.

"Let's go back downstairs and tell the others about this," Secilia decided.

"I'm way ahead of you." Marianne grabbed Secilia, leaped over the railing, and flew to the ground.

Ivan and the others had joined up again and looked like they were discussing why the forces attacking them suddenly stopped. It seemed they hadn't seen Anthony and Brianna yet. Of course, those two were still behind enemy lines, so you couldn't see them from the first floor. That was why Secilia explained what she saw.

"So their flank is being attacked." Ivan actually looked pleased when he heard about what was happening. "That boy seems to be more capable than I gave him credit for."

"He seems like quite the man." Alexandra smiled. "I'm becoming even more interested in him."

Ivan twitched when his daughter expressed an interest in Anthony, but he was at least smart enough not to say anything about it right now. Secilia thought he might lecture his daughter after this was over.

"It isn't just Anthony," Marianne said. "It looks like the Academy Island Private Security Forces have joined him. They are pushing their way toward us right now."

"Ara, ara. In that case, I believe we should lend them a hand." Gitsune placed a hand on her cheek and turned to Elizabeth. "Don't you?"

"I do," Elizabeth said. "Now that they are too busy protecting their backs to send people after us, we should use this opportunity to attack."

"Hmph. Then what are we waiting for?!" Ivan shouted. "Let's go!"

Secilia and Marianne stood back as Ivan, Alexandra, Svetlana, Elizabeth, and Gitsune left the safety of the convention center and charged the enemy lines.

"I guess all we can do now is wait here," Secilia muttered.

"You hate being left behind, huh?" Marianne asked.

"Of course. Don't you?"

"Yeah... I do." Marianne smiled, but it was a little more brittle than normal. "I'm always the one being left behind... Always..."

Secilia didn't know what Marianne meant by that, and even when she asked, her fellow bondmate wouldn't tell her a thing.

***

The battle ended after Anthony, Brianna, and the remaining Academy Island Private Security Forces mobilized and attacked the large force arrayed against the convention center from behind. Anthony and Brianna had led the charge. They cut a large swath through the enemy forces and broke their lines. Once they joined up with Ivan, Elizabeth, and the others, the battle had basically been won.

"Hmph. You're a lot stronger than I gave you credit for, but don't think that means anything! I'm still not giving my daughter to you, even if you are strong! Even if you were the strongest man in the entire world, I would not give her to you!"

Despite Ivan's newfound respect for his strength, the man continued to obstinately dislike him because Sasha had expressed an interest in Anthony. He couldn't really understand. Anthony had never once expressed an interest in Sasha, so Ivan should not have been taking this matter so personally.

"Dear... you're being obstinate again," Svetlana said with a smile on her face. While her smile looked pleasant, the dark shadows cast on her face gave her an ominous appearance.

Ivan looked away.

Their group was standing in the middle of the lobby, surrounded by the hundreds of foreign dignitaries who had survived the attack. Gitsune Hagaromo's daughter had also joined them. She quietly stood behind her mother and peered at Anthony. He did his best to ignore her. Anthony still remembered when her mother tried to pawn the girl off on him.

"Thank you for your assistance," Elizabeth said to Anthony. "This situation would have been much worse if you hadn't been here."

Anthony shrugged. "You're welcome. I'm glad I could help."

"Still, though, I have to wonder what happened here." The smile left Elizabeth's face. "Why did all those people turn traitor? I don't understand. And this attack was clearly something they had been planning for a long time now."

"From what I understand, the person who was responsible for this attack is Felton," Anthony said.

"Felton?!" Elizabeth looked startled. "You mean the man who was in charge of the Academy Island Private Security Forces?! That Felton?!"

Nodding, Anthony began explaining what he knew. "I received a message from Professor Inca—erm, from Lucretia Incanscino. She said Felton was part of the Sons of Liberty. He's been gathering these forces ever since he came to power. His original plan was to initiate a hostile takeover of Academy Island and eradicate the demons living here, but when it was decided that the peace conference would take place here, his plans changed to destroying the peace between humans and demons by killing the world leaders responsible for creating the Demonic Covenant."

"So that's how it is." Ivan crossed his arms and glared at nothing. "It seems you guys were fools. How could you allow such a man enter a position of power?"

"Don't look at me." Anthony shrugged. "I'm not responsible for what the Board of Directors decides on, and I've only been living on Academy Island for a little over a year. Felton has been in the position as the head of the Academy Island Private Security Forces for at least five years—long before I ever came here."

Ivan had no retort to that, so all he could do was huff and look away.

"It's a shame Felton got away," Gitsune said as she placed a hand on her cheek.

"He didn't." When those words left Anthony's mouth, everyone looked at him, causing Anthony to give them a bright grin. "He might have escaped from us, but there is one person he can't escape from."

EPILOGUE

"DAMN THAT INCUBUS!"

The sound of Felton slamming his fist against the armrest of his chair echoed throughout the airplane. An attendant who was standing off to one side flinched at the noise. She didn't say anything, however, as that would only invite his wrath.

"I cannot believe all of my plans were ruined because of one fledgling demon!" Felton continued to rant. "I spent five years building up those forces! Five! Nearly an entire third of the Academy Island Private Security Forces had become my pawns! It should have been more than enough to deal with the likes of Ivan, Elizabeth, and their ilk—and yet... and yet...!"

Felton had never been so infuriated in his entire life. Years ago, he had infiltrated the Board of Directors for Academy Island with the purpose of eradicating the demons there and taking control of the many research companies who made that island their home. He plotted with the Sons of Liberty, planned out numerous strategies, and even initiated an attack against all the most powerful world leaders suing for peace.

But none of it had amounted to a damn thing.

While Felton had disappeared during the chaos and never saw the conclusion of the battle, he had received reports on what happened. He knew who was responsible for the destruction of his army. That knowledge caused his blood to boil and his vision to see red.

"That fucking... Anthony Amasius! I'll make sure you regret ever being born!"

Felton reached for the communication console on the chair's armrest, but just as he was about to open a holographic screen, his body froze. He tried to move. He couldn't. Felton couldn't move anything, not his fingers, his hands, his mouth, or even his eyes. It was as if his body had suddenly been frozen solid.

Just as he was about to panic, someone spoke beside him.

"Who are you going to make regret being born?"

If his eyes could have widened, they would have, for sitting in the chair in front of him was none other than Lucretia Incanscino. She wore her normal white lolita outfit. Her blonde hair was done in the usual ringlets. With her hair, cute dress, and vibrant eyes, this woman looked like a middle schooler. No one would have ever suspected that she was actually a five-hundred-year-old witch nicknamed the Time Witch.

Felton knew otherwise.

He tried to speak, tried to say something, anything. Yet no matter how hard he tried, he could not say a word.

"Do not bother trying to speak," Lucretia said as she crossed her left leg over her right one. "I have currently sealed off your time. Everything except your brain and your ears are currently frozen." Felton's blood would have run cold, but it felt like even that had been frozen solid. "I bet you're wondering why I've frozen you like this." Lucretia smiled at him. It was such a terrifying look that Felton would have pissed himself if he could. "You see, I'm rather... angry right now. I discovered someone infiltrated Academy Island, used our forces to disrupt the peace conference, and tried to kill one of my precious students. Now I am going to have so much paperwork on my hands dealing with this disaster, I doubt I will be able to sleep for at least a year. Whose fault do you think that is?"

The question was completely rhetorical. Felton couldn't have answered even if he wanted to.

"I doubt you realize what kind of trouble you have caused..." Lucretia trailed off for a moment, tilted her head, and then began again. "Actually, you probably do, but you're going to listen to me complain anyway. It's the least you can do to repent for your sins before you die."

Felton didn't think he'd ever been so frightened in his entire life, yet even though he was terrified enough to release all the content in his bowels, he couldn't move a single muscle. All he could do was sit there and listen as this old woman who looked like a little girl complained about how much trouble he had caused her.

"Thanks to you, Academy Island is currently being attacked from all sides. Many people are blaming us for the attack on the peace conference. Of course, it's not as if they don't have the right to complain. One of our most important members on the Board of Directors betrayed us, helped the Sons of Liberty infiltrate our ranks, and was directly responsible for the deaths of several foreign dignitaries. I can see why people would pin the blame on us, but that does not make it any easier to accept."

Felton didn't want to listen to this woman. He didn't want to be here anymore. He was already beginning to regret what he'd done. Had he known this was what the outcome would be, he'd have never launched an attack on the peace conference.

"Academy Island's current government will have to be completely restructured. I don't think I can trust anyone on the Board of Directors now. After all, they were the ones who let you join. I'll need to find some means of making them disappear."

It was pretty terrifying how easily this woman spoke of making people "disappear." Felton didn't know if she intended to kill them or not, but a woman of her power could easily make it so someone never existed. She had never used that power so flagrantly before. However, given what happened, Felton wouldn't be surprised if she decided to turn back everyone's time so it was like they'd never been born.

"I think I'm going to have Anthony help me out." Lucretia uncrossed her legs, then recrossed them. "He's becoming a lot more reliable these days. Hm. He's not as reliable as Yokumaru yet, but he has more potential than anyone I've ever seen. I think he'd be able to help me. What do you think?"

Another rhetorical question. Felton couldn't even open his mouth.

"We're awfully high up." Lucretia turned her head to look out the window, which offered a view of blue sky and clouds. "Did you know this entire airplane is currently frozen in time? I figured it would be easier that way. I don't want anyone interrupting us." She turned back to him. "Well, I suppose I have ranted enough. Goodbye, Felton. I hope you enjoy your time in hell. That's where assholes like you always end up."

Felton wanted more than anything to be able to speak, to plead for his life and promise to help her if she just let him live, but the words wouldn't come. His time was still frozen.

Lucretia stood up and tapped her foot against the floor. She stared at him for a second, then slashed out with her hand. It was just a casual movement, but the moment she made that action, Felton's throat split open like someone cutting an overripe fruit with a butcher's knife. Blood spilled from his throat. It hurt. It hurt so much. Yet he still couldn't move even as his life bled out.

It was not long before Felton died. Lucretia continued to stare at the corpse for several long seconds before she disappeared. After that, the airplane began moving again as its time was unfrozen. Felton, his time also unfrozen, slumped in his chair as blood gushed from the wound on his neck.

The attendant who had been standing to the side screamed when she saw the man's corpse.

To be Continued...

AFTERWORD

I can't believe I was finally able to publish Incubus 4. I hope you all enjoyed reading it. This volume marks the conclusion of the first and hopefully only two volume arc of the series. While I thought volume 3 was okay, I was very unsatisfied with the cliffhanger ending. Unlike WIEDERGEBURT: Legend of the Reincarnated Warrior, which is an epic saga that continues with a massively complex and constantly expanding storyline, Incubus is more like pulp fiction. I wanted each volume to contain its own story. This arc ended up being too long for a single volume, so I had to divide them.

Anyway, we got to see of the fruits of Anthony's training in this volume. How did you enjoy watching him tear through the enemy army at the end? Was it fun to read?

Marianne and Anthony also finally got together. I think she makes a nice contrast to Secilia and Brianna, both rather busty women. The legal loli vampire trope is pretty widespread in Japanese media. While I personally wouldn't call Marianne a loli because she's simply petite instead of childlike, I know a lot of people will probably not share my views. Either way, I hope you guys enjoyed that moment where she becomes Anthony's bondmate.

This arc introduces a number of important antagonistic characters: Selene and the Son's of Liberty—an anti-demon organization similar to The Sons and Daughters of Humanity from my American Kitsune series—will play important roles later in the story. I don't know how yet since I haven't written that far, but give me some time and I'll work my magic.

As always, I really want to thank my editor and proofreaders for lending a hand and fixing my grammar. And I also need to thank Orendi Laran for the amazing artwork. That cover was perfect. Like, geeze! I just can't get over how gorgeous Brianna is on the front cover! And all the interior artwork is super cute too.

I also want to thank you for reading this volume. I really hope you enjoyed it, and I hope even more that you'll join me for the next volume. I have a feeling it's gonna be an even more intense volume than this one.

~Brandon Varnell

ANTHONY AMASIUS

A 19 year-old college student. He just happens to be the world's only incubus.

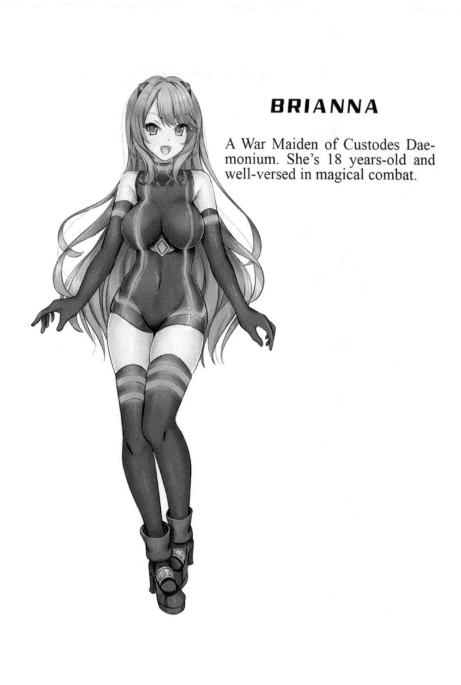

BRIANNA

A War Maiden of Custodes Daemonium. She's 18 years-old and well-versed in magical combat.

SECILIA

Anthony's friend. She attends the same college as him. Well-known for her sarcasm and sharp tongue.

LUCRETIA INCANSCINO

Known to her students as the lolita teacher because of her youthful appearance, Lucretia is also an Attack Mage working for the Academy Island Private Security Forces.

MARIANNE TEPES

The daughter of Elizabath Tepes, one of the three Vampire Lords, who rules over all vampires. She tries to present a brave front, but she's honestly very timid and meek. Likes to cook, clean, and do laundry.

DID YOU KNOW THAT BRANDON VARNELL IS ADAPTING THE AMERICAN KITSUNE SERIES INTO A MANGA ON PATREON?

Hey, did you know?
Brandon Varnell has a Patreon
You can get all kinds of awesome exclusives
Like:

1. The chance to read his stories before anyone else!
2. Access to sketches, artwork, and more!
3. The American Kitsune Manga adaptation!
4. Exclusive SFW and NSFW artwork!
5. His undying love!

Er...maybe we don't want that last one, but the rest sound pretty cool, right?

Join Brandon and get all his exclusive content at:
https://www.patreon.com/BrandonVarnell!

WIEDERGEBURT
LEGEND OF THE REINCARNATED WARRIOR
HE RETURNED TO THE PAST IN ORDER TO CHANGE THE FUTURE.

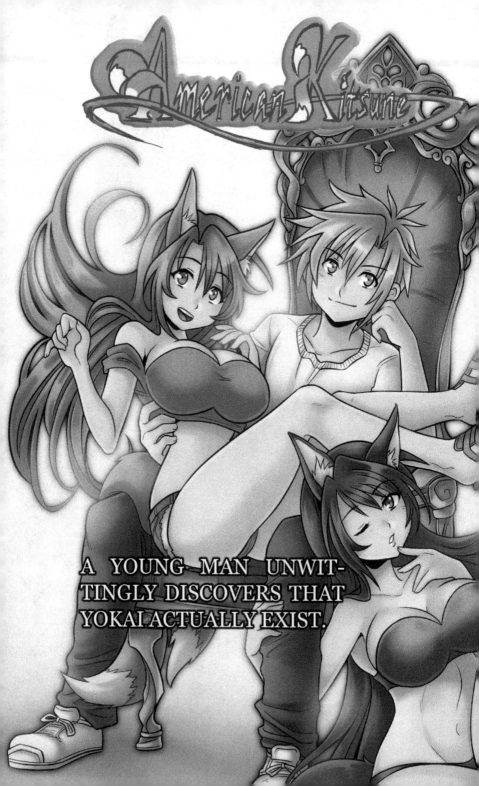

A YOUNG MAN UNWIT-
TINGLY DISCOVERS THAT
YOKAI ACTUALLY EXIST.

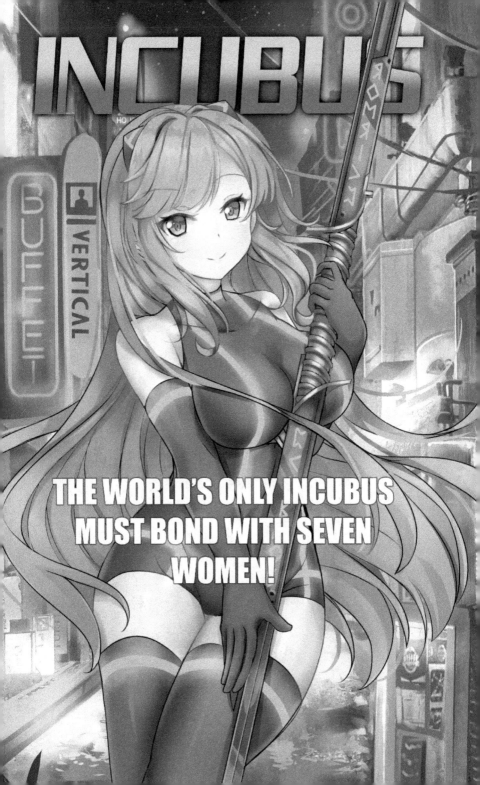

catgirl doctor

THE STORY OF A YOUNG DOCTOR-IN-TRAINING AND CATGIRLS.

MMG:001

A MAN DESPERATE TO SAVE
HIS LOVER JOINS FORCES
WITH A WOMAN LOOKING
FOR A WAY OUT OF AN UN-
WANTED MARRIAGE.

MAN MADE GOD

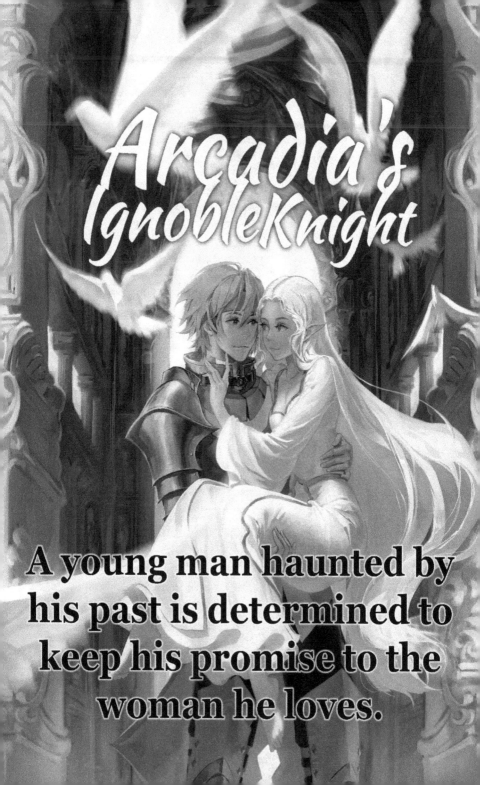

A former Marine running from his past.
An angel with nothing left to lose.
A succubus at the bottom of the food chain.
What do these three have in common?
A goal: To escape the hellish nightmare
they've found themselves in. Together.

Swordsman
Of the
Rift 2

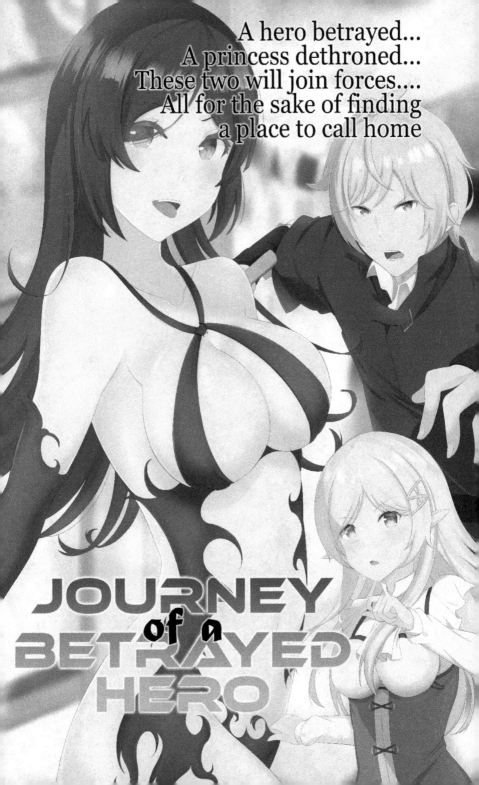

A hero betrayed...
A princess dethroned...
These two will join forces....
All for the sake of finding
a place to call home

JOURNEY
of a
BETRAYED
HERO

Want to learn when a new book comes out?
Follow me on Social Media!

 @AmericanKitsune

 +BrandonVarnell

 @BrandonBVarnell

 http://bvarnell1101.tumblr.com/

 Brandon Varnell

 BrandonbVarnell

 https://www.patreon.com/
BrandonVarnell

CPSIA information can be obtained
at www.ICGtesting.com
Printed in the USA
LVHW051512180222
711470LV00007B/172

9 781951 904463